DARK
PASSAGE

ALSO BY M. J. PUTNEY

Dark Mirror

DARK PASSAGE

M. J. Putney

 St. Martin's Griffin ⚑ New York

DARK PASSAGE. Copyright © 2011 by Mary Jo Putney, Inc. All rights reserved. Printed in the United States of America. For information, address St. Martin's Press, 175 Fifth Avenue, New York, N.Y. 10010.

www.stmartins.com

Library of Congress Cataloging-in-Publication Data

Putney, Mary Jo.
    Dark Passage / M. J. Putney.—1st ed.
        p. cm.
    Sequel to: Dark mirror.
    ISBN 978-0-312-62285-5
    [1. Magic—Fiction. 2. Boarding schools—Fiction. 3. Schools—Fiction. 4. Aristocracy (Social class)—Fiction. 5. London (England)—History—19th century—Fiction. 6. Great Britain—History—George III, 1760–1820—Fiction. 7. World War, 1939–1945—France—Fiction. 8. France—History—1945–1958—Fiction.] I. Title.

PZ7.P98232Dav 2011
[Fic]—dc23

2011019840

First Edition: September 2011

10 9 8 7 6 5 4 3 2 1

To my wonderful editor, Sara Goodman, and my agent,
Robin Rue, who helped me become a YA author

DARK
PASSAGE

PROLOGUE

France, Autumn 1940

Tory had almost reached her destination when a machine gun blasted crazily from the farmhouse ahead. As Lady Victoria Mansfield in her own time, she'd been taught to dance and manage a household and embroider, rather badly. As a mageling and a member of Merlin's Irregulars, she'd learned to dive for cover when she heard gunfire.

She hit the ground hard and took refuge under the hedge on her left, grateful for the darkness. Clamping down on her fear, she peered out from under the hedge.

The machine gun was being fired in bursts. Sparks spat from the muzzle that stuck out of a window on the upper floor. The weapon wasn't aimed in her direction, which was good. But damnably, it was aimed at the small barn that sheltered the people she'd promised to protect.

Another thing she'd learned in 1940 was swearing. She muttered some words that would have shocked her parents, the Earl and Countess of Fairmount, speechless.

She had to stop that rain of death, and quickly. But how? She was no warrior. She was an undersized sixteen-year-old girl who looked even younger. She wouldn't know what to do with a gun if it was handed to her fully loaded.

But she was a mageling, and she could draw on the magical power and talent of her friends. She studied the small stone house. It was old and simply constructed, two stories high. Probably just two rooms downstairs and two on the upper floor.

The building was dark except for the room where the machine gun was placed. Likely the inhabitants of the place had fled when their home had been commandeered.

If she was able to get into the house and come up behind the men with the machine gun, she should be able to do—something. Exactly what would depend on what she had to work with.

Cautiously she worked her way around the house, glad she was carrying her stealth stone. It didn't make her invisible, but it would make the men less likely to notice her. Bullets were brainless and harder to mislead.

Like most old houses, the windows were few and small. She tested the back door. Locked. On the floor above was a casement window that looked large enough for her to climb through. Since it might also be locked, she selected a rock the size of a large man's fist from the stone border around a flower bed. Then she turned her mind inward to focus her special magic.

Click! She began to rise, skimming her left hand along the stone wall until she hovered next to the window. She tried unsuccessfully to open it.

Could magic muffle the sound of breaking glass? She hadn't tried that before, but it should work. Doing magic was mostly a matter of focusing magical power on the desired result—and Tory had a great deal of power.

She concentrated on silencing the sound, and for good measure she waited for the next burst of machine-gun fire. Smashing the rock into the right-hand casement sent shards of glass flying, nicking her wrist.

The breaking glass made very little sound, but even so, she waited to hear if she'd been noticed. Coarse laughter came from the front of the house. A man spoke. French, not German. Collaborators of some sort, perhaps police working with the Nazis. Their raucousness suggested that they were drunk and amusing themselves by shooting up the flimsy barn that sheltered helpless people.

One of them made a sneering remark about killing filthy Jews. For a red-rage moment, Tory wished she had a gun and knew how to use it.

But magic was her weapon. She felt inside for the window latch. It was badly stuck, so she gave it a little blast of power. The lock opened but her hovering bobbled as she diverted energy. She was using up power at an alarming rate.

She wrenched the casements open and glided into the dark room. After catching her breath, she cautiously created the dimmest possible mage light. The room was a simply furnished bedroom. The bed looked rumpled, as if the sleepers had left in a hurry. That would also explain why the door had been left ajar, enabling Tory to hear the voices.

As she'd guessed from outside, the primitive cottage would have been old in her own time. Gnarled beams ran across the ceiling. Good.

The door opened to a short corridor that led to the stairs and the other bedroom at the front of the house. The door to the other room was open, revealing three men in French police uniforms, the machine gun, and bottles of wine or spirits.

With only the barest of plans, she walked softly toward the front room. She had just reached the doorway when one of the men turned and looked right at her. He blinked uncertainly, but the stealth stone wasn't enough to conceal a direct stare.

He lurched to his feet. "It's a little girl! Must have hidden here when the rest of the family ran."

A second man turned, then smiled nastily. "Old enough that we can use her."

He lurched toward Tory. Even six feet away she smelled the alcohol on his breath. Her rage flared again. These men shot at the innocent and were ready to assault a female they thought to be a child. Drawing her focus to blazing intensity, she drew masses of power from her friends, most of all Allarde's special talent.

When she'd gathered her strength, she made a furious sweeping gesture with one arm at the beams. *"Enough!"* she cried as she pulled down the front half of the roof.

The massive beams smashed into the men and their horrible gun. Tory threw herself out the door in a rolling tumble as the male shouts abruptly cut off. The remaining roof beams began to groan ominously.

Devil take it! The whole cottage was collapsing!

She scrambled to her feet and raced to the back bedroom, diving out the open window before the roof could crush her. Something hard crunched into her left arm and she barely managed to catch herself before crashing into the ground.

With the last of her power, she managed to roll and turn her fall into a safe landing. She folded into an exhausted ball, panting. Her left arm hurt like Hades and blood was saturating her sleeve, but at least she'd escaped. The three shooters hadn't.

She rested her head on her bent arms as she fought the pain and the horror of knowing that she'd just killed or seriously maimed three men. They were beasts, but she hadn't wanted their lives on her head.

She drew a shuddering breath. She had *sworn* that she would never return to the future again. Why the devil was she here?

Because she had no choice.

CHAPTER 1

England, June 1940

Traveling through time was not for the faint of heart. Lady Victoria Mansfield wiped damp palms on her skirt as she contemplated being torn into screaming pieces, dragged through a magic mirror, and dropped one hundred thirty-seven years in the past, exhausted and ravenous. But this was the only way home.

She surveyed her friends. "Everyone ready to brave Merlin's mirror again?"

There was a mutter of assent, with Lady Cynthia Stanton's edgy "I want to get this over with!" the clearest comment.

Elspeth, flaxen-haired and fey, said to Cynthia, "Since you had the most difficult time coming through the mirror to get here, take my hand and I'll see if I can send you extra energy to make the trip easier."

Cynthia nodded ungraciously—she was often ungracious—and took Elspeth's hand on one side and Allarde's on the other. Allarde,

6 · *M. J. Putney*

dark-haired heir to a dukedom and a powerful mage, gave Cynthia an encouraging smile. Though he was jaw-droppingly handsome, Tory loved his kindness even more than his looks.

He laced the fingers of his other hand through Tory's. Energy sparked between them. She always felt calmer and stronger when they were together.

The last of her group, Jack Rainford, clasped Elspeth's hand to complete the line of magelings. "Lead on, Tory!" He wiggled his blond brows at her. "But if you take us to the wrong century, I'm going to be very, very cross."

She smiled innocently. "Do you want to lead us through the mirror, Jack? I'll be happy to defer to you."

He looked horrified. "I'll stick to weather magic, thank you. You're the expert on traveling through time."

A wise choice on his part. Jack was surely the best weather mage in England in 1940, and quite possibly would be the best when they returned home to 1803. But Tory seemed to have the most talent for moving through the mirror portal to other times—and taking others with her.

Tory gave a last smile to the four twentieth-century friends who had come to see them off. "Good luck and stay safe."

"If you ever come back, we'll find beds for you," Nick Rainford said with a grin. His family was descended in some way from Jack's family, and he and Jack shared similar blond good looks. They could easily pass as brothers.

Tory smiled, but they all knew it unlikely they'd ever see each other again.

She turned to the end of the chalk tunnel and raised her right hand. Though the time travel portal called Merlin's mirror wasn't yet visible, she could feel the burn of its magic. Summoning all her power, she visualized the time and place of their destination.

Take us back through time. Return us to Lackland Abbey in 1803. Take us to just a few minutes after we left. Take us home . . .

Magic was mostly a matter of will, and she had plenty of stubbornness as well as a talent for invoking the time portal. As she concentrated, a tall silver mirror shimmered into view. For an instant she saw the five of them reflected, somber and dressed in the clothing of their own time rather than the strange garments of 1940.

Stepping forward, she laid her palm against the mirror. The silver surface turned black—and she pitched into the abyss, dragging her friends behind her.

Passing through time was getting a little easier with practice, though not by much. Tory still felt as if she were being torn into small pieces and reassembled. But for the first time her mind was clear enough that she sensed other pathways through the dark screaming chaos. Other portals leading to . . . different places? Different times?

Allarde's hand held hers in a death grip. Through him she felt the energy of the others, like notes of music.

Tory returned to normal space with wrenching abruptness. She collapsed on a cold chalk floor, the others crumpling down behind her. She almost passed out, but this time she managed to stay aware.

After a dozen gulping breaths, she sat up and surveyed her surroundings. Mage lights glowed on the ceiling. She may actually have succeeded in bringing them home the same night they'd left.

"That is a really terrible way to travel," Jack groaned as he sat up.

"A massive understatement," Elspeth said raggedly. "Are you all right, Cynthia?"

There was no reply. "Cynthia? Cynthia!" Elspeth rolled to her knees and laid her hands on the other girl's forehead and midriff. "She's not breathing!"

Terrified, Tory scrambled to her feet. She was still dizzy from the transit and lurched toward the wall. Allarde caught her before she crashed into it. She drew a steadying breath, then moved to Cynthia's side.

For an instant, Tory had the horrible impression that Cynthia was melting, her features distorted by the difficult passage. But then she blinked and Cynthia was her normal beautiful self, except for her corpselike pallor.

As Elspeth poured in her powerful healing energy, Jack grabbed hard on to Cynthia's hand, resting his other hand on Elspeth's arm. Tory and Allarde gripped Elspeth's shoulders, each of them adding their power. Tory couldn't see the magic, but she could feel its fierce potency, like a river of white fire.

Learning how to combine their powers was a vital part of what they learned down here in the secret underground school known as the Labyrinth. The aristocratic outcasts of Lackland Abbey studied as equals with talented locals like Jack. Collectively, they were Merlin's Irregulars, sworn to use their magic to defend Britain.

Tory had a special gift for blending different magics, and she'd needed that as the five of them pooled their power and varied skills to control weather over the English Channel. They'd been aided by twentieth-century Rainfords who were descendants of Jack's family. Together, they'd enabled the evacuation of hundreds of thousands of Allied troops desperate to escape the Nazis.

This time, their combined power was channeled through Elspeth, the best healer. After an agonizing moment, Cynthia choked, gasped, and breathed again. Opening dazed eyes, she snarled, *"I. Am. Never. Going. Through. That. Horrible. Mirror. Again!"*

Tory laughed and sat back on her heels. "You don't have to. None of us do. We're heroes and heroines of Britain, even if we can't tell anyone." Nor would anyone believe them if they did speak. "Now we settle back into our normal lives."

She tugged Cynthia's skirt down so the other girl's trim ankles weren't exposed. Probably it was silly to worry about that when all three girls had worn shockingly short skirts and even trousers in the twentieth century. But here, it mattered.

"I've had enough adventure for now." Jack slid an arm under Cynthia's shoulders to help her sit up. As soon as she was sitting, Cynthia batted his hand away with a scowl. Jack grinned at her. "You're recovering well, I see." Which made her scowl even more.

Jack got to his feet, moving with less than his usual bounce. "The mage lights are the same as when we left, so I think you successfully brought us back to the same night, Tory. I'll see if there's anyone still in the hall."

Elspeth made a face. "If this isn't the same night, we'll have a lot of explaining to do to the Lackland masters."

Allarde looked thoughtful. "What would happened if we returned before we left? Could we meet ourselves then?"

Cynthia looked horrified. "That would be awful!"

Tory frowned, wondering how she'd feel about meeting herself. The idea made her stomach queasy. "I'm not sure that could happen. It doesn't feel possible."

"I hope you're right. The idea is just too strange," Jack said. "I'll report back as soon as I've checked out the hall." He walked swiftly down the passage, conjuring up a mage light to illuminate his path as he turned the corner.

Cynthia attempted to stand and made it up with the aid of Allarde's hand. She'd always had her eyes on him. Even though she grudgingly recognized that it was Tory Allarde wanted, she still looked for excuses to touch him. Tory was confident enough of the bond between her and Allarde that she didn't mind. Much.

As Cynthia leaned against a wall, a small object came flying through the mirror. They all jumped, then stared as a paper-wrapped stone clattered along the passage and stopped near Allarde. He scooped it up, undid the paper and grinned. "It's for you, Tory."

She took the paper and called down a mage light from the ceiling to help her read. "It's a message from Nick," she said with surprise. "He wanted to see if it's possible to send messages through the portal."

"Apparently it is," Elspeth said. "And much easier than traveling in person!"

The rock and paper looked perfectly normal, unchanged by their journey through time. Tory asked, "Does anyone have a pencil?"

Allarde pulled one from inside his coat. "As my lady wishes."

She gave him a private smile before scrawling, *"It worked! We all got back safely and never want to travel through the mirror again! Tory."*

After neatly retying the paper around the rock, she faced the mirror and concentrated on the destination she wanted to reach. *1940, Nick Rainford . . .*

When the goal was crystal clear in her mind, she tossed the rock through the mirror. The missile touched the surface of the shining energy and vanished. "We'll have to check here regularly in case he sends more messages."

Elspeth frowned. "With such a huge war going on, there will be other crises where someone will think our magic is useful. They might want us to come back."

"They can ask," Cynthia said tartly. "We don't have to agree."

"I don't intend to. But I'm glad we can communicate with our friends," Elspeth said softly. "We all became so close when we worked together. I feel like all of the Rainfords are family."

"So do I," Allarde agreed. "But I'm another who is in no hurry to travel through Merlin's mirror again!"

Cynthia straightened up from the wall, looking frail but noble. "I still feel weak, but I want to get back to my own bed." She glanced hopefully at Allarde.

"Let me help you," Elspeth said, taking the other girl's arm. "I can add some healing energy if you need more." The mischievous spark in her pale green eyes showed that she knew what Cynthia had hoped for.

Cynthia accepted the other girl's arm with a martyred air and the two of them headed toward the main hall. Allarde offered Tory his arm. "My lady?"

She took a firm hold of his arm with a mixture of pleasure and wistfulness. "I'm going to miss the freedom to be together that we had in 1940."

"So will I." The two girls ahead were out of sight, so he paused and cupped her face with his free hand. "But the Lackland authori-

ties can't keep us here forever. At twenty-one, we'll be free to leave."
He bent into a kiss.

His lips were warm and full of longing. Tory had to blink back
tears or risk disgracing herself. More than four long years to wait
before she could leave . . .

Chaos!

The passageway dissolved into darkness and gunfire. She was in
some high, frightening place with a vicious wind tearing at her clothes
and deadly peril threatening her. She cried out in terror, "Justin!"

"Dear God, Tory! What just happened?" In the space of a heart-
beat she was back in the Labyrinth, shaking in Allarde's arms while
he stared at her, his gray eyes shocked.

Using his Christian name instead of his title was a mark of how
upset she was. She struggled for composure. "I had a . . . a vision, I
guess."

"I saw it, too," he said grimly. "It was night and you were in a high
place with bullets blazing around you. I think I was near, but not
with you."

"Nick's war again." She swallowed hard. "You're better at foretelling than I am. Is that a glimpse of the future?"

He closed his eyes, his face smoothing into detachment. After a
dozen heartbeats, he said, "As you know, the future usually appears
as possibility, not certainty. I think that scene has a strong chance of
coming to pass. But not certain."

Her mouth twisted. "Do I live to tell the tale?"

"I didn't feel your death." He opened haunted eyes and smoothed
back her hair with a warm hand. "But that might be too great a horror for me to see."

She gave a choke of near-hysterical laughter. "Justin, sometimes I
wish you were a little less honest and honorable. What I really want
right now is for you to pat my back and say, 'Don't worry, Tory, that's
just a faint possibility, or maybe a memory of Dunkirk. You don't
ever have to go back to 1940 again.' "

"Don't worry, Tory, that's just a faint possibility," he said promptly as he began stroking her back. "Maybe a memory of Dunkirk. You don't ever have to go back to 1940 again."

"That's *much* better." She managed a smile. "I prefer to think that wasn't a vision, just a memory."

His arms tightened around her. "No one can force you through the mirror without your cooperation."

"It's hard to imagine what circumstances might change my mind." She rested her head on his shoulder, feeling tired. "But I suspect that I should never say never."

"You're probably right. But for tonight, we're home and happy, and we were part of a very great deed." He kissed her forehead, then resumed walking, this time with his arm around her shoulders.

Tory wrapped her arm around his waist so they were as close as humanly possible while still able to walk. She'd nearly lost him, but she hadn't. There was no point to worrying about the future so much that she couldn't enjoy the present.

"Do you hear those voices?" Allarde asked, his voice threaded with excitement.

"Yes!" Tory exclaimed.

They quickened their pace. The heart of the Labyrinth was a wide hall furnished like a shabby but comfortable drawing room. Here the Lackland students and the locals studied and mingled. Now it sparkled with mage lights and happy chatter.

They'd arrived back only minutes after leaving because the people who had seen them off at the mirror hadn't gone home yet. Jack was in a three-way hug with his mother and his younger sister, Rachel, all of them talking and laughing at the same time.

Cynthia and Elspeth were talking excitedly with Miss Wheaton and Mr. Stephens. The teachers were both powerful mages, and they risked their jobs by tutoring students secretly in this mass of ancient tunnels that ran below the abbey. They looked fascinated and deeply relieved to have their students back safely.

Tory sighed happily and leaned into Allarde. They'd had the adventure of a lifetime and made it home. She hoped she never had such an adventure again.

But as she thought back to her chaotic vision, she felt dark certainty that Merlin's mirror wasn't done with her.

CHAPTER 2

Bong . . . bong . . . BONG! Tory awoke in her Lackland bedroom as
the bell boomed from the chapel tower. Usually the sound was jar-
ring, but this morning the familiar clanging made her happy. So
much nicer to hear a chapel bell than Nazi bombers.

"I'm so glad to be home," she said as she threw the covers back,
wincing at the bruises she'd acquired when she landed on this side of
the mirror.

It was cold at the end of November, and would be colder soon.
She swung her feet to the floor, glad for the rug her mother had sent.

Cynthia was already out of bed, brushing out her glorious golden
hair. By the time they'd finished their work in 1940, she'd looked pale
and exhausted, though still beautiful. A good night's sleep had completely restored her looks.

"How do you do it?" Tory asked enviously. "Always look so
perfect."

"It's a gift," Cynthia said smugly.

Tory almost laughed. Though Cynthia had proved herself a trouper in 1940, it was too much to expect humility. As a duke's daughter, Cynthia was the highest ranking girl at Lackland, a fact she was not shy about pointing out. Tory also ranked high as the daughter of an earl—but not as high as Cynthia. "Now that we're back, it's hard to believe we were away, much less that we had such adventures."

"Like a dream, or a nightmare." Cynthia made a face. "But I'm glad I wasn't born in such a vulgar era."

Tory sighed as she brushed out her straight dark hair. Her older sister, Sarah, said that Tory's petite figure and exotically slanted blue eyes made her very winsome and attractive, but next to Cynthia, Tory always felt plain as a muffin. Thinking of Sarah, she said, "I wonder what Lackland is like over Christmas. I thought I'd be going home for the holiday, but . . . that won't happen."

She splashed icy water from the china washbasin on her face to cool her stinging eyes. Her father had told her she couldn't return to Fairmount Hall even though Sarah was to be married at Christmas. Tory hated knowing she'd miss the wedding.

"There's a long, boring church service in the boys' chapel since it's larger than ours. That's followed by a joint Christmas dinner for both schools. It's one of the few official occasions when boys and girls mingle." Cynthia rolled her eyes. "Under the gimlet gaze of the teachers, of course. But the food is usually decent, and there are some students who are brothers and sisters, so they get to visit."

"You've been here for Christmas?" Tory asked, surprised. She'd always had the impression that Cynthia's father would want her home when possible.

Cynthia turned away to select a gown from her clothespress. "My family's seat is too far north to make returning for Christmas practical."

There was a note in the other girl's voice that made Tory wonder if the duke was as fond a father as Cynthia claimed. Not a subject she dared ask about, especially before breakfast. "After the other students leave, we can go into the woods and gather holly and ivy and other greens to decorate the room. I'll ask my mother to send a Christmas pudding. We can also leave the abbey through the Labyrinth and visit some of the Irregulars who live in the village."

"They are *commoners*," Cynthia snapped. "Why would we want to visit them?"

"Because they're our friends?" Tory asked mildly. "Jack is a hero, and I've learned so much from others like Alice and Rachel." She'd learned not only magic, but that being wellborn was less important than character and personality.

Cynthia coiled her hair at the nape of her neck and stabbed in a long hairpin. "That doesn't mean one joins such people for Christmas dinner."

There was no point in arguing with Lady Cynthia Stanton when she was in this mood. Changing the subject, Tory asked, "Do you need help fastening that gown? We'll have to hurry to get to chapel on time."

"Please," Cynthia said grudgingly. Tory's Lackland wardrobe contained only garments that she could put on without help, while most of Cynthia's clothing required the assistance of a maid. Usually one of Cynthia's adoring acolytes, Lucy, came to help her dress, but Tory remembered that the other girl had a streaming cold and had stayed abed for the last several days. Strange to think that Tory had lived over two eventful weeks between her today and her "yesterday"!

Tory tied and pinned the back of Cynthia's gown. When her roommate started to fuss with her hair, Tory said, "I'll see you later. I'm off for the chapel now so I can find a seat in the back."

She donned her dark red cloak and headed out into the drafty corridor. Other girls were emerging sleepily from their rooms to go to the chapel. Being late for the morning service would call down the Reverend Hackett's wrath.

A plump girl stepped out of a room near the stairs. "Good morning, Tory," she said with a cheerful smile. "I fear that winter has arrived!"

Tory wistfully remembered the June warmth they'd left in 1940. "The wind from the North Sea would freeze a goose in its tracks, Nell."

Like most Lackland students, Nell Bracken's greatest dream was to be cured of her despised abilities so she could go home. Tory had been like that until the siren call of magic had lured her to the Labyrinth and she had discovered the Irregulars.

But she was still friends with Nell, a motherly sort who looked out for all the new students. Tory would never forget Nell's kindness when she first arrived, shocked and disoriented at being exiled from her home.

Nell frowned as she fell into step beside Tory. "You have great circles under your eyes and I swear you seem to have lost weight between yesterday and today. Do you think you're sickening for something?"

"I feel fine, it's only that this dress is loose," Tory replied, though she'd indeed lost weight in 1940. Using so much magic literally burned a person up. "Plus I slept badly last night."

"Cynthia?" Nell nodded knowingly. "I don't know how you manage with her as a roommate."

"She's not so bad now that I'm used to her," Tory said offhandedly. Nell would never believe it if Tory said she'd grown rather fond of her impossible roommate.

Nell looked skeptical but refrained from further comment. They descended the stairs and walked outside onto the chapel path. A blast of wind hit them and the air was so cold their breath came out in white puffs.

"I'm so much looking forward to going home for Christmas," Nell said confidingly. "I've been corresponding with a young man back home. We have . . . much to discuss." Her smile was mischievous.

"If he's wise, he'll offer marriage," Tory said. "Miss Wheaton said you'd be able to leave Lackland soon, and no one would make a kinder or better tempered wife."

Nell made a face. "You know that magic reduces our value on the marriage mart." Her voice dropped. "But George and I have reached an understanding. His father's the local doctor and George is studying medicine, too. My family would never approve such a match if I hadn't been cursed by magic, but George doesn't mind."

"How wonderful!" Tory said with delight. Too often girls were released from the school but not welcomed back by their families. They faced a grim future of teaching or becoming companions. But some were lucky, and no one deserved it more than Nell.

Girls who managed to find husbands invariably married down into a lower social level. Even though students were considered "cured" of magic, children could still inherit their power, making them undesirable mates within their own class.

Once Tory thought that marrying down was unfortunate, but no longer. A good, loving husband who accepted his wife's nature was a treasure.

The ancient stone chapel had a lovely sense of peace, but managed to be even colder than outdoors. Though there was always competition for seats in the back of the room, Helen and Penelope, two other members of Nell's group, had arrived early enough to save half a pew. Tory sat beside Nell and tried to look unobtrusive.

The pews were miserably hard, but she'd learned early that the daily services were a good time for her to practice mental exercises to improve her magical control. With her focus turned inward, she could usually ignore Mr. Hackett's condemnation of mages and magic and wicked young girls cursed with sinful abilities.

Tory's happiness about being back at Lackland was fading by the end of the service. For one thing, she was freezing. Away from the school, she'd be able to warm herself with hearth-witch magic, but power was smothered in the abbey by a huge magical suppression spell. That spell was why the abbey had been chosen for the school.

The school authorities liked to think that monks and nuns of centuries gone past had suppressed magic because they hated it. Actually, the ancient order who had built the abbey had done so to train mages. Power was driven belowground and intensified in the Labyrinth. In the abbey proper, only the most powerful mages could use any magic.

Tory was so cold that she couldn't concentrate on her mental exercises, so she heard too much of Mr. Hackett's angry rant. In 1940, magic had been largely forgotten, but at least people like Tory weren't despised for their talents.

Breakfast in the refectory was also familiar, though not in a good way. The long room wasn't much warmer than the chapel and the porridge had chilled. Nell frowned as she and Tory collected their bowls. "It's always like this the first really cold day of the year. Tomorrow the room and porridge will be somewhat warmer."

"I certainly hope so," Tory said as she regarded the congealed mass and thought wistfully of the huge, tasty breakfasts the weather brigade had been fed to keep up their strength when they were calming the seas.

At least the tea was steaming hot. Tory suspected the students would riot if the tea wasn't decent.

Sipping her tea, Tory watched the girls split into their usual three groups. Cynthia fit seamlessly back into her circle of haughty, angry girls who deeply resented their exile at Lackland. They were a difficult lot.

The smallest group was Elspeth and her friends, the students who embraced their magic. They were resigned to staying at Lackland until they turned twenty-one. Then they would leave and become practicing mages. Though the girls who loved magic were avoided by other students, they were relaxed and happy with what they were.

The largest group centered around Nell Bracken. These were the girls who wanted nothing more than to be cured so they could leave Lackland and try to reclaim what they could of their old lives. They considered themselves the most normal students at the school.

Tory had been happy to be taken under Nell's wing. Nell and her friends were pleasant and easy to like.

But Tory no longer belonged here. She should be sitting at the far table with Elspeth and the others who embraced their abilities. If she moved across the room and sat with them, she would be politely dropped by Nell and the others, who abhorred any suggestion that they approved of magic or mages.

If Tory publicly declared herself a mage, there would be no going back. Even her brother and sister, who accepted her now on the assumption that she wanted to be cured, might change their minds if she revealed herself to be an unrepentant mage.

Tory had never liked the rigid separations between the groups, and now she liked them even less. Why shouldn't Tory publicly be friends with Cynthia and Elspeth as well as Nell? But that wasn't how the school worked.

With a sigh, she applied herself to her cold oatmeal. She was home after terrifying adventures—and her old problems were still here waiting.

At least they were small problems compared to being shot.

The day got worse when Tory went to her Italian class. The teacher was Miss Macklin, a fervent hater of magic and not fond of young ladies, either. Since Tory's father was a firm believer in education, even for daughters, Tory had done very well on her entrance evaluation when she started at the school. Miss Macklin had never forgiven her for that.

Tory's French was better than Miss Macklin's so she'd been placed in the Italian class instead. She would have enjoyed learning a new language if not for Miss Macklin's constant criticism.

Besides being angry all the time, Miss Macklin wasn't a very good teacher. She managed to make a beautiful language boring. Today the classroom was cold and the chairs were almost as hard as the pews in the chapel.

Tired from her fortnight of exertion, Tory dozed a little toward the end of a boring set of grammar exercises. Her hands were neatly folded on her desk and she was sitting upright, but her eyes drifted shut. Her whole body was saturated with fatigue. . . .

"Abominable girl!" Miss Macklin's furious words jerked Tory to full awareness an instant before the teacher's brass ruler smashed across the back of Tory's hands.

Tory cried out as pain stabbed through her hands, particularly the left, which took the worst of the blow. Miss Macklin had struck her twice during her initial evaluation, but not since. Tears in her eyes, she shoved her chair away from her desk, distancing herself from the triumphant teacher.

Mercifully, the bell rang to end the class. Tory grabbed her notebook with her less-bruised right hand and bolted from the room, wondering if her fingers were broken.

The corridor was full of girls changing classes. Elspeth, who was also a student of Italian, murmured at Tory's shoulder, "Go into that room ahead on the left. It should be empty now. Maybe I can reduce the pain."

Blinking back tears, Tory obeyed. Though most magic was suppressed inside the abbey walls, very strong mages like Elspeth could use some of their power.

When they were in the small, unoccupied office, Elspeth closed the door to give them privacy, then took Tory's left hand gently between her palms. "Your hands are like ice!" she exclaimed.

"This is a very cold building," Tory said gloomily. "I'm not looking forward to January. The wind off the North Sea must freeze people solid. I wish I had enough hearth-witch magic to really warm myself up, but inside the abbey, I can barely manage to take the worst of the chill off."

"That must hurt like blazes. I hope I can draw enough power to help." Elspeth closed her eyes and concentrated. White heat surged through Tory's hand, warming her fingers as well as smoothing away the pain.

"That's wonderful!" Tory removed her left hand from Elspeth's grasp and examined it. Apart from fading red marks, there was no sign of the vicious blow, and all the pain was gone. "I'm surprised you could do so much within the abbey."

Elspeth's brow furrowed. "So am I. Give me your other hand."

"It's not as bad," Tory said as she complied. "I really think she broke some bones in my left hand. The right is just badly bruised. You don't need to tire yourself out with more magic."

Ignoring that, Elspeth clasped Tory's right hand and sent another long wave of healing energy. When she was done, she asked, "How's that?"

Tory flexed her fingers in surprise. "As good as new. I'm impressed!"

"So am I," Elspeth said thoughtfully. "Try hearth magic to warm yourself up."

Tory closed her eyes and visualized warmth sweeping through her. So much heat surged that she felt feverish. Startled, she released the magic. "Good heavens, I've never been able to create so much warmth inside the abbey!"

Elspeth examined her own hands as if they belonged to a stranger. "Remarkable. I can draw major power in spite of the suppression spell."

Tory used the hearth-witch magic again, more carefully this time, and found she could make herself comfortably warm with little effort. "So can I."

"This must be a result of working so furiously for days on end," Elspeth said. "I used more magic during the evacuation than everything I'd done in the previous five years put together."

"I suppose it's like playing the pianoforte. The more we practice, the stronger our skills become." Tory cocked her head. "Now that I think of it, I'm not feeling as crushed by the Lackland magical suppression spells as before. I'm still aware of them, but the feeling is nowhere near as smothering."

"This is worth all the grueling work we did!" Elspeth said. "Now it's time to get along to the next class. I'll leave first."

She peeked out the door, then left. Tory sighed, wishing they could leave together. Elspeth said she didn't mind being publicly ignored.

But Tory minded.

CHAPTER 3

Three nights a week study sessions were held in the Labyrinth, and there was one that night. Despite her fatigue, Tory looked forward to seeing the other Irregulars. Especially Allarde. She and Cynthia went together, quietly slipping through the concealed entrance in the cellar of the classroom building.

As they closed the door behind them, Tory was stropped on the ankles by a tabby she'd befriended. She bent to scratch the cat's neck. "Yes, puss, I brought you a bit of ham from dinner." The tabby daintily took the tidbit from her fingers.

"Why do you spoil that cat?" Cynthia asked.

"Cats keep the tunnels free of rats and mice," Tory said as she straightened and created a mage light to guide them through the Labyrinth. "Besides, I like cats."

"I'd rather have a horse."

Cynthia set off and Tory fell in beside her. The ancient chalk tunnels were centuries old, and the floors were worn by the passage of countless feet. First nuns, now students. The passage was just wide enough for two girls to walk abreast, if one of them wasn't very large. "Have you found that your magic is stronger since you returned?"

"I don't use magic in the abbey because the suppression spell is so irritating. Let's see what happens." Cynthia held out a hand and created a ball of light on her palm. It flared blindingly. She squeaked and let go of the light. The globe hovered in front her, dimming as she reduced her power. "Good heavens! Usually I have to concentrate to make a mage light, but that was easy."

"Elspeth and I have both noticed that we have more power," Tory said thoughtfully. "I was able to use enough hearth witchery to warm myself in the abbey, and I've never managed that before."

"I'm glad to hear that we might get some benefit from going through the mirror!" Cynthia exclaimed as they resumed walking. When they turned a corner, the sounds of many voices echoed down the corner. She frowned. "Do you think it's another raid?"

"I certainly hope not!" Tory had been fleeing a raid by the school authorities when she discovered Merlin's mirror. Not a pleasant experience, even though it had worked out well. She cocked her head. "They're happy voices. Celebrating?"

A slow smile spread over Cynthia's face. "Return of the heroes! That's us."

They reached the main hall where groups of people were laughing and talking and eating. They seemed to be the last to arrive. Tory was used to being last when she waited for Cynthia to ready herself.

Jack Rainford approached them, a grin on his face and a tankard in his hands. "About time you two appeared! We've been telling the other Irregulars about our adventures. I brought in a cask of cider so we could celebrate."

"Is this the kind of cider that can flatten an ox in its tracks?" Tory asked warily.

"Have a taste." He handed her the tankard. "It's fresh made a few weeks ago from our own apples and hasn't aged long enough to have much kick. My mother wouldn't let me bring the ox-flattening cider."

She sipped and found that the cider had just a light alcoholic tingle amidst fizzing apple flavors. "Very nice!" She handed the tankard back. "Has everyone heard the story of Dunkirk?"

"Indeed they have." Allarde approached them, his gaze warm when it met Tory's. "We've been telling everyone what a wonderful job the two of you did."

"We all worked together," Tory said uncomfortably. "Those of us who traveled through the mirror couldn't have done what we did without all the study sessions here."

Cynthia elbowed her in the ribs. "Relax and enjoy the appreciation, Tory. We did something quite wonderful, and it wasn't easy!"

"True, but Tory's right, too," Allarde said thoughtfully. "When we joined the Irregulars, we swore an oath to use our abilities to protect Britain. Now we've proved that magelings can make a difference. Our success is everyone's success. That's particularly important for those of us who were raised to be ashamed of our magic."

"Not like us lucky locals, whose families celebrated when we showed talent," Jack said cheerfully. "But enough theory. Come along, your ladyship. Time to collect your applause."

He set a light hand at the back of Cynthia's waist and guided her into the middle of the celebrating students. Despite Cynthia's snobbery, she had become more relaxed with Jack, Tory noticed. As the two most talented weather mages, they'd worked closely during the evacuation. Perhaps Cynthia was beginning to realize that one could be a good person without aristocratic bloodlines.

Now it was just Tory and Allarde. Not really private with so many people across the room, but a private moment. She gave him a wry smile. "In 1940, it was easy to joke about me ruining my reputation. Here the subject is serious."

He nodded. "That wasn't where we belonged, so we didn't have reputations. Here, our actions have real consequences."

She was relieved that he felt as she did. Before returning through the mirror, they'd done some kissing that was rather beyond what was acceptable for a young lady in 1803, though well short of ruination. "Here holding hands is rather bold."

"But acceptable." Eyes alight, he extended his hand.

She clasped it, interlacing her fingers as warmth and connection flowed through her. With a quiet sigh, she moved close and leaned against him. The top of her head barely cleared his shoulder. With Allarde, she felt . . . safe. And justly so. When they'd been under fire, he had twice protected her with his own body.

He caressed her with his other hand, skimming lightly from the back of her neck down to her waist, where his warm palm rested for a moment. Exhaling roughly, he moved away a step. "I've just moved a bit beyond the bounds of propriety."

"I started it." Her smile was crooked. "I'd like more, but—being with you is enough."

"Indeed it is," he said huskily. "Ever since we returned, I've been aware of you all the time, but it's a distant shadow. Not like when we're down here." He squeezed her hand. "Not at all as strong as when we touch."

"I always feel a thread of connection with you, too," she said slowly. "Elspeth and Cynthia and I have all found that our magic is stronger now. Have you noticed that?"

Allarde looked surprised, then thoughtful. "Let's see. My strongest talent is moving objects . . ." He turned and gazed at one of the worn sofas scattered about the hall. It was set near a wall and currently unoccupied.

The sofa shot up in the air. "Good God!" He stopped the sofa just short of bashing into the ceiling. A few people glanced at the floating piece of furniture, then returned to their socializing. Such sights weren't uncommon in the Labyrinth.

"A good thing I picked a sofa no one was sitting on," he said as he lowered it to the floor. "Now that I'm aware, I can feel the difference in my magic."

"Our theory is that we used our magic so intensely that we

strengthened it," Tory said. "Even up in the school under the suppression spell, I have more power."

"Miss Wheaton and Mr. Stephens will be interested to know that." Allarde's warm hand tightened over hers as they walked deeper into the hall. Tory was very aware of his clasp. Holding hands was an open declaration that they were a couple.

Allarde was handsome, admired, and, as the heir to a duke, the highest-ranking student in the school. In short, he was what a matchmaking mama would call a great catch. Before Tory, he'd never become involved with a Lackland girl, never even flirted.

No wonder other girls looked envious. Tory suspected they wondered what he saw in her. Though she was passably pretty, she was no beauty. Not like Cynthia. But after their adventures on the other side of the mirror, she and Allarde knew each other far better than if they'd been normal young people meeting in London ballrooms.

As they moved across the room, Allarde said, "I'm going to miss you over the Christmas holiday, but I'm sure you'll be glad to return home. I always look forward to being there despite the complications of . . . what I am."

She bit her lip. "I won't be going to Fairmount Hall. My father won't allow it. I . . . I'll miss my sister's wedding."

"You can't go home?" He hesitated, his gray eyes dismayed. "I can stay, too. We'll be able to spend more time together since there won't be any classes."

Though it was a tempting offer, she shook her head. "You're very generous, but I don't want you to miss your visit home. I'll manage here very nicely."

He looked unconvinced. "You're sure?"

"I'm sure." Since he could sense her emotions as she could sense his, she projected conviction and contentment. His expression smoothed out.

She could indeed manage without him. But it would be a long three weeks.

The days leading up to the Christmas holidays quickly fell back into the usual Lackland pattern of classes and meals and walks on the walled grounds. Tory liked peering through the holes in the stone lattice fence that divided the girls' school gardens from the boys' playing fields.

The fence carried a spell that made it impossible to brick up the holes. The spell also made it impossible to climb over the fence, but boys and girls could talk through it, and even touch. When the boys were playing the endless ball games that occupied much of the time they weren't in classes, the girls watched.

The first time Tory had seen Allarde had been through the fence. She'd noticed him instantly. Even then, his height and strength and swiftness had mesmerized her. She and Allarde tried to meet at the fence every day. Just touching their fingers through the lattice made any problems melt away. When she wasn't with him—the cold stone buildings made her grateful that her magic was strong enough to keep her warm.

In her regular classes, Tory managed to avoid being struck by Miss Macklin again. The teacher had enough targets among students who were so excited to be going home that they didn't pay attention to their lessons.

Study sessions in the Labyrinth were serious work, so she and Allarde didn't spend much time together. But at least they were breathing the same air.

Before the sessions began, the two of them would walk to the tunnel containing Merlin's mirror. Tory tried not to block her awareness of the portal. If the blasted thing appeared, it might decide to sweep them to a different time. Best to let it sleep.

Once or twice a week, there would be messages from Nick or Polly Rainford. Their father had been given a fortnight's home leave after being rescued from Dunkirk. To his family's delight, he was then assigned to British intelligence based near London rather than sent back into combat.

Britain had adjusted to the prospect of a long and difficult war that they were determined to win. The American president was making good on his promise to send military aid. Tory read the newspaper clippings of the future somberly, and gave thanks that the current war against Napoleon was much more distant than what the Rainfords were experiencing. She tried not to think of a high dark place with bullets flying.

After, she and Allarde would share a good-night kiss before heading back to their rooms. Tory memorized each and every kiss. She'd need them while Allarde was gone.

CHAPTER 4

On the day the holiday break began, the chapel service was longer than usual and particularly virulent because Mr. Hackett wouldn't be able to vent his spleen to the whole girls' school for three weeks. Already some students had left, including Allarde, and classes hadn't accomplished much in several days.

After the midday meal, Tory returned to her room, trying not to feel sorry for herself because she would be spending her first Christmas without her family. Cynthia was sitting by the window for the best light as she beaded a small purse.

Tory was competent with a needle. Lessons had been mandatory since it was considered a ladylike "accomplishment." But she didn't particularly enjoy sewing and avoided it when possible. Cynthia actually liked needlework and did exquisite work.

"That purse is coming along well," Tory said. "The gold thread sets off the design perfectly."

Cynthia stretched complacently. "It *is* one of my best pieces."

Tory looked out the window, which showed the English Channel in the distance beyond the abbey grounds. The sea was winter gray today. On the opposite side of the channel, Napoleon Bonaparte blustered and plotted to invade England.

She prayed that never happened. She'd seen enough of war in 1940. "I am so tired of girls talking about all the exciting things they'll do over the holidays. It will be a relief when they're all gone."

"So much chatter!" Cynthia agreed. "I'll be glad when we have quiet. With fewer students to feed, the meals are a bit better as well."

Quiet sounded good, but three weeks of quiet would be excessive. Tory planned to leave the school via the Labyrinth tunnels so she could visit with some of the Irregulars who lived in Lackland village. Jack and Rachel Rainford had already invited her to come. If Cynthia didn't choose to come with her, it would be her loss.

"I'm looking forward to sleeping late," Tory remarked. "That will give the room more time to heat up after Peggy builds the fire."

"If that lazy maid started at this end of the corridor, we'd be warm sooner every morning," Cynthia grumbled.

True, but a girl at the other end of the corridor had weak lungs and needed the heat more. Knowing better than to appeal to Cynthia's better nature, Tory said, "I must work on my hearth-witch skills. Perhaps I can learn how to heat the whole room without using too much power."

Cynthia frowned. "Hearth-witch magic is so vulgar."

Tory grinned. "But very practical."

A maid knocked on the door, calling, "A package for you, Miss Mansfield."

"Maybe it's the Christmas pudding I asked my mother to send," Tory said hopefully. She opened the door and saw Peggy carrying a small latched wooden box. "Maybe it's two Christmas puddings!"

"There's a letter, too, miss," the maid said. "Where would you like me to set this?"

"On my desk." Tory rapidly stacked her books on the floor so there would be room for the box. "Thank you, Peggy."

She accepted the letter, but set it down, more interested in what the box contained. As she removed the crushed newspapers and rags that were used as packing, Cynthia joined her, drawn by the delicious scents of exotic, expensive spices. "Surely we don't have to wait until Christmas to sample?" she asked hopefully.

"We must wait," Tory said firmly. She lifted out a dark bottle and pulled the cork. After sniffing, she said, "Here's the brandy to flame the pudding when the time comes." She tilted the bottle for her roommate to smell.

"Very nice French brandy," Cynthia said approvingly.

"Here's a pot of brandy butter to serve on top." Tory pulled out a small crock. "And here's the pudding!" She flourished the pudding high in the air, no small feat given its size. The pudding had been wrapped in layers of cheesecloth for steaming, and had the weight, shape, and density of a cannonball.

"That's large enough to serve every girl still here with enough left for the next day," Cynthia observed. "Perhaps we should have some now to reduce the size."

Tory grinned. "It will taste better with more aging. But my mother would know we would be tempted." She dug into the box again and brought up a tin box. "If this is what I think it is . . ."

She pried the tight tin open to reveal a box packed with dense shortbread bars dusted with nutmeg. On top of the bars were two shapes wrapped in paper stained by the butter used in the rich shortbread. Tory unwrapped one to reveal a shortbread cake cut in the shape of a star with bright sparkles of sugar on top. "She knew we wouldn't want to wait, so these are for now." She handed one star to Cynthia, then unwrapped the other.

"She did this for me?" Cynthia's voice sounded vulnerable instead of imperious. "That was very kind of her."

Tory knew her roommate's mother had died, though not when or how. If she'd grown up without maternal warmth, it explained a great deal about her. "My mother is very kind," she agreed. "Except about standing up to my father about my magic."

"Standing up to fathers is very difficult." Cynthia bit into the rich, crumbly star cake and sighed with pleasure.

Tory's mother had some magic herself. Fear that she'd be discovered prevented her from supporting her daughter. Tory understood, but it was hard to forgive. She took a bite of her own star. "Lovely. My mother and sister and I would always spend a day doing Christmas baking down in the kitchen."

"You know how to *cook*?" Cynthia's tone would have been the same if Tory had just confessed to murder.

"My mother thought we should know cookery because someday we'd be running a great household." Tory took a second small bite, wanting the shortbread to last as long as possible. It melted in her mouth with luxurious richness. "I rather like cooking, just like you enjoy embroidery."

"Needlework is ladylike." Cynthia finished the star and took one of the shortbread bars from the tin box. "Cookery is for servants."

"One can't eat a reticule, no matter how beautifully it's embroidered."

"Food gets eaten. People will admire my stitchery long after I'm gone."

Since Cynthia was eyeing the tin box again, Tory took out a last bar for herself, then snapped the lid back on. She belatedly reached for the letter that had been delivered. "This is from my sister," she said, recognizing the lovely penmanship. "She's probably writing to express her regret that I'll miss the wedding." Tory broke the wax seal and began to read.

Dearest Tory,

When Papa announced that you will not be allowed to come home for Christmas and my wedding to Lord Roger, I was Outraged!

How dare he forbid you to return to your own home! It would make more sense if he was forbidding you London, where reputation must be watched more closely. But the wilds of Somersetshire???

By this time all the world knows that there is magic in the family. I've had people look at me oddly and perhaps move away. Since the damage has already been done, why not let you come home?

Since our distinguished Papa is being so stubborn, I have devised A Plan: Roger and I will marry at Geoffrey's estate in Shropshire.

Geoffrey and Cecilia are delighted to host the wedding, particularly since it means you will be there. They haven't forgotten that you saved Jamie's life. I shall never forget the Terror I felt when he fell over the cliff.

So I am sending this message in Lord Roger's coach, along with a maid to accompany you to Shropshire, and a trunk of your best gowns. I'm so looking forward to seeing you, little sister! It seems like an age. I want you to be there when I'm married.

Your favorite and only sister,
Sarah

Tory gasped with delight. "Cynthia, wonderful news!"

Her roommate had drifted back to her embroidery, but glanced up quizzically. "Your father is embracing magery and says you can come home."

"That isn't going to happen," Tory said wryly. "But my sister is so exasperated with him that she's moving her wedding to my brother's estate so I can come. I'll be able to spend Christmas with my family! Part of my family, anyhow. My sister sent a carriage with the message. Heavens, it must be waiting! I can leave right away."

Swift shock and pain flashed through Cynthia's eyes, gone almost before Tory saw it. She realized that her roommate had been looking forward to the two of them spending the holidays together. And from the way Cynthia crushed the purse in her hand, Tory realized it had been meant as a gift for her.

Dropping her gaze, Cynthia said nastily, "Good! I can have my room to myself again. It's such a nuisance to have you here all the time chattering nonsense."

Tory felt as if she'd been slapped. She had thought they were friends now.

She was about to snap back that it would be a relief to get away from Cynthia, but she reminded herself that her roommate was feeling hurt and betrayed. With Tory leaving, Cynthia would be left alone and unwanted. "I wish you could come with me," she said in a soft voice. "It would be more enjoyable that way."

Cynthia raised her head and glared. "Why would I want to go to a stupid wedding with people I don't know?"

"I would enjoy your company," Tory said mildly. Her remark was even mostly true. Should she invite Cynthia to go with her?

No, Tory wanted to be able to concentrate on her family and Sarah's wedding, not spend her time dealing with Cynthia's prickly moods. "But it would be wearying to bounce across England in a carriage just to be with strangers. You'll find it more amusing to celebrate with the others who will stay through the holidays."

"Most people staying are stupid magic lovers," Cynthia said sourly. "My particular friends are all leaving."

Cynthia would not appreciate having it pointed out that she was an Irregular and a "magic lover" herself. Nor would she welcome hearing that the snobby girls could not be very good friends if Cynthia couldn't be honest with them. Only with the Irregulars could Cynthia reveal her mageling talents. A pity that she was torn between what she was—a powerful mage—and what she wanted to be.

Tory was in the same position. If she lived to be a hundred, she would never forget the shock and pain of seeing her friends and neighbors turning away when her magic was revealed. They treated her like a plague carrier. She would have given anything to make her magic disappear.

Yet now, she wanted to use her magic and keep her mage friends. Every student at Lackland had to face this dilemma. Telling herself to be patient with Cynthia, Tory said, "I'd better pack. The carriage will be waiting."

She flung open the doors of her clothespress. Her school wardrobe was serviceable, but not suitable for a wedding. Since clever Sarah was sending her best clothes, there was no need for her heavy trunk. Her rugged canvas carrier bag would do.

After packing a few necessities, she jotted a quick note to Elspeth, who was still at the school but would be leaving the next day to spend Christmas with her former governess. *"Elspeth, I'm going to my sister's wedding! I shall explain after the holidays. Have a safe journey with much roast goose and gingerbread. Tory."*

She folded the note and crossed the room to give it to her roommate. "Tell everyone where I've gone and wish them happy Christmas for me."

Cynthia shrugged, not looking at her. "If you're going to go, *go!*"

Her rudeness would make it easy to be cross, if there hadn't been a glint of tears visible in Cynthia's eyes. Feeling uncomfortable, Tory said, "I'll leave you the Christmas pudding and brandy butter. I'm sure you'll enjoy it. The Fairmount cook is wonderful."

Her roommate gave her a seething glare. "Why would I want a stupid great cannonball pudding like that?"

Patience finally exhausted, Tory snapped, "You could try sharing it with other students, if you're capable of thinking about anyone but yourself!" She slung the long strap of the carrier bag over her shoulder, swept up her cloak, and stalked out.

When she returned, she should talk to the headmistress about moving to another room the next time there was a vacancy. When Tory first arrived at Lackland, the only bed available had been in the room Cynthia had to herself. Cynthia had not been pleased to be landed with a roommate.

Tory had admired the work Cynthia had done in 1940. There were times when Tory genuinely liked her roommate. But most of the time, Cynthia was just too much work. It was time for a change.

Cynthia managed to control herself until Tory left. Then she broke down into tears of rage. How dare Tory just run off like that? They had made plans for the holidays! Christmas would have been rather enjoyable if she and Tory had been able to gather greens and eat pudding and talk about their adventures.

Furiously she knocked the box of holiday treats from Tory's desk. The box crashed to the floor and the great ball of Christmas pudding bounced across the floor, protected by the layers of cheesecloth it had been steamed in.

Cynthia kicked the pudding with all her might, then gasped with pain when she bruised her unshod toes. The pudding rolled smoothly across the room and came to rest against the wall with a dull thud. The stupid thing wasn't even dented.

Her anger collapsed and she folded into the center of her bed, her arms wrapped around her as she sobbed uncontrollably. It wasn't *fair*! Tory had everything. She wasn't beautiful like Cynthia, but she had a sparkling charm that made everyone like her.

Allarde, who by rights should want Cynthia, couldn't take his eyes off Tory. And not only did Tory have lots of friends at Lackland and the handsomest beau in the school, she even had some family members who loved her despite her magic. *It wasn't fair!*

But maybe it was fair. Tory was much nicer than Cynthia. Even though she knew that her sharp tongue drove people away, Cynthia couldn't seem to stop.

Since she hated herself, it was only right that other people hated her, too.

CHAPTER 5

Tory scampered down the steps and outside the student quarters, moving as fast as she could without being a complete tomboy. She didn't slow her pace until she'd crossed the cloister garden and entered the main building.

Mrs. Grice, the headmistress, was waiting in the front hall, her lips pursed disapprovingly. "You certainly took your time," she snapped.

Tory cast her eyes down and assumed her most humble expression. "I'm sorry, Mrs. Grice. It took time to prepare for the journey since I didn't expect to leave today."

"This is irregular," the headmistress grumbled. "Most irregular. Lord Fairmount should have given me proper notification."

Tory concealed her surprise that Mrs. Grice thought Tory's father had summoned her. Sarah must have forged a note claiming to be from the earl. Clever sister. "I was taken by surprise also."

"Try not to disgrace the school while you're away," the headmistress said sourly.

Doing her best to look angelic, Tory bobbed a meek curtsy, then scooted out the door before anything could stop her.

The carriage that waited carried the family crest of Sarah's fiancé, Lord Roger Hawthorne, and the footman by the door was a stranger. But Tory's eyes widened at the sight of the girl waiting with downcast eyes and a smile she couldn't suppress. Molly Fulton had been Tory's maid when she lived at Fairmount Hall, and she'd offered warm comfort when Tory was disgraced and exiled to Lackland Abbey.

"Allow me to take your bag, Lady Victoria," the footman said, looking surprised at how little Tory was carrying.

She found it odd to be addressed by her title after months of being called Miss Mansfield. She climbed into the carriage, and Molly followed. The footman closed the door and climbed up onto the box with the driver, and the carriage set off.

As soon as they were private, Tory clasped the maid's hand with an enthusiasm that young ladies were not supposed to show to servants. "Molly, I'm so glad to see you! How did you get assigned to accompany me on this trip?"

Molly, a cheerful girl with sandy hair and freckles, replied, "I volunteered. The other maids didn't want to spend Christmas away from their families, but I wanted to see how you were doing, my lady."

Touched, Tory said, "How kind of you. It was difficult at first, but I've made friends. I enjoy most of the classes, and we're treated fairly well." She thought of Miss Macklin. "Most of the time. How have things been at Fairmount Hall?"

" 'Twas very quiet after you left, miss." Molly shook her head. "The house just isn't the same. Your father never speaks of you, your mother looks ready to cry, and Lady Sarah has already gone to your brother's house to prepare for the wedding."

Perhaps Tory should feel gratified that everyone else was unhappy, but mostly she was just sad. The happy home she'd grown up in was gone forever, shattered by the revelation of Tory's magical ability.

Ironically, her mother had power and Sarah had more or less admitted that she did, too. Only Tory was unlucky enough to be caught.

With a sigh, she settled into the cushioned seat. "I'm glad Sarah made it possible for me to come to her wedding."

"I can see why, miss!" Molly stared out the window at the gray stone buildings receding behind them as the carriage rattled down the long, curving entrance road. "As soon as the carriage came through the gate, I felt that I was being smothered." She shivered. "I'll be that glad to be away from here, miss. I don't know how you stand it."

Tory came alert. She'd felt the magical suppression spell the instant her father's carriage brought her inside Lackland's tall, forbidding walls. In fact, she'd felt—smothered. "Molly, that last night before I left Fairmount, you told me you had a touch of the sight. Have you ever felt other signs of magical power?"

Molly bit her lip. "I . . . I'm not sure, miss. Sometimes it feels like I might know something more than I should, but it's hard to be sure. Sometimes I have dreams that seem to be true, but they're not clear." She glanced out the carriage again. They were approaching the outer wall of the abbey. "Maybe I just imagine things."

Tory studied the other girl thoughtfully. "Did you volunteer for this journey because I might help you understand if you have magic?"

"That was part of the reason," Molly admitted, her cheeks pinking. "But I did want to see how you were faring, and it's also a chance to travel a bit. I've never been out of Somersetshire before, and now I've seen half of England."

Though the maid was striving to sound lighthearted, her uncomfortable glances out the window at the receding abbey suggested that she was very aware of the magical suppression. The real test would be when the carriage left the abbey grounds.

"How long will it take us to get to my brother's home?"

"This morning the driver said it would be two or three days if the weather holds."

Tory wondered if she'd learned enough weather magic to ensure that the weather stayed fair. She didn't want anything to delay her journey.

The carriage paused while the gatekeeper swung the great iron gates open, then the vehicle rumbled through. As they turned onto the road, Molly sighed with relaxation and leaned back in her facing seat. "I feel ever so much better now that we've left. I don't know how you bear that place, my lady."

"Molly, the fact that you reacted so strongly when entering and leaving the abbey suggests that you have magical ability," Tory said seriously. "A fair amount, judging by how much the suppression spell bothered you."

Molly's face lit up. "You really think so, miss?" When Tory nodded, Molly continued, "You've learned about magic even though Lackland exists to cure it?"

Tory didn't blame the other girl for being skeptical. Since she couldn't discuss the Irregulars, she said only, "Learning to control magic so it can be eliminated means teaching us a great deal about magic. I've done reading on the subject as well."

"Can you help me understand what power I might have?" Molly's hands twisted nervously together.

"Of course. We have a long ride ahead of us, and that's perfect for studying." Tory settled in her seat, amused that she would be able to act as a teacher on their journey. "Tell me about those dreams you have."

After two and a half days of swift, smooth travel, they were almost at Layton Place. Tory had abandoned her tutoring to stare out the window and watch for landmarks to appear. Soon, soon . . . "There!" she said excitedly. "See the ruined castle on top of that hill? We'll turn into the drive of Layton Place in just a few minutes."

"Have you been here often, miss?" Molly was bright-eyed with interest. She maintained the politeness required of her position, but with the intensive teaching and practice they'd done during the trip, the relationship had changed. They were no longer mistress and maid, but mageling and eager student.

"Only once, after Jamie was born. My parents were very excited and wanted to see the next generation of the Earls of Fairmount." Tory swallowed against the tightness in her throat. She'd been fourteen then and never dreamed how her family would be shattered. "It's a new house, only about forty years old. Very comfortable."

"Will there be many guests?"

"I'm not sure. Probably just the families, and perhaps a few very close friends." Tory knew her father wouldn't come, but she couldn't imagine that her mother would miss Sarah's wedding.

"This will give me a chance to practice reading other people's possessions," Molly said, eyes gleaming.

"Just remember what I said about respecting people's privacy, and not gossiping about what you learn, or think you've learned," Tory cautioned.

"Yes, my lady." Molly's words were proper, but she was still fizzing with anticipation. "I've learned as a maid to be discreet. But this is the most exciting thing that has ever happened to me!"

"And you get to enjoy discovering your power without being sent into exile," Tory said wryly.

Molly's expression sobered. "It was cruel how you were sent away for doing what was right. But you're better and stronger for it."

Her comment wasn't a guess. During their hours in the coach, Tory had determined that Molly's ability was not foretelling, but a talent for reading personalities and events from objects that a person had handled extensively. The night before Tory had been sent to Lackland, Molly had helped her pack. While handling Tory's clothing and other possessions, she'd made the prediction that Tory would do well, despite the shock and pain of being exiled from everyone and everything she knew. She'd been right, too.

Tory smiled. "Why is it that the events that improve our characters are so often unpleasant?"

"Because if we're happy, there's no reason to grow and change."

Tory blinked, startled by the clarity and truth of Molly's comment. "Have you thought about becoming a village counselor?"

Molly's eyes rounded. "Do you think I could? That is the most wonderful thing I can imagine for myself!"

Counselors offered guidance and comfort, particularly in matters of the heart. Young lovers would bring in something handled by their objects of affection. A good counselor could determine if the potential mate was healthy, honest, loyal—or not.

Counselors were also good listeners who helped people sort out their problems. Even small villages usually had at least a part-time counselor, though sometimes they might be paid in chickens or other forms of barter. Most counselors were women, and it was an occupation that could be practiced even after marriage and children.

Some counselors were particularly gifted in matters of commerce. Merchants, bankers, and others in trade would use them to determine if a potential buyer, seller, or borrower was honest and reliable.

"I think you'd make an excellent counselor," Tory said. "You have the ability to read objects, you're kind, and you have common sense."

"I'd need to serve an apprenticeship," Molly said uncertainly. "I'm not sure I could afford the fee."

"I could help you with that. You helped me a great deal when I was in need of kindness and understanding," Tory said quietly.

"You'd do that, my lady? That would be wonderful! I always felt I wouldn't spend my life in service, but I had no idea what I could do instead."

"Life can send us on new paths at any time." Certainly Tory's path was unexpected.

Molly said earnestly, "You may command my services as a counselor forever, my lady. As soon as I return home, I'll find a counselor who needs an apprentice."

Tory smiled, pleased with Molly's decision. She might make a good counselor herself.

CHAPTER 6

Tory couldn't control her impatience when the carriage halted under Layton Place's porte cochere. Molly said, "You go along inside, my lady. I'll arrange for your trunks to be brought in and I'll press your gowns. I brought your nicest outfits."

"Thank you. I look forward to wearing something that isn't practical!" The footman who had watched over them through the journey opened the door and let down the steps. Moving so quickly that her feet barely touched the stone drive underfoot, Tory skipped into the house.

She was greeted by her brother's butler, who bowed deeply. "Welcome, Lady Victoria. Your sister requested that she be notified as soon as you arrived." He glanced at a footman, who immediately set off. "If I may take your cloak and bonnet, my lady?"

Tory could hear the chatter of strange voices in nearby rooms. By the time she'd removed her outer garments, Sarah appeared, her face alight. Tall and blond and very lovely, she looked a bit like Cynthia, but with a better disposition. "Tory!"

They hugged each other hard. Tory was on the verge of tears. She'd missed her family *so much.* Ending the hug, she said, "I used to dream that someday I'd be as tall as you. It hasn't happened."

Sarah grinned. "Resign yourself to shortness. I think it's too late for you to catch up with me."

Tory had inherited her petite frame and dark hair from her mother's Russian grandmother, Viktoria Ivanova. She'd also received her name and probably her magic from the woman. "Someone has to be the runt of the litter," she joked.

"You're do appear a bit too thin," Sarah said critically. "But otherwise you're in good looks. Do they feed you well enough at Lackland?"

"The food isn't bad, but it's not like home."

"You must be hungry after that long journey. Dinner won't be until rather late, so come up to my room and we'll have tea and cakes." Sarah glanced at the butler. "Would you take care of that, Simpson? And ask Lord Roger up also."

The butler bowed acknowledgment and Sarah swept Tory away. "This will give us some time to catch up before Roger arrives."

As the sisters climbed the stairs, Tory asked, "Is Mama here yet?"

Sarah's levity vanished. "She wanted to come, but Father forbade it."

Tory bit her lip, painfully disappointed. Sarah had to be equally disappointed. "I'm sorry. It's costing you a lot to have me at your wedding."

"It's worth it." Sarah darted a worried glance. "But—there's a cost to you also. Remember we'd always assumed we'd stand up for each other at our weddings?"

Tory braced herself. "You're saying I can't be your maid of honor."

"I'm afraid not." Sarah sighed as she opened the door to her room. "Roger's family isn't thrilled that he's marrying a . . . a Mansfield."

"Because the Mansfields are tainted by evil mage blood," Tory said helpfully as she stepped into the comfortable bedchamber and moved to the small sitting area.

Sarah winced. "The Hawthornes are more tolerant than Father, but they aren't exactly approving. Do you mind terribly?"

"Do I mind that I'm here on the condition that I stay mum and don't draw attention?" Tory's smile was crooked as she recognized how much her life had changed. "The situation doesn't please me, but I'm very aware that it would have been much easier for you to ignore my existence and have a grander, less complicated wedding at Fairmount. I'll behave, and I appreciate what you've sacrificed to have me here."

Sarah's face stilled. "You've grown a lot these last few months, Tory."

Had Sarah expected Tory to make a scene about not being in the wedding? Apparently. Tory shrugged. "I didn't have much choice."

Sarah sank onto the small sofa and gestured for Tory to sit. "Is Lackland dreadful?"

Tory took a chair opposite, considering her reply as she smoothed her skirts. "It's rather like a female version of Eton, only without the beatings that Geoffrey had to endure. Most of the girls are nice and I've made good friends. I enjoy most of my classes and teachers." Except Miss Macklin. "The hardest part was being wrenched away from Fairmount and feeling as if I was a worthless criminal being sent to Newgate Prison."

Her sister relaxed a little. "I'm glad it's not worse. If only you hadn't had to reveal your magic in front of everyone important in the county!"

"You know I didn't have any choice." Tory decided to ask something she'd been curious about. "When you visited me the night before I was sent to Lackland, I got the impression that you also have some magical ability."

Sarah looked away. "A little, perhaps. Hardly any at all."

"You have enough that it worries you," Tory pointed out. "Have you ever experimented to see what you can do?"

"Well," Sarah said reluctantly. "I've found that if I concentrate on someone making a journey, they usually have a safe, fast trip with no bad weather."

Tory's brows arched. "Did you do that for me?"

Sarah nodded. "I wanted you to arrive as soon as possible, not get bogged down somewhere like Worcestershire."

"It worked," Tory said, impressed. "So you're a weather mage, like Mama."

"Our mother is a weather mage?" her sister gasped, eyes rounding.

"She won't admit it, but haven't you ever thought it odd that the weather for her outdoor fetes and entertainments is always good?"

"I . . . I never realized. So I came by my ability from her." Sarah shook her head. "It isn't fair that she and I were able to escape unscathed while your life was ruined."

Tory gave a bittersweet smile. "Though my life has been drastically changed, it wasn't ruined." She thought of Allarde. Should she tell Sarah about him? No, it would require too many explanations. "There are some splendid compensations."

"You aren't just saying that to make me feel better?" Sarah asked, wanting to believe but not yet convinced.

Tory laughed. "I'm your little sister. Have I ever tried to make your life easier?"

That made Sarah laugh, too. "I wonder if Geoffrey has any magical talent?" Tory said thoughtfully. "Since you and I do, there's a good chance he does also. Though he might not realize it."

Her sister looked startled. "I never considered that."

"Magic is the great forbidden subject for the wellborn," Tory said dryly. "Since I'm already an outcast, I can think and talk about it. But I won't while I'm here at Layton Place. Mustn't make the other guests feel uncomfortable. So fortunate that I'm so small and harmless looking."

Sarah grinned. "No one who knows you would think you harmless, but you should be able to fool the Hawthornes while you're here."

A footman entered with a large tea tray. As he was setting up the teapot, tiny sandwiches, and cakes, Lord Roger arrived. "Tory, I'm so glad you're here."

He seemed to mean it, too. Lord Roger Hawthorne was the youngest son of a marquess, a Member of Parliament, and as intelligent as he was amiable. Though not as strikingly handsome as Allarde, he was attractive and good-natured.

Sarah had had several seasons in London without finding a man she wanted to marry, though she hadn't lacked for offers. Then she met Lord Roger. The two of them started talking and hadn't stopped since. Sarah would make a wonderful political hostess. Tory was sure that Roger would end up in the cabinet, maybe even be Prime Minister someday.

But now he was about to become her brother-in-law, and his smile was wide and welcoming. Tory rose and clasped his hand. "Thank you for letting me come, Lord Roger. It would have been safer for your career if you hadn't."

As he kissed Sarah's cheek and accepted a steaming cup of tea from her, he said, "Sarah wanted you at the wedding, and what Sarah wants, Sarah gets."

They exchanged besotted smiles before sitting and giving the cakes and small sandwiches the attention they deserved. Tory was ravenous and tackled the food with gusto. Her appetite had been robust since leaving Lackland.

As she ate a third miniature sandwich, she realized her hunger was because she was using her power more now that she was away from the school. Magic was a constant extra sense observing the world, like hearing and smelling. As she polished off the last of the triangular sandwiches, she said rather guiltily, "I've eaten more than my share."

"We haven't been traveling and aren't as hungry," Lord Roger said. He'd eaten lightly, but was on his third cup of tea. "Tory, I don't want you to think that your presence will damage my career. Rather the contrary, I suspect. Remember that the vast majority of Britons approve of magic. The men of the district I represent will think better of me for accepting my mage-born sister-in-law."

"Most people think aristocrats are mad for condemning magic," Sarah added. "I've thought about this a great deal since your abilities were revealed, and I agree. Magic is so useful. People like us are fools for not embracing it."

"I think Parliament could use an advocate for magic who comes from the nobility," Roger said seriously. "Thanks to my great uncle, I'm financially independent, so I can buck the disapproval of other aristocrats if I choose." He took a ginger cake from its plate. "There is a great deal of hypocrisy about magic among our kind. The Mansfields can't be the only family concealing magic."

Tory looked innocent. "Not the Mansfields in general. I'm the black sheep. Practically a changeling. I don't look like anyone else in the family."

"Roger knows of my modest ability, so there's no need to claim you're a changeling." Sarah nibbled thoughtfully on an iced cake. "After you were revealed as a mageling, he and I had a long talk." Her fingers tightened on the delicate china of her cup. "Honesty was necessary if our betrothal was to survive."

If Lord Roger had broken with Sarah, no one would have blamed him. Many would have said he'd done exactly the right thing. "I'm very glad you two decided to marry in spite of my scandalous abilities," Tory said quietly. "I'll do my best not to embarrass you."

"I'm a politician. I don't embarrass easily," Roger said, a twinkle in his eyes. "Someday you might even be an asset to my career."

"I hope our children will grow up in a world where there is more tolerance of magic," Sarah said. "But enough of that! For the next fortnight, Cecilia and I intend to see that you have a splendid time, Tory. There will be a ball to celebrate the wedding, and Cecilia has promised she'll invite every attractive young man in the neighborhood for you to flirt with."

Tory laughed. Though she didn't have much interest in flirting with anyone but Allarde, a ball would be delightful. "My first ball! You know I love to dance. How many guests are staying here at Layton Place?"

"Most of the men are out hunting at the moment," Sarah said, "but the house is full up, not counting everyone's servants. Your room is tiny, and Molly will be sleeping on a pallet on your floor. Several of the neighboring estates are hosting guests, too. It's the largest house party at Layton Place since Geoffrey and Cecilia moved in."

"She must be frantic!" Tory said. "It's time I paid my respects to her." She eyed the almost empty plate of nut balls. Should she . . . ?

She should. Sweeping up the last two nut balls, she said, "I'll see you at dinner." She curtsied gracefully, then left in search of her hostess. Geoffrey would be hunting with his guests. Where might Cecilia be?

Tory visualized her sweet-natured sister-in-law, then searched the house for that energy. Ah, the stillroom, of course. Cecilia was an expert at making medicines and cosmetics and other concoctions used around the house. Plus, the stillroom was a good place to hide from her guests if she wanted some peace.

Since the servants' stairs were nearby, Tory descended that way. She emerged in the hall next to the kitchen. It was full of tempting scents and busy servants. Presiding over the staff was a tall and majestic cook who had trained at Fairmount and followed Geoffrey to Shropshire when he married and established his own household.

Tory poked her head in the door and said to the cook, "The ginger cakes were particularly fine today, Mrs. Lane."

Mrs. Lane looked up from the sauce she was stirring with a broad smile. "'Tis fine to see you, Lady Tory! But you're looking too thin. Don't be shy about coming down here for a bit to eat between meals. You need fattening."

"I shall take you up on that," Tory promised before heading down the flagstone passage to the stillroom. She opened the door and stepped into a chamber warmed by a fire and redolent with the scents of herbs.

Thick bunches of sage and savory and lavender hung from the ceiling, along with braids of onions and garlic. Cecilia was perched on a stool by the worktable and carefully measuring a dark liquid to add to a bowl of some waxy substance. "Cecilia?"

"Tory!" Her sister-in-law looked up with pleasure. "I'm so glad you made it here safely."

Before she'd even finished speaking, her two-and-a-half-year-old son, Jamie, buzzed around the corner of the worktable. "Aunt Tory!"

She scooped up his warm, solid little body. "Goodness, how you've grown since I last saw you!" Which had been on the fateful day that had made her an outcast. But as she held her nephew, she couldn't be sorry for what she'd done.

"I won't be able to lift him much longer." Cecilia came around the table and gave Tory a hug. Fair and soft-spoken, she wasn't a great beauty, but she had a quiet charm that had captured Geoffrey's heart the first time they danced at a London ball.

Tory set her wriggling nephew on the floor. "Did you mind when Sarah asked if the wedding could be held here with my scandalous self as a guest?"

"I was the one who suggested it," Cecilia replied. "Sarah wrote about how difficult Lord Fairmount was being, so I told her she could be married from Layton Place." She lifted a bottle from a shelf behind her. "Would you like to taste my elderberry cordial? This year's batch turned out well. It's very good for coughs and colds, so you should have a few sips after your long journey."

"I'd love some." The cordial was sweet and tangy, with a strong kick of alcohol. As its warmth curled through her, Tory held Jamie in her lap and chatted with her sister-in-law. Lackland Abbey seemed a very long way off.

Relaxed and happy, Tory headed upstairs through the main part of the house. The enclosed staircase led up to the ground floor, and she found herself behind two women she didn't know, presumably Hawthorne relations. They were chatting about the weather and activities planned. Tory didn't pay attention until the older of the women said in a hushed voice, "My maid tells me that Lord Smithson has invited the other sister, the mageling. She was sent to Lackland, you know."

The younger woman squeaked with delighted horror. "He *didn't*! I hope she has the decency to stay at Lackland rather than come here to ruin the wedding!"

Tory gasped, feeling as if she'd been drenched in ice water. The warm reception from her family had made her temporarily forget how deeply most aristocrats despised mages.

"If she comes, I don't suppose we can give her the cut direct since she's sister to our host," the first woman said with regret. "Her parents aren't coming to Lady Sarah's wedding because they refuse to stay in the same house with a creature like her."

"Very proper of them," her companion said. "Do you know the girl's name?"

Tory's icy shock turned to hot fury. Controlling her voice with effort, she said brightly, "Lady Victoria Mansfield. Alas, I didn't have the decency to stay away."

Startled, the two women swung around to stare at her. Tory spent an instant thinking of the various ways she could justify their opinions of magelings before giving them her sweetest smile. "Don't worry. Magic isn't contagious."

Head high, she swept past the women, glad that she hadn't embarrassed her family by misbehaving.

But, oh, she'd been tempted!

CHAPTER 7

Tory tapped her foot to the music, thinking wistfully that this wasn't what she'd imagined for her first ball back in the days when she'd thought herself normal. She'd dreamed of being presented to the beau monde in London. Her debut would have been held in the splendid ballroom of Fairmount House with her parents standing beside her.

Her ballgown would be both innocent and dazzling. The handsomest, most eligible young men in Britain would beg for dances. One or two would probably be inspired to offer marriage by the end of their dance, though Tory would cast her eyes down demurely and say something like, "Sir, you honor me, but this is so sudden!"

Unless that first dance was with Allarde. She might have been ready to accept him at the end of a single dance. She smiled to herself at the thought.

This Christmas country house ball in honor of Sarah and Roger did not match her dreams. There was less formality and half the people present were trying to ignore her existence without actually giving her the cut direct.

She didn't have a dazzling new gown, either. With private defiance, she wore the pretty sprigged muslin with sapphire blue ribbons she had worn only once, on the fateful day that had sent her into exile. She'd thought the garment ruined, but Molly had fixed it up as good as new. The gown was very becoming, so why not wear it tonight?

Tory sat out the first two dances since her brother and Lord Roger were obliged to dance with Cecilia and Sarah and no one else asked. But Lord Roger partnered her for the third dance. He was an excellent dancer and he made her laugh.

Her brother appeared to claim her for the fourth dance. Large and blond, Geoffrey looked quite a bit like Sarah and not at all like Tory, but he'd always been an excellent brother. "May I have this dance, Lady Victoria?" he asked with a formal bow.

She curtsied in return. "It will be my pleasure, Lord Smithson."

Formality ended as he led her to where a country dance was forming. "You've been holding up very well, Tory," he said quietly. "I couldn't blame you if you clawed some of these vicious tabbies."

"It's been a near thing," she admitted. "But I didn't want to embarrass my family any more than I already have."

"I will never be ashamed of you." The longways dance called for a line of men to face a line of women. As they took their positions, Geoffrey glanced at the door. "I'm expecting a few more guests. Ones you should enjoy."

The music began and Tory concentrated on the dancing. Geoffrey had often been her partner when she was learning, so they danced well together. As they moved down the lines of dancers, she was pleased to see that the men didn't shrink from taking her hand and whirling her around. They didn't seem to think she was contagious.

The atmosphere eased enough that she was asked for the next dance by a male who wasn't related to her. Her partner was a shy young fellow from the neighborhood, and not a very good dancer, but his gaze was admiring.

The dance was just ending when the door opened and Geoffrey's late guests arrived. First was a tall, distinguished man of advanced years, but his back was straight and his gaze shrewd. On his arm was an elegant silver-haired woman. Behind walked . . .

Allarde! Tory was so startled that she tripped over her partner's feet and almost pulled them both down. She apologized without taking her gaze from Allarde.

Seeing him unexpectedly made her freshly aware of his striking handsomeness. She'd first seen him playing ball with the other Lackland boys. His chiseled features and perfectly proportioned body were like a Greek sculptor portraying a great athlete, or even a god. But better because he radiated life and strength.

Sensing her regard, he turned. His face lit with the same surprise and pleasure Tory felt.

She recovered her wits enough to thank her partner for the dance. By the time she'd dismissed him, her brother was approaching, Allarde at his side. Geoffrey said, "Allarde was one of my fags at Eton, Tory. Now he's at Lackland Abbey."

Tory offered her hand and Allarde bowed over it. "I have seen Lord Allarde in the Lackland playing fields," she said demurely. "There are viewing holes in the fence that divides the schools. One of the favorite occupations of the girls is watching the boys. Lord Allarde is much admired."

Her brother laughed. "Human nature in action. I must go speak to his parents, but I wanted you two to get acquainted."

When her brother moved away, Tory said mischievously, "I assume you won't be afraid to dance with me for fear my magic is contagious, Lord Allarde."

Laughing, he proffered his arm. "Indeed not. May I have the next dance, Lady Victoria?"

She slipped her hand into the crook of his elbow. "It would be my great pleasure, sir." Though both of them used formal manners as if they'd just been introduced, under the surface they bubbled with delight.

Allarde led her to a quiet corner of the ballroom. "This is wonderful! As we drove over here, I thought how unfortunate it was that I'd be in your brother's house when you weren't."

"My sister moved her wedding here so I could attend," Tory explained. "I didn't receive her letter until you'd left the school. I never expected to see you, though. I thought your family seat was in Worcestershire?"

"It is, but Layton Place is right on the county border. Kemperton Hall is only a few miles away. Closer if you ride cross country." The musicians struck up a tune for the next dance. They joined a square of four couples that was forming.

"We can't really talk here," Allarde said under his breath. "On the day after Boxing Day, can I take you on a ride to Kemperton Hall? I'd like you to see the estate."

"I'd love that." As she took her place beside him in the square, she said with a smile, "The dance after this is the supper dance."

"Then I shall claim that, too," he murmured, his gray eyes warm.

It wasn't like the first ball that Tory had expected. It was much, much better.

CHAPTER 8

Christmas Day was dark and damp and *cold*. Cynthia lay on her back and stared gloomily at the crack in the ceiling. Her bedroom was dim in the pearl-grayness of an overcast winter afternoon, and a biting wind from the channel rattled the windowpanes. She should rise and put more coal on the fire, or at least pull a blanket over herself, but she felt too dismal.

This was her third Christmas at Lackland, and the worst. There were only a handful of girls left in the school, none of them friends. The first day after the school emptied out, she'd arrived in the refectory for breakfast and moved to join the table where all the other students were.

As soon as she touched a chair, the other girls had stood en masse, pivoted sharply, and moved to another table so smoothly that they must have planned it in advance. Cynthia gasped, humiliated.

If only Tory had stayed! Everyone liked Tory. If she'd been with Cynthia, no one would have moved away.

That night, she took Tory's stupid steamed pudding and carried it down into the Labyrinth. She'd hoped that some of the Irregulars might be there. Even magelings from the village whom she hardly knew would be better than nothing. Among the Irregulars, she was respected for what she'd done on the other side of Merlin's mirror.

But the hall and maze of passages were empty and echoed like a tomb. She left the pudding on a table with a note offering it to anyone who wanted it, and good riddance. The stupid pudding would probably still be there when everyone returned from holiday. Christmas puddings not only had the shape, size, and density of cannonballs, they were almost as durable.

Even without being heated, she had to admit the stupid pudding smelled very good, with tantalizing hints of spice and dried fruit and fine brandy. But Christmas puddings weren't meant to be eaten alone, and there was no way Cynthia would share it with the awful girls who'd given her the cut direct.

There wasn't much to do at Lackland over the holidays. The only teacher left on the girls' side was horrid Miss Macklin. Cynthia took a book to the refectory so she could read during her solitary meals. The only volume she could find was a beastly collection of sermons, but at least it gave her something to pretend to read.

She whiled away her days with embroidery and walking the spacious grounds. Once she stood on the edge of the cliff and watched the crashing waves of the English Channel below. Would anyone miss her if she fell? Tory would have the whole room to herself, so she'd probably be happy.

Turning away, she reminded herself that Napoleon loomed on the far side of the channel like a great hungry beast, making plans to invade England. If the little tyrant tried, he'd have to get past *her*. In her present mood, she could destroy any number of stupid tyrants.

Occasionally she considered leaving the school through the

Labyrinth, but where would she go from there? Lackland village was small, and none of the Irregulars who lived there were particular friends.

There was Jack Rainford. She'd worked with him very closely in the weather brigade because they were by far the strongest weather mages, but he was the most *annoying* boy. Still, they were friends, more or less. She'd never had a boy for a friend.

Christmas Day began with a long, boring service in the chapel, where Cynthia had a whole pew to herself. Then a decent midday dinner, for which she had little appetite. Now all the other girls were gathered in one of their bedrooms to have a party. They'd discussed within Cynthia's hearing all the cakes and sweetmeats they'd share, along with good sherry and brandy.

She hoped they all *choked* on their stupid hazelnuts!

The room was so dark she could barely see the crack in the ceiling. Shivering from the chill, she sat up and swung her legs over the side of the bed. She'd never studied hearth witchery because it was vulgar, but she was cold enough to reconsider.

She concentrated on the coals in the tiny fireplace, imagining them burning hotter and brighter. The coals brightened faintly, but not enough to warm the room. She'd have to replenish the coal.

As she added a shovelful of coals, someone tapped at the door. She ignored it. Probably one of those stupid girls had decided to practice some Christian charity because it was a holiday. Well, Cynthia didn't need any of them.

The door swung open. Catching the motion from the corner of her eye, she glanced over. Good heavens, a *man*! She scrambled to her feet, wondering wildly what spells she might use to drive him off.

The newcomer stepped forward into the room. Jack Rainford, tall and broad-shouldered in a heavy cloak, his fair hair catching the firelight. As disgustingly handsome as always. "What are you doing here!" she exclaimed. "Boys aren't allowed in the girls' school! Not *ever*!"

He gave his usual infuriating Jack Rainford grin. "There's no one around to notice or care." He opened his hand to show a small, water-polished pebble. "I brought a stealth stone so no one would see me, but I didn't need it. Your reputation is safe."

"*I* care! Get out of my room *right now!*"

"I'll leave," he said with a wicked smile. "But you're coming with me."

"You have lost your mind," she said with conviction. "Your grasp on sanity was always weak, and now you've descended into sheer madness. Why would I want to leave the school with you?"

"To have a nice Christmas dinner in good company," he said. "We should get to my house about the time the goose is done."

"I've already had Christmas dinner," she snapped. "It was served to the students from both schools, and it was the best meal the abbey serves all year."

His brows arched. "That's not saying much."

Too true. Voice starchy, she said, "I can't accept an invitation from a man."

"The invitation is from my mother. I am but her emissary." He gave her a warm, almost irresistible smile. "I guarantee that our dinner will be much better than what you had here. We'll end with that splendid plum pudding you left in the Labyrinth."

She frowned. "Why were you in the Labyrinth when there were no classes?"

"I like to check every few days to see if Nick Rainford has sent a message. His life is a lot more interesting than mine." Jack looked a little envious. Leave it to a stupid boy to think it was "interesting" to be in the middle of a catastrophic war!

Jack frowned. "I'm getting worried. There hasn't been a message from Nick in over a fortnight. One can't help but wonder . . ."

Cynthia shuddered as she remembered the menacing roar of the heavy guns as the Nazis and Allies pounded away at each other. Lackland was right on the Straits of Dover and could easily be bombed from horrible airplanes or pounded by artillery. Her imagination produced a ghastly vision of a Nazi bomb smashing into the Rainford home. The whole family could be dead.

She really liked the Rainfords, even though they were commoners. Mrs. Rainford and Polly had been very welcoming, and Nick was less annoying than Jack. "I'm sure he and his family are fine," she said, trying to convince herself. "He's probably just too busy to walk out to the abbey."

"Probably you're right," Jack said. "But if there's no message from him in another fortnight, I may go through the mirror to find out if they're all right."

Appalled, Cynthia asked, "Could you travel there without Tory's help?"

"Nick made it back here on his own. I think I could manage the return journey. Probably." Dismissing the topic, he said, "Come along now. The goose is waiting."

"Why would I want a second Christmas dinner?" Except that she did. She'd been too miserable to eat much, and she'd finished Tory's shortbread days ago.

"Because the abbey is a flat bore over the holidays. Another day or two and you'll be kicking the walls." He grinned. "In a very ladylike way, of course. My mother thinks that since you provided the pudding, you should share in it."

"Lady Fairmount sent the pudding, and Tory left it for me when she got an unexpected invitation to her brother's house. I couldn't eat that great thing so I left it to the Labyrinth. I thought the Irregulars would share it after the holidays."

"Well, I took the pudding home. I promise that a Rainford Christmas dinner will be far more amusing than sulking here in a cold room."

"I'm not sulking!" Cynthia scowled, privately admitting that he was right. This was such a ghastly holiday that even joining a family of commoners sounded good. Jack's younger sister, Rachel, was pleasant, and his mother seemed nice.

A thought struck her. "Your mother is the best hearth witch around, isn't she? Could she show me how to keep this room warm in spite of the suppression spell?"

"She could probably teach you a few tricks," Jack said. "Rachel is good, but she hasn't anything like Mum's experience."

"Very well, I'll join you for dinner," she said ungraciously.

He beamed, and she realized he hadn't been as confident about persuading her as he'd pretended. "Then grab a cloak and come along. It's cold out there."

She gave a horrified thought to her appearance. She was wearing her plainest gown, and her hair fell in slatternly tangles around her shoulders. "I'm not going out to dinner even in a farmhouse dressed like this!" she exclaimed. "Go wait in the corridor until I change."

He rolled his eyes. "You look fine as you are. If you must change, do it quickly. I'm hungry."

"Out!" she ordered. "And no peeking!"

Smiling, he ambled from the room while Cynthia considered what to wear. She was tempted to change slowly just to irritate Jack, but she was hungry, too.

She didn't have any choice, actually. Her most fashionable garments needed the assistance of a maid, and all the servants had been given a half day off because it was Christmas.

After her visit to 1940, Cynthia had reluctantly conceded that Tory was right about having clothes that could be put on without assistance. A letter to her father's secretary had produced two gowns that were easy to wear, if not very fashionable. The garments had arrived after most students left for the holiday. She was wearing the plainer gown now since none of the other girls would help her dress.

The second new dress was a little prettier, so it would have to do. She certainly couldn't ask Jack Rainford to fasten the back of her gown.

The fabric was a shade of blue that enhanced her eyes and there was a rich band of embroidery on the hem and bodice. Though too simple for a dinner with her own kind, it would do for a farmhouse. She donned it quickly, ran a brush through her hair and pinned it up, then put on her heaviest cloak and a warm bonnet.

Jack was lounging in the corridor, juggling small mage lights.

Like the other members of the weather brigade, his power had increased during their marathon of magical work. "You didn't take quite as long as I expected." He tossed her one of the lights. "Most girls need more time to pretty themselves up than you do."

"Is that a compliment?" she asked suspiciously as they headed toward the stairs.

"I guess it is," he said thoughtfully. "Even when you worked endless hours and looked like something the cat dragged in, you looked like a *pretty* cat."

She was tempted to hiss like a cat, but settled for tossing her head as she led the way downstairs.

As Jack said, the abbey was so quiet that stealth stones weren't needed. They used the tunnel in the cellar of the refectory to enter the Labyrinth. It was a relief to move out of the abbey's suppression spell.

The Labyrinth felt a lot less empty with Jack at her side. Say what one would about his social status and appalling sense of humor, Cynthia grudgingly admitted that he did have presence. When Jack was around, he was impossible to ignore.

They crossed through the main hall into the tunnels that connected to the boys' school. Cynthia had never been on this side of the Labyrinth.

As they entered a tunnel on the left, Jack touched the small magical patch high on the corner. It flared purple. "This is the route I always use for coming and going from the Labyrinth. The tunnel comes out in a beech wood near the road to the village."

"I wonder why none of the tunnels on the girls' side lead off the abbey grounds."

"To protect you frail creatures," Jack said with a laugh. "Whoever dug these tunnels obviously couldn't imagine warrior women like you."

There was real admiration in his voice. Surprised, Cynthia said, "I'm no warrior woman. If some horrible soldier attacked me, I wouldn't know what to do."

"You'd call lightning down on his head and fry him like an egg," Jack said promptly. "Even Boadicea couldn't do that when she fought the Romans."

"You know I can't call lightning unless I have a storm to work with."

"You'd come up with something." His voice turned serious for a change. "We could never have controlled the weather over the channel without you. I have more experience and perhaps more raw ability, but you're inventive. You came up with some clever ways of shifting winds that I'd never thought of. We were good partners."

Stupidly, she felt a warm glow of satisfaction. Why did it have to be Jack Rainford who fully appreciated what she'd done?

They walked steadily until the tunnel ended in a flight of stairs leading up to a door. "Time to dim our mage lights," Jack said as he touched the magical patch on the frame at the top. The door swung silently open to reveal the beech wood and a blast of cold, damp night air.

Cynthia was surprised to see a saddled horse placidly munching hay nearby. "We don't have to walk?"

"I wouldn't ask a fine lady to walk all the way into the village on such a cold night," he explained. He patted the padded contraption behind the saddle. "You'll have to ride pillion, though. I dug out the old seat my great-grandmother used when they rode to market."

"That is the ugliest horse I've ever seen." Cynthia brightened her mage light to confirm what she was seeing. "Walleyes, a mule nose, lop ears, and he's pigeontoed. Have I missed anything?"

"He's long-backed, too." Jack stroked the beast's neck affectionately. "Pegasus had a hard life, but he has good heart. He'll get us to where we're going."

"Pegasus?" she asked incredulously. "Could you possibly have picked a less appropriate name?"

"I thought he needed a name to live up to." Jack mounted, then reached down to give her a hand. Cynthia hesitated. She was a good rider in a proper sidesaddle, but perching on a horse's rump was a different matter. "Is that contraption safe?" she asked as she studied the pillion seat dubiously.

"As long as we aren't galloping away from armed highwaymen. The pillion seat is attached to my saddle and there's a girth and a tail strap."

"It probably hasn't been used since your great-grandmother's day," Cynthia muttered. But she didn't want to go back to her cold, lonely room, and annoying as Jack was, she trusted him to keep her safe. Even a horse moving at slow speed would be quicker and warmer than walking.

"I cleaned it just for you," he assured her.

She took Jack's hand and stepped on his stirruped, booted foot. With his help, she managed to swing around awkwardly and perch sideways behind him.

"All settled?" he asked.

"Well enough." The padded seat was surprisingly comfortable and the back edge turned up to help keep her safely in place. The footrest was set for a shorter woman, but it did give her a place to rest her feet. She slid her arms around his waist, very aware of the hard, strong body under his heavy cloak. "Just don't let highwaymen find us."

Chuckling, he set Pegasus into a smooth walk. "If that happens, we'll just have to call down the winds to blow them out to sea!"

CHAPTER 9

Cynthia hadn't been riding since she was sent to Lackland. As they moved through the night toward the village, she realized how much she enjoyed being on a horse again, even perched on the broad rump of the ugliest horse she'd ever seen. This was much more amusing than staring at the crack in her ceiling.

"Here we are," Jack said as they turned into a lane a little short of the village. As Pegasus carried them smoothly up a hill, Cynthia saw the outlines of a sprawling house take shape. Sometimes inns had lights in every window as a welcome to travelers. Here balls of mage light glowed with equal welcome.

As they drew closer, she realized that the weathered stone structure was as large as a manor house, though the shape was irregular from having been built over centuries. It looked like the home of a prosperous yeoman family.

Cynthia stared at the well-kept house and grounds. Jack had always given the impression that his family lived in modest circumstances. Tenant farmers, perhaps. Instead, they must be very nearly gentry.

She was so irritated by his deception that she was tempted to push him off the horse. Except, since this was Jack, he might not have deceived her deliberately.

Before she could decide whether to push him off, they'd ridden around the house. The faint sounds of music and laughter could be heard. This was not a small gathering.

Jack pulled up by a mounting block in front of the stables, steadying her arm as she stepped onto the block. "You can go into the house and get warm while I give Pegasus a quick rubdown."

"I'll wait for you." There was no way Cynthia would walk alone into a house full of strangers who were not her kind. She pulled her cloak tight and regarded the house warily, kicking herself for having agreed to come. Yet spending Christmas alone had been driving her into flat despair.

Grooming finished, Jack joined her. "These are friendly folk," he said quietly. "You won't regret coming, I promise."

She raised her chin. She was the daughter of a duke, a descendant of great ladies who'd held castles against attackers when their husbands went to war. She could face down a house full of farmers.

They entered the house through the kitchen. That would never happen in the home of a nobleman, but the long room was irresistibly warm and bright. Cynthia sighed with pleasure. She hadn't been this comfortable in weeks.

"Nothing like a warm kitchen on a cold night!" Jack said with appreciation. "Try one of these." He scooped up a pair of mincemeat tarts.

Cynthia's wariness vanished as soon as the warm tart landed in her palm. It was a traditional mince of venison and dried fruit and spices, and she ate it in three bites. The tart was the best thing she'd tasted since the fish and chips in 1940.

"Out of the kitchen with ye, Master Jack," a gravel-voiced woman ordered. Her tone changed. "I see you brought the young lady back. Welcome to Swallow Grange, miss."

Cynthia turned and saw the cook, a round, smiling woman with twinkling eyes. Unable to resist that smile, she said, "The mincemeat tarts are delicious."

The cook nodded, pleased. "You won't find finer on a duke's table." She chuckled. "And I'll wager you know dukes' tables firsthand. Here, my lady. Have another tart." She offered the platter. When Jack also reached for one, she swatted his hand. "That's enough for you, my lad! If I left you alone with these tarts, the whole batch would be gone quicker than the cat can lick her ear."

He tried to look wounded. "You're a cruel woman, Mrs. Brewster."

"And you, my lad, are a biblical plague of locusts that devour everything down to bare ground." She made a shooing motion with one hand. "Go join the family so we can start getting dinner on the table."

"Yes, ma'am," he said meekly. "Cynthia, let me take your cloak. If it hangs here, it will be warm when you leave."

If they departed through the kitchen, perhaps Cynthia could collect some food to sustain her at Lackland. She'd learned early that sincere appreciation was very successful for charming food from a cook.

Jack took her cloak from her shoulders and hung it on a hook by the door. Then he removed his own cloak. She blinked. Instead of his usual casual clothing, he wore coat and breeches whose tailoring would not disgrace a London gentleman.

She tried not to stare as she removed her bonnet and hung it on another hook. He had really excellent legs and shoulders. In fact, he was downright . . . handsome.

After hanging his cloak, he took Cynthia's arm and led her from the kitchen. A short passage emerged into a large drawing room lavishly decorated with greens and berries. Mage lights clung to the ceiling and a blazing fireplace warmed the space and brought out the tangy scents of the greens.

There were at least thirty people present, probably more, and they came in all ages and sizes. Some looked like laborers, a few were as refined in appearance as Jack. Though the furnishings and the clothing lacked the elegance she was used to, the gaiety was contagious. She found herself smiling as Jack escorted her to his mother.

They'd met the night the Irregulars had gone through the mirror. Lily Rainford was fair-haired like her children. Even when she'd known she might never see her son again, her composure had been impressive.

When Lily saw Jack and Cynthia approaching, she smiled warmly and offered her hand. "I'm so glad you've come, Lady Cynthia. Your plum pudding is magnificent."

Her hand was as warm as her smile, and both touched a dark, shriveled place in Cynthia's soul. She hadn't seen a smile like that since . . . since her mother died. "The pudding really isn't from me. Lady Fairmount sent it to Tory, and I inherited it when she was invited to her brother's house."

"I know, but you're the one responsible for the pudding reaching Swallow Grange!" Lily released Cynthia's hand. "Jack, get our guest a cup of mulled wine."

"Yes, ma'am," he said cheerfully. "More for you, too?"

His mother shook her head. "It's too early in the evening for the hostess to let her wits be scrambled. Run along now."

As Jack headed to the fireplace, where a great cauldron of spiced wine was steaming, Lily said in a quiet voice that only Cynthia could hear, "I wanted to thank you for what you did for Jack on the other side of the mirror. No one could have controlled so much weather for so long, but knowing Jack, he would have died trying. If not for you, that's exactly what would have happened."

Startled by the older woman's intensity, Cynthia said, "There were five Irregulars and three other Rainfords contributing magical power. It wasn't only Jack and me."

"Everyone was needed," Lily agreed. "But power alone wasn't enough. Another first-class weather mage was required. And that was you."

Cynthia remembered how Polly Rainford, who was younger and almost entirely untrained, had burned out her magic and collapsed after pushing too far beyond her limits. Scarily, she recognized that Jack might have done the same or worse. Annoying though he could be, she didn't want him dead.

"We all did our best. I'm glad it was enough." A thought struck her. "If you'd like to express your appreciation, could you show me how to make the fire in my room at the abbey warmer? It's freezing there!"

Lily laughed. "I'd be delighted. Hearth magic is very ancient and has its own rules. I can show you how to work around the suppression spell, but not tonight." She raised her voice as her daughter, Rachel, approached with several other girls. "Rachel, will you introduce Lady Cynthia to your friends?"

Rachel was a couple of years younger than Jack, pretty and fair-haired like her mother. She and Cynthia had seldom worked together in the Labyrinth, but her smile now was welcoming. "I'm so glad you came, Lady Cynthia. My friends have heard you're a very powerful mage, and they're perishing to meet you. You know Alice from the Irregulars, of course, but here are Margie and Rose."

Margie, the shorter girl, said worshipfully, "Cousin Jack says you're a wonderful weather mage!"

The other girl, Rose, a little older and a lot taller, added, "Jack says you're one of the most powerful magelings at Lackland Abbey."

"Perhaps," Cynthia admitted. "But there are many strong mages around. Jack for one. Both Rachel and Alice." She tried to think of the names of other Irregulars from the village, but couldn't. She usually stayed among the wellborn students from the abbey.

"Being a hearth witch is much less romantic than doing weather magic," Rachel explained wryly. "They want to hear your tales of calling the winds."

"Really?" Cynthia said, wondering if she was being quietly mocked.

"Really," Jack said as he came up behind her. He placed a warm mug of mulled wine in her hand. "Did you know how rare female weather mages are?"

She sipped the wine, enjoying the warmth and the heady scent of spices. "Oh? I've never heard that."

"Tell us how you discovered you could work weather!" Margie begged.

Cynthia regarded the eager young faces with bemusement. They really did think the talent that had wrecked her life was exciting and enviable. But despite their ignorance, it was impossible not to be flattered by their interest.

"I accidentally blew the hay outside the stable halfway into the next county," she began, mentally editing the story for their tender ears. "My father was *not* amused. . . ."

Jack was right. The Rainford Christmas dinner was much better than the one served at Lackland Abbey. Cynthia was seated next to Lily Rainford as guest of honor, with Jack on her other side taking pains to ensure that she lacked for nothing.

The climax of the feast was the ceremonial entry of the Fairmount Christmas pudding. The mage lights were dimmed to a faint glow while Mrs. Brewster proudly carried in the blazing pudding on a great platter. The blue flames from burning brandy flickered out as the cook set the pudding in front of Lily Rainford.

The size and richly spiced scents of the pudding were greeted with *ooohs* and *aaahs*. Lily removed the slightly charred sprig of holly from the top. "We must thank our special guest Lady Cynthia Stanton for this magnificent pudding."

Several guests who'd clearly had more than enough mulled wine broke into a chorus of, *"For she's a jolly good ladeee, for she's a jolly good ladeee . . ."* while others applauded enthusiastically.

As Lily began serving the pudding, Cynthia ducked her head, embarrassed but also deeply pleased. She had never in her life been in a place where so many people liked having her present.

Conversation lulled as everyone dug into their pudding. Servings were small but incredibly rich, particularly since pitchers of cream and brandy butter and custard were being passed around. For those who didn't like plum pudding or who needed more sweets, there were also splendid cakes and trifles.

The only sounds were the clink of spoons on plates, and occasional exclamations of pleasure as guests discovered the silver tokens hidden in the pudding. Here as in her ingredients, Lady Fairmount had been generous. There were sixpenny pieces for wealth in the year ahead and rings to symbolize marriage. Someone happily held aloft a silver thimble for thrift, another person welcomed a tiny silver wishbone for luck. The real luck was that no one broke a tooth biting on a silver token. Such accidents were not rare.

Cynthia poured thick cream over her pudding, and tasted it. Though very good, it was similar to what her father's cook made, and she was too full to want more. Beside her, Jack polished his serving off and looked wistfully at the empty platter. "I suppose it would be bad form to see if there are any crumbs left."

"Very bad form indeed." Feeling mellow, she added, "Take mine if you like. I've eaten enough."

"Thank you!" Jack stealthily exchanged their dessert dishes, then consumed her pudding more slowly to make it last.

As people finished the sweet, conversation resumed and some guests began to rise from the table. "I suppose it's time to go home," Cynthia said, a little wistfully.

Jack shook his head. "The evening has just begun. By tradition, the small children are put down to nap on various beds, the older men go into the study to play cards, the older women retire to the kitchen and trade horrifying gossip with Mrs. Brewster, and the younger folk go to the music room to dance."

Cynthia brightened. "Dancing?"

"Not a grand ball," he assured her. "Just a bit of music and some country dances. That's where you and I belong."

Cynthia had been taught by a dancing master, of course, but she'd still been in the schoolroom when she was condemned to Lackland. She'd never done real dancing with real people. "I don't know any country dances."

"You'll learn then quick enough." He got to his feet. "I can take you home now if you wish, but why not try at least one set?"

Though it was foolish to involve herself further with a bunch of farmers, Cynthia had drunk enough mulled wine that she didn't care. "Very well, one dance. But you'll have to show me the steps."

"With pleasure, my lady." He offered her his arm, his voice deliciously husky.

Furniture in the music room had been moved to the walls and the rug rolled up to make space for dancing. A very *enceinte* young matron was seated on the pianoforte bench and leafing through sheets of music.

Jack suggested, "Lolly, since Lady Cynthia is unfamiliar with our dances, play 'Apley House.' That's simple enough that by the end she'll be ready for anything."

"That's a good one to start with," Lolly agreed. Her pleasant-looking young husband hovered over her, ready to turn pages. Seeing Cynthia's gaze, Lolly laughed. "Be careful, Lady Cynthia. Christmas dancing can lead to Christmas kisses."

"What do you mean?"

The pianist patted her rounded abdomen. "George and I grew up almost next door to each other. But it wasn't till we met under the Rainford kissing bough two years ago that we really saw each other!"

"Remind me to avoid the kissing bough," Cynthia said dryly.

The others laughed. They thought she was joking.

CHAPTER 10

Dancing was *wonderful*! Cynthia had never felt so exhilarated. "Apley House" was as simple as Jack said, a longways dance with men and women facing each other. Couples worked their way up the lines with steps and turns and swings. The movement and general exuberance stirred her blood and made her want to laugh out loud.

She had the heretical thought that this informal dance was far more fun than a London ball. There critical eyes would be watching and knives would be waiting to slice the reputation of any girl who set a foot wrong.

Here the only danger was the kissing bough, which hung by the doorway. A globe formed of vine, it was decorated with holly and ribbons and bright oranges. A giant bunch of mistletoe was tied below with golden ribbon. The bough was getting steady traffic as couples came from other rooms to stand under it. Jack certainly took advantage, kissing any female between the ages of twelve and eighty.

Cynthia made sure to keep her distance. She was happy to dance with the locals, but kisses were quite another matter.

At the end of the first dance, Jack said with a grin, "Are you game for more?"

Her hair was falling down around her shoulders, but she didn't care. "Yes!"

An ancient man, at least fifty, approached her. "May I have the next dance, Lady Cynthia?" the old fellow asked. "I've always wanted to dance with a real lady, and you must be the prettiest lady in England!"

"Who could turn down such an invitation?" she said with a laugh. It was a square dance, and the old fellow turned out to be very spry despite his advanced years.

Her next partner was a gangling boy younger than she, and even more ignorant of dance steps. They still had a fine time.

After a particularly energetic circle dance, she waved off an invitation to dance the next set. "I'm exhausted," she panted. "I need to recover."

"I can help with that," Jack said, laughing as he approached. "Come, I'll give you some energy."

He caught her hand and spun her under the kissing bough. His arms circled her waist and she found herself drawn against his broad chest. He was strong, and taller than she'd realized.

She turned up her face and started to say, "Enough of this nonsense!" Before she could get the words out, his mouth descended on hers.

Energy blazed through her like raw lightning. Her sense of who she was vanished as she clung to him, her knees too weak to support her.

Dear God in heaven, not Jack Rainford! Please, not Jack Rainford! As wits and strength returned, she jerked away from him, wanting to flee fast and far.

Jack, the charmer who flirted with all the girls, was staring at her as if he'd just been clubbed. He swallowed hard. "S . . . sorry, I forgot how much power you have. I sent too much energy."

Retaining barely enough sense not to run and make a spectacle of herself, Cynthia said tightly, "I'm going home *now*."

"It's almost midnight," he agreed. "Time to collect our cloaks."

Ride again on that ugly horse with her arms around Jack's waist? That was *not* going to happen! "I'll walk. It's only a couple of miles."

"You are not walking that far alone in the middle of the night!" Accurately guessing her thoughts, he continued, "We'll take the gig."

The seat should be wide enough for her to keep her distance, and Cynthia privately admitted that she didn't want to walk home alone at this hour. "Very well."

She pivoted away and stalked through the house, uncomfortably aware that Jack was just behind her. Was there anyone else she could ask to take her home? Not really. Jack was the only one she knew well, and much as she wanted to avoid him, she knew he wouldn't cause trouble. If he did, she'd . . . she'd call down lightning to fry him!

Most guests had gone home already. The dancers were staying the latest. Music and partners for dancing were rare. No one wanted to waste the opportunity.

In the kitchen, Mrs. Brewster and Lily Rainford and another woman Cynthia didn't recognize were chatting over cups of tea. The cook glanced up when Cynthia and Jack entered. "You looked like you enjoyed the dancing! Lady Cynthia, would you like to take some food back to school?"

"How kind of you." Cynthia donned her cloak without waiting for Jack to help. "I would like that."

Jack lifted his own cloak. "I'll go harness the gig."

As he moved toward the door, Lily said, "If you're still interested in being tutored in hearth-witch magic, Lady Cynthia, midmorning the day after tomorrow would be good for me. Things will have quieted down by then."

Cynthia almost said no, but a long, cold winter stretched ahead. "Thank you. I shall look forward to the lesson."

Mrs. Brewster found a basket and began to pack sweets and

savories and even a small jug of cider. The basket was brimming by the time she finished.

When it could hold no more, she tied a red ribbon on the handle and set it on the table by the door. "That was one mighty fine plum pudding, Lady Cynthia," she said. "It gave me ideas for the ones I'll make next Christmas."

Cynthia was certainly getting great benefit from Lady Fairmount's pudding. "Thank you for inviting me, Mrs. Rainford. It's been a lovely evening."

"Please come again. Schools have their uses, but they aren't a home." Lily's eyes were compassionate.

Cynthia turned away sharply, afraid of what the other woman might see. "Till day after tomorrow, then. I'll walk over."

"It's a pleasant walk in good weather, and I know you can assure that weather is good," Lily said with a chuckle.

Jack entered and lifted Mrs. Brewster's basket. "I'll have you home in no time."

Silently she accompanied him outside. The gig had a folding hood which Jack had pulled up to protect them from the wind. Even for weather mages, sometimes simple solutions were best.

Jack had attached several mage lights to the gig to illuminate the road. The light also showed that the skewbald pony between the shafts was almost as ugly as Pegasus. Besides splotchy coloring, it was cow-hocked and mule-eared. Refusing his hand, she climbed into the gig, moving as far to the edge of the seat as she could. "Are all your horses ugly?"

"Most of them." He climbed in and collected the reins. As he did, a dog galloped up and leaped into the gig. It landed in front of their feet with an impact that made the small carriage shake.

Cynthia instinctively drew away. "What is *that*?"

"Rex." Jack scratched the dog's jaw. Rex moaned with pleasure. "He likes riding in carriages."

The beast had a flat, wrinkly bulldog face and an irregular patch over one eye, and half his left ear had been chewed off. Staring at Rex with horrified fascination, she asked, "Do you *collect* ugly animals?"

"Damaged creatures need love more than the beautiful ones do." He scratched Rex's ears. "Treat a wounded animal like Rex well, and you'll have a friend forever."

As Jack set the gig into motion, Rex flopped over Cynthia's feet. At least his warm, chunky body would keep them warm.

The night was very silent. Houses were dark as the inhabitants slept off the celebrations of Christmas. As they turned onto the road that led back to Lackland, Jack said, "I'll pick you up at the Labyrinth day after tomorrow to bring you to the Grange for your lesson with my mother."

Cynthia scowled. "I'll walk."

"I'd be happy to collect you. The walk is going to be cold until you get better at hearth witchery."

"I'll walk!"

He glanced at her, his eyes narrowed. "Why are you so angry with me?"

"You have to ask?" she asked incredulously.

"I'm guessing it's because I kissed you, but I don't know why you're so upset." Jack slowed the gig for a sharp turn. "It was just a Christmas kiss under the kissing bough. Everyone does it. I kissed every girl there."

"I noticed that," Cynthia said frostily.

"As the senior male of Swallow Grange," he explained, "it was my duty to make sure that no female guest was neglected."

"I doubt that any other kisses were the same," she snapped.

"That's true," he admitted. "I really did only intend to give you some energy and a kiss would be a pleasant way to do it. I didn't expect . . . what happened. It's the first time I've kissed a girl who was such a strong mage."

"If you want to try that again, kiss Tory or Elspeth."

"Allarde wouldn't like it if I kissed Tory, and Elspeth would laugh in my face if I tried," he said with a grin. "None of the other female Irregulars are as strong."

"As long as you don't kiss me!" She felt on the verge of weeping.

Jack halted the horse and looked at her with a frown. "What's wrong, Cynthia? Did that energy flare hurt you? Or do you just hate kissing me?"

She stared down at ugly snoozing Rex. "It didn't hurt, though it was upsetting. It's just . . . I thought you were my friend, and friends don't kiss."

"Why kiss a girl who isn't a friend?" He sounded genuinely puzzled. "I wouldn't want to kiss a girl I *didn't* like!"

She pulled her cloak as tightly as she could. "You're not a girl."

He laughed. "I'm glad you noticed. That doesn't explain why you were so upset."

She bit her lip, suspecting that he'd keep asking until he got an answer. She must give him part of the truth. "Starting when I was about twelve, too many men have tried to kiss me when I don't want them to."

Jack winced. "I should have realized that a girl as beautiful as you might attract too much male attention. I'm really, really sorry I became another irritating man who tried to take something I wasn't entitled to."

"So am I," she whispered.

He swore under his breath. "I don't want to lose you as a friend, Cynthia. Would it even the score if you slapped me for an improper advance? I'll hold still for you."

She glanced up and saw real remorse on his face. "I'd have trouble striking you in cold blood, so let's just pretend it never happened." His gaze was so shrewd that she turned away.

He set the gig in motion. "Since that never happened, how about I collect you for the trip to Swallow Grange day after tomorrow?"

She sniffed. "Riding pillion was interesting once. Twice would be excessive."

"I can bring the gig. Better yet, if you have a riding habit, would you like to ride? We have a couple of good hacks in the stable."

"Real riding with a proper sidesaddle?"

"Haven't you noticed that I'm always proper?" he said grandly.

That was so absurd that a reluctant smile escaped her. "If you have a decent horse that isn't too ugly, I'd love to ride."

"Then I'll meet you in the Labyrinth around ten o'clock."

Cynthia nodded. They didn't speak during the rest of the trip to the beech wood. Jack tethered the horse and walked her to the boulder that concealed the tunnel entrance.

He touched the underside of a stone edge and violet light flared. As the heavy door swung open, he said, "I should walk you back to the school, but I don't want to leave Cleopatra standing in a cold wind for long."

"Cleopatra." Cynthia rolled her eyes. "The perfect name for a mule-eared skewbald. Don't worry, I'm in no danger." She stepped into the tunnel. "Thank you for inviting me. The evening was indeed more amusing than staying in my room."

"Are we still friends, Cynthia?" he asked quietly. "I don't want to be at odds with the only other decent weather mage in Kent."

His soft voice curled through her. She paused and looked back. He looked very solid. Misleadingly reliable. Her hands clenched under her cloak. Within limits, he could be trusted. And she didn't want him to travel through the mirror and perhaps become lost forever. "We're still friends. Good night, Jack."

Conjuring up a mage light, she moved swiftly down the steps. There were other things Jack might be, in theory.

But only friendship was safe.

CHAPTER 11

Tory borrowed Cecilia's well-mannered mount, Primrose, for her ride with Allarde. He showed up to collect her with a groom behind him. She had one of her brother's grooms in attendance. All very proper.

But as soon as they headed over the hills toward his family's estate, she gave a whoop and urged Primrose into a gallop, her dark red cloak flaring behind her. The sky was a brilliant blue and sunlight blazed off the light dry snow that had fallen in the night.

The mare's hooves kicked up little white clouds. Tory felt wonderfully free. It was almost like flying.

Laughing, Allarde followed a couple of lengths behind. "I should have guessed you'd be a neck or nothing rider!"

The grooms followed at a distance, giving them the illusion of privacy. After the first glorious blaze of speed, Tory slowed the mare to a more moderate pace. Allarde fell in beside her. She gazed at the rolling hills, crisp and beautiful in the sparkling snow. "I've only visited Layton once before this trip, when my nephew was born. I didn't see enough of the area to realize how beautiful it is."

"There is no lovelier place in England." He pointed with his riding crop. "As soon as we cross that stream, we'll be on Westover land."

They trotted over the stream on a old humped stone bridge. As they continued up the opposite hill, he said, "I don't suppose that Kemperton Hall is that different from your father's estate, but I'm glad to have the chance to show it to you."

Tory glanced toward Allarde and was surprised to see a faint glow of magic around him. The power had a flavor unlike any she'd seen before. It seemed to flow from the land itself, humming in tune with his nature like a harp string.

"Justin," she asked, amazed, "did you know that there's a magical bond that ties you to this land? A glow of power appeared as soon as we rode over the bridge."

His dark brows arched. "I didn't realize the connection is visible to anyone, but it doesn't surprise me. My family's roots go centuries deep here, to well before the Norman conquest. A Norman lord married the Saxon heiress to the land. How long her family was here before that, I can't even guess."

All Lackland students lost a great deal if they embraced magery, but she realized uneasily just how great Allarde's loss would be if his father disinherited him. He would lose not only the title and vast fortune, but the land to which he was mystically connected. His father didn't want to disinherit him—Allarde was an only child so there was no younger brother who could step in. But if Allarde embraced his magic openly, the duke would have no choice.

They continued riding. Over the next hill, they met a man dressed as a farmer strolling with his dog and puffing his pipe contentedly. Allarde pulled to a halt and dismounted. "Good day to you, Mr. Hatter." He bent and ruffled the dog's ears. As the dog sighed blissfully, Allarde continued, "You and Roddy seem to be in fine fettle."

"Aye, Lord Allarde, we are. 'Tis the most restful time of the year for a farmer." Mr. Hatter grinned. "And I'm still walking off the Christmas feast my good wife provided." He glanced at Tory and gave her a polite nod.

She smiled back. It was clear that Allarde and his family were liked and respected by their tenants.

After a few minutes' chat which ended when Hatter asked Allarde to pass a message to the estate steward, they resumed their ride. When they were out of earshot, Tory asked, "Do you know everyone on the estate by name?"

"Most of them." He grinned. "Though one of the tenants recently married a girl from Shropshire and I haven't met her yet."

He really did belong here. It was lovely to see how connected he was to the land, but the knowledge knotted Tory's stomach.

Allarde turned into a lane leading up another hill. "I want to show you one of my favorite places on the estate."

"Anywhere you want," she said cheerfully. As long as they were together, she was happy. "When we get there, perhaps we can stretch our legs a bit. I can feel that I haven't been riding in months!"

The lane led to a hilltop that gave a breathtaking view over the snow-frosted estate. "How beautiful!" she exclaimed.

Allarde dismounted and tethered her horse, then raised his arms to help Tory down. She descended slowly, taking teasing advantage of their nearness.

Smiling, he guided her to the edge of the hill. "I never tire of this," he said softly.

Tory gestured. "That's the hall over there? It's too large to be anything else."

Allarde nodded. "The snow makes the hall look like a fairy palace." He smiled apologetically. "If you don't think that sounds too fanciful."

"Not at all." The wide hall could be considered a palace, with beautifully designed grounds and a lake beyond. "No wonder you love it so."

Ka-bang! Tory dropped to the ground even before she consciously identified the sound as a gunshot. For a brief, horrific instant she was back in her vision of a high place and lethal bullets. By the time her knees hit the snowy ground, she was aware again. And embarrassed.

"The gamekeeper," Allarde said as he offered his hand to help her up. "I had the same reaction the first time I heard a gunshot after I returned for the holidays."

She scrambled to her feet with his help. Brushing the snow off her knees, she said, "I wonder how long it will take to get over that?"

"Maybe we never will. We've been in combat. Our mission was to save, not kill, but we would have been just as dead if the bullets hit us."

"I hope never to have bullets fired in my direction again." Tory smiled wryly. "But if the French invade, ducking quickly might prove useful."

"Perhaps the Irregulars will help other mages foil Napoleon's invasion, when and if it comes." He tucked her hand in his elbow and they strolled back toward the horses. "At least our weapons today are less lethal than the ones we saw in 1940."

She caught something from him. A feeling, perhaps. "What's wrong?"

"There are drawbacks to the way we're connected," he said ruefully. "As we talked, I had a feeling that I haven't seen the last of twentieth-century weapons."

She bit her lip. "You think you'll go through the mirror again."

"Yes. That doesn't mean you must, though."

"You think not?" She hated the idea of going back, but if her presence might help protect Allarde or her other friends, she'd have to go. "Let's put the future out of our minds and talk about something pleasant. For example, have you ever thought about how we both have strong talents for lifting that are similar, but not identical?"

"I have thought about how odd it is that I can lift sizable objects, like that boulder." He gestured and the massive rock lifted a foot into the air, startling two rooks that had been perched on top. As they flew away with angry caws, he continued, "Yet I can't raise myself or other living creatures. You can't lift as much, but you can fly."

"Not fly, really. Just float. Like this." Tory concentrated until she felt the internal click that meant her power was engaged. She swirled gracefully into the air so she was facing him at eye level.

He laughed with delight. "Just the right height for kissing!" He leaned forward, brushing his lips against hers. They were warm in contrast to the wintry day. "I wish I could fly. It looks delightful."

"It is rather fun." Tory drifted back to the ground. "But I can't move large objects like you do. Odd indeed."

"Can you lift living people?"

"I was able to carry my two-year-old nephew, but it was a strain. Of course, I'd not had training then. I could probably lift more now."

"I wonder what we could do if we blended our magic," Allarde said thoughtfully. "Would I be able to fly?"

"I have no idea, but it's worth trying." She turned to face him and they clasped each other's hands. "Let the magic flow," she murmured.

She focused her lifting magic on Allarde, pouring it into him. Her power blended with his, becoming stronger, lighter . . .

His hands pulled free and he swept into the air. Knowing how startling that was, Tory called, "Think yourself still or you'll end up above the trees and that's alarming!"

Allarde's ascent halted about fifteen feet above the ground. High enough to injure him if he dropped, so she concentrated on keeping her magic steady. Combined with his magic, the strain wasn't too great, though she'd rather not do this for too long.

Face wreathed with delight, he said exuberantly, "This is wonderful! So much more enjoyable than tossing sofas around." He tucked his body and rolled forward, somersaulting in the air. He came out with his arms outstretched, cruising like a bird.

"I never thought of doing acrobatics!" she exclaimed. "Of course, that's easier when not wearing skirts."

He swept down toward her. "Dance on the air with me, Tory?"

After a startled moment, she caught his hands and let her floating magic sweep through her. With a little more effort, they rose into the air together.

He slid one arm around her waist and clasped her hand and swirled her into an aerial waltz. She laughed with delight as they spiraled upward. "This is marvelous!"

When his laughter joined hers, she felt the rumble where her chest pressed against his. Her skirt fluttered wildly and her bonnet went flying, but she didn't care.

They had shared wonder and danger and fear, but never such pure, uncomplicated playfulness. They spun and swooped giddily, free to move in all dimensions.

They had whirled up to treetop level when Allarde's energy faltered. They began to fall toward the frozen earth.

"Justin!" Tory grabbed fiercely at her magical reserves and slowed their descent some, but she couldn't stop it altogether. After a few moments that felt much longer, Allarde's energy picked up again and they came down in a graceful, controlled landing.

She glanced at his face, wondering what had gone wrong. He was staring at the edge of the clearing. She followed his gaze and saw . . .

The Duke of Westover. Allarde's father sat on a fine gray horse, looking old and tired. He had the saddest eyes Tory had ever seen.

Allarde drew a deep breath, then took Tory's arm and led her across the clearing to the duke. "Good day, sir. You were out for a ride?"

His father nodded. "I saw you rising above the trees. It was a remarkable sight."

"Allow me to present Lady Victoria Mansfield."

"Lord Smithson's sister." The duke studied Tory's face as she dropped a polite curtsy. "I saw you at Layton Place."

"Yes, your grace."

"You and Allarde danced there, though less dramatically." Face grave, he said, "Come to the house and have some refreshments."

They had planned a winter picnic, with Allarde bringing food and Tory some of her brother's cider, but they couldn't refuse the duke's invitation. Besides, Tory was now feeling the cold.

She was no foreteller. But she had a bad feeling about the visit.

CHAPTER 12

The ride to the great house was quiet, apart from the duke asking Tory occasional questions about her family. She could see where Allarde got his grave courtesy. He resembled his father greatly in both appearance and manner, though the duke was so old he looked more like Allarde's grandfather.

Tory could see a faint glow of connection between the duke and his land. But that seemed to be the only touch of magical power Westover had. Allarde had that connection, and a great deal more.

His life would have been much simpler if he had less power.

The house was as magnificent and intimidating as it had looked from the other side of the valley. Even Fairmount Hall, where Tory had grown up, looked modest by comparison.

But the Duchess of Westover was a delight. Fragile and lovely with silver hair, she was younger than her husband, though far from young. She had a warm smile and quiet charm in abundance. Allarde had inherited that as well.

The four of them shared a light meal in the family dining room, which was high-ceilinged and immense and far from relaxing. They were all achingly polite, the food was exquisite, and it tasted no better than ashes in Tory's mouth.

The sword she had been expecting fell when they finished eating and the duchess said to her son and husband, "You gentlemen run off for a bit so that Lady Victoria and I can become better acquainted."

The men obeyed, though Tory sensed that Allarde's usual calm expression hid tension that matched her own. The duchess rose from the table. "We can have our tea in my morning room, Lady Victoria. It has a lovely view over the lake."

The room was lovely, too, furnished with feminine colors and dainty furniture. "How splendid!" Tory crossed to the window. "Are those swans in the lake?"

"Very likely. The gamekeeper has standing orders to make sure they have enough to eat." The duchess joined Tory at the window. "I've lived here almost forty years, and even so, sometimes the beauty of Kemperton catches me in the heart."

"Lord Allarde has that same feeling for the land," Tory said.

"You saw that?" The duchess turned to Tory, but before she could say more, a maid arrived with a tea tray.

After the clinking of silver spoons on porcelain and the pouring of fragrant China tea, Tory said, "I think your desire to speak with me was not casual, your grace."

"You are as perceptive as you are pretty." The duchess placed her cup in the saucer. "Direct, too. I like that. Very well, we shall be direct. Do you love my son?"

Direct indeed. Her throat constricted, Tory replied, "I do. I will not bore you with a list of his perfections since you know them already. But as soon as I saw him, I wanted no one else."

"I will not insult you by saying that is mere calf love," the duchess said gently. "Love is real and always precious, no matter what one's age. One's first love has matchless purity and intensity." The older woman smiled nostalgically. "But one's first love is seldom one's last love."

Tory's hands began to shake, causing the fragile cup to chatter in its saucer as she set it down. "You want me to turn away from Allarde."

"Yes." The duchess's expression was sorrowful. "I know that I ask a great deal of you. But I believe you have the courage and intelligence to understand why."

"Because of my magic." Tory was proud that her voice was almost steady.

The older woman nodded. "Justin is our only child, born long after we had given up hope. He is the joy of our lives."

Tory could barely keep her voice steady. "Naturally you want the best for him."

"In another time or place, the best might be you, Lady Victoria. You have all the qualities one could hope for in a Duchess of Westover." The duchess sighed. "But this is not that time and place."

"Because here and now, my magic would ruin him," Tory said dully.

The duchess nodded. "You know our world. If Allarde leaves Lackland Abbey 'cured' and marries a girl with no power, his father won't have to disinherit him. Though his time at Lackland will be considered somewhat scandalous, scandals fade."

"But only if he is not seen to associate with magic in any way."

"Exactly. If his power is seen as a minor, youthful weakness, people will accept him as the Duke of Westover. He will be able to perform the duties and responsibilities he was born to." There was a faint tremor in the duchess's voice. "Not all members of the nobility are truly noble in their souls, but Justin would make an exemplary duke."

Tory silently agreed. A peer of the realm was personally responsible for the prosperity of his lands and tenants. Through his seat in the House of Lords, he was also a steward for the nation. Allarde was intelligent, conscientious, and a natural leader who was good at

reconciling differences. As a duke, he'd be able to use all those qualities. And yet . . .

"Is it right that Allarde have no say in such an important decision?"
Tory protested. "A relationship is two people, not one. Perhaps you
don't realize how important his magic is to him."

She thought of his willingness to give his power and his life to
protecting Britain. "Much as he loves his parents and Kemperton, he
also loves magic, and perhaps also me. It should be his choice which
path he takes."

"I can feel the strength of the bond between you." The duchess
smiled sadly. "Allarde is too loyal and honorable to break that bond.
Only if you set him free will he actually be able to choose between
magic and his heritage."

Feeling kicked in the stomach, Tory realized the older woman
was right. Allarde had never expected to become involved with a
Lackland girl. He'd deliberately avoided the teasing and flirtation
that most of the Irregulars indulged in. If not for Tory, he would
still have years ahead in which to decide which path he wanted to
take.

She must end their relationship or he would certainly lose Kemperton. He might still choose magic when he left Lackland, but at
least he would do it freely, not because loyalty to Tory made it impossible to choose his heritage.

"I will think on what you have said, your grace." Numb to the
bone, she rose. "But now it is time to return to Layton Place."

The duchess took her hand. "Thank you for listening, my dear.
Believe me when I say that life can hold many loves."

Perhaps. But there was only one Allarde.

Blindly she left the room, felling ill. If she truly loved him, she
must set him free. She must use the privacy of the ride back to speak
to him and end their romance.

Easier to cut out her heart.

Allarde emerged from his meeting with his face and emotions so locked down that he might have been carved from marble. But whatever was going on behind his controlled façade didn't affect his flawless manners. He helped her onto her horse, waited until their grooms were summoned and mounted, then rode beside her from the Kemperton stable yard.

He rode so close that she could touch him if she tried. Tory fought the impulse as she wondered how to begin an impossible conversation.

Allarde said tightly, "My mother asked you to leave me, didn't she?"

Tory swallowed hard, hoping her better self was strong enough for this. "Yes, and she was right to do so. We are too young, and you have too much to lose. It is better if we . . . we walk separate paths."

"Do you think you can end *this* with a handful of words?" He leaned over and caught her hand. The full power of their attachment blazed between them. Love, need, understanding deeper than mere words.

She wanted to dissolve into that sweet heat that connected mind, body, and soul. For an instant, she almost did.

It took all her will to jerk her hand and emotions away. Voice shaking, she said, "Our connection is too strong to break entirely, but we can't let it become stronger." She drew a ragged breath. "We can't be a couple. We can't touch." *We can't kiss.*

"How can we see each other in the Irregulars and not want to be together?" he retorted. "One of us would have to leave."

"No!" she exclaimed. "We are both sworn to serve Britain. We need the training and the friendship of the other Irregulars. We can learn to be . . . separate. We *must*."

His eyes narrowed. "My mother must have been very persuasive."

"She was. Your parents love you deeply. Your father doesn't want to disinherit you. But he would feel that he must if you attach yourself to another mageling."

"I know all that," he said impatiently. "If I must choose, I choose *you*."

She wiped at the tears that were spilling down her cheeks. "I am honored beyond words that you say that. But can you survive if you don't have Kemperton?" In the darkening afternoon, the glow that connected him to his land was even more visible. "Your roots sink so deep into this soil that you might wither if you are torn from it. You mustn't throw away your heritage for what might be only a . . . a passing infatuation."

He stared at her. "I owe you my *life,* Tory! How can I put Kemperton above you?"

"Saving your life didn't come with cost or obligation, Justin," she said softly, seeing how right his mother had been. "As comrades, we risked ourselves for each other. That doesn't mean you must give up the life you were born to because you feel you owe me anything."

His mouth twisted. "What we have is much more than obligation, isn't it?"

She wished she could lie convincingly, but she couldn't. Not to him. "Yes. But we have known all along how much uncertainty lies ahead of us." She sighed. "I have never been sure that we would have any kind of future, Justin."

"Nor have I." His hands were white-knuckled on his reins. "But I thought we would at least have the time until leaving Lackland. Why can't we have that?"

"Because the longer we are together, the deeper the bond between us. It's almost impossible to end things now." She saw with absolute certainty if she wasn't strong enough to break with him now, she would never be able to do it later. "I can't bear to cost you the certainty of the land you love for the uncertainty of me. Of *us.*"

They rode in silence for the space of a dozen heartbeats before he said in a voice of flint, "Perhaps you are right, though I don't think so." He turned to her, gray eyes blazing. "But if you are hell-bent on destroying the priceless gift we've been given, I can't hold you against your will."

"Staying would not be against my will," she whispered. "But it would be against my best judgment." And because she loved him, she must leave him.

Unable to bear another moment, she turned and beckoned for her brother's groom to approach. "No need to take me all the way home. I'll be safe enough."

Allarde started to protest, then clamped his mouth shut. He looked like marble again. Cool, impossibly handsome, remote. And under the surface, searing anger. As they stared at each other, Tory felt something tearing deep inside her spirit.

Wordlessly he wheeled his horse and headed back to Kemperton at a furious gallop. She stared after him, one hand pressed to her aching chest. Was it possible to die of a broken heart?

But her breathing continued, her pulse still hammered in her temples, and her horse continued forward as if the world had not changed irrevocably.

She knew she was doing the right thing. And she would pay for it the rest of her life.

By the time Tory arrived back at Layton Place, it was dusk and flurries of snow were blowing past her. She felt like a bubble of blown glass that would shatter at a touch.

Wishing she had her stealth stone so she wouldn't be seen, she slipped into the house. The wedding was to be day after tomorrow, and the hum of happy excitement in the air made her feel even worse.

Giving a sigh of relief that she'd reached her room unseen, she darted inside—and found Molly seated by the lamp and singing happily under her breath as she hemmed a garment. The maid glanced up. "Good evening, my lady. Did you have . . . ?" Her face changed and she rose, setting her sewing aside. "Miss Tory, what happened?"

As Tory stared at the maid's round, good-natured face, she began to shake. She felt cold down to her very marrow.

"Oh, my lady," Molly said compassionately. "That young man of yours has decided he had best avoid any expectations so he's turning away?"

"No," Tory whispered. "I turned from him because if we stay together he will lose—too much."

Seeing her expression, Molly enfolded her in an embrace, more like a sister than a maid. But Molly wasn't really a servant. They were magelings together, and the older girl was a reader.

Remembering that, Tory asked brokenly, "What do you see of him and me?"

Molly frowned and closed her eyes, focusing her talent. "He is good, your young lord. Honorable to the bone. You and he would fit forever if you were born to a different station. But as you are"—she shook her head—"there is so much to keep you apart. You were born to be a heroine, my lady. To put others first. You do the right thing with Lord Allarde, just as you did with your nephew."

"Does the right thing always hurt so much?" Tory whispered.

"Not always. But often." After a thoughtful pause, Molly added, "As much as it hurts now, I think it would hurt more if you betrayed your nature. Now you sit down here and I'll ring for a nice hot cup of tea."

Tory sank into the nearest chair, grateful for Molly's care in tucking a warm shawl around her trembling shoulders. The other girl was right. Ending things with Allarde hurt beyond anything she'd ever known, even worse than her exile to Lackland.

But selfishly leading him to lose his heritage would hurt even worse.

CHAPTER 13

Cynthia eyed Jack Rainford warily when she met him in the Labyrinth the morning of her lesson with Lily Rainford, but his greeting was perfectly proper. "Good morning, Lady Cynthia. Your horse awaits." His eyes sparkled. "You see I am being very well-behaved."

"You can say all the right words and still sound impertinent," she said tartly as she caught up the long skirts of her riding habit. It was deep sky blue and she knew she looked very fine. She'd never had a chance to wear the outfit, with its dashing shako hat.

Though she'd outgrown the habit she'd worn when she was exiled to Lackland, she refused to be without proper riding gear. Sending her measurements to her father's secretary always produced a fine and fashionable ensemble. What she hadn't been able to acquire was a horse.

"Impertinence is a gift," he said modestly. "I come of sturdy yeoman stock, you know. We own land but aren't noble, and that makes us independent."

As they fell into step down the violet tunnel, he continued, "I have cousins in America, in their new United States. I like their democracy. All men being equal."

She stared at him, genuinely shocked. "You really believe all are equal?"

"Equal in the eyes of God and the law," he said seriously. "Not equal inherently, of course. You and I and the other Irregulars are all special because of our power." He glanced at her. "You are also above average in beauty."

"And you are above average in insolence," she said, but she had to smile.

"As I said, it's a gift."

They continued along the passage in silence, but a comfortable one. She'd had two days to recover from that strange, harrowing energy surge when he'd kissed her under the bough, and had decided he was right. It was merely a matter of misapplied energy between two powerful magelings. As they neared the end of the tunnel, she remarked, "I wonder how ugly this horse will be."

"Prepare yourself for a shock," he warned as he opened the door to the outside.

She stepped out and was immediately swept up by storm energy. "Some fierce weather coming in from the North Sea!" she said, exhilarated.

"Wonderful, isn't it?" They shared a weather mage smile.

Still smiling, she followed him to the edge of the grove. As he'd warned, the horse tethered beside Pegasus was a shock. Cynthia stopped with a gasp. "She's beautiful!"

The sweet little gray mare's flawless conformation would bring a queenly price at the fashionable Tattersall's horse market in London. Cynthia moved to the mare's side and stroked the silky neck. "How did such a beauty end up in your stable?"

"She was born to one of our ugly mares," Jack said with a grin. "Though she is unfortunately beautiful, she's Rachel's mount, so we have to keep her."

"If I don't see Rachel later, please thank her for letting me ride her horse." Cynthia had always loved horses. She could safely tell them her secrets. "I wish I had a treat for her."

Jack reached into his pocket and produced an irregular white lump. "Your wish is my command, my lady. Sylph loves sugar."

"She's a spirit of the air?" Cynthia offered the mare the sugar on her palm. Sylph delicately lapped it up.

"Because she rides like the wind. Ready to be off?"

When Cynthia nodded, Jack laced his fingers together to create a foothold to help her up. "Careful, there's an extra horn on the saddle," he warned. "My mother added it. She says it gives a more secure seat for jumping."

Cynthia studied the extra horn with interest. "I like the look of this." She set her foot in Jack's joined hands and he tossed her into the saddle. By the time she adjusted her long skirts to fall modestly over her ankles, Jack had mounted Pegasus.

They set off toward Swallow Grange. Once they were clear of the woods, Cynthia set Sylph into a gallop, glorying in the speed and the lovely horse and the burning power of the approaching storm. "This is as good as dancing!"

Jack answered her with a laugh and matched his speed to hers. Pegasus might be ugly, but he had good gaits and power. They slowed their pace when they reached the road into Lackland. "Main road or coast trail along the cliffs?" Jack asked.

"The cliffs, by all means." Cynthia's eyes sparkled. "So we can feel the approaching storm." She'd never taken the coast path before, and the churning seas and biting wind were stimulating.

"It's going to be a fine storm," Jack said, his voice pitched above the crashing waves. "If it gets too bad, you might want to spend the night at the Grange. Or will they miss you at the school?"

Cynthia shrugged. She didn't want to think about Lackland. Even the churlishness of the girls there couldn't ruin her mood. "If I don't show up for dinner, no one will come looking."

"The advantage of having a reputation for temper?" he asked shrewdly.

"Exactly," she said, surprised that he had recognized that. "It's very useful." And often she was in a bad mood. She had been for over two years, since her magic had been discovered.

Swallow Grange came into view, sturdy against the winds. They rode around to the kitchen door and Jack dismounted so he could help Cynthia down. His touch was entirely proper, yet she was very aware of the heat of his body only a few inches away.

She was tall, but he was taller, and he had a fine set of shoulders. She moved away quickly, not wanting to be too aware of his body.

"My mother will probably be waiting for you in the kitchen," Jack said. "She thinks you might have a good deal of hearth-witch talent."

Cynthia was unsure whether to be flattered or insulted, since hearth witchery was the magic of commoners. But useful. "I hope she's right. I'd like to be able to stay warm at the abbey." Like Tory, who had made a point of studying hearth witchery with the Irregulars who were particularly talented in it.

"I'll take care of the horses now," Jack said with a smile. "Until later."

Thinking the blasted boy had a smile almost as warm as hearth witchery, Cynthia caught up her skirts and sailed into the kitchen. Jack Rainford was a commoner, and practically a radical who believed all were created equal. But Cynthia couldn't help remembering scandalous tales of grand ladies who kept personal footmen who were lowborn but notably good-looking.

Lily Rainford was indeed in the kitchen. It was a frightfully vulgar scene—the lady of the house having tea with the cook! But undeniably homey.

Lily rose, her smile as warm as the fire. "Good morning, Lady Cynthia. Would you like a cup of tea and some ginger cakes just out of the oven? That will warm you from the ride while I explain hearth-witch magic."

"That would be lovely, Mrs. Rainford." Cynthia removed her bonnet and cloak and hung them on the pegs by the door. There was no footman to take the garments in a farmhouse kitchen.

So why did she feel more welcome here than anywhere else in her life?

Once Cynthia was settled in a cushioned Windsor chair by the fire with tea and delicious cakes beside her, Lily Rainford said, "You've probably learned much of this in the Labyrinth, so forgive me if I go over what you know."

"Please start at the beginning," Cynthia said, not wanting to say that she'd never paid attention to hearth-witch lessons since she'd considered them beneath her. But she'd had enough of being cold. "I want to know everything."

"Hearth witchery is the most ancient and basic of magics," Lily explained. "It deals with temperature and the elements around us. Water, fire, air. The primal powers that helped our ancestors survive."

She gestured at the fireplace. Flames leaped a yard high. With a snap of her fingers, the flames curled into a circle of dancing light. Cynthia caught her breath in delight.

Releasing the fire, Lily continued, "Traditionally, hearth witchery is more of a woman's power, though most mages have at least a little of the talent. It comes from a different, deeper place in the spirit than other magical abilities." She hesitated. "The quickest way for me to teach this is if you'll allow me to enter into your mind."

Cynthia stiffened. "Read my thoughts? I should think not!"

"Not that," Lily said soothingly. "The power to read thoughts is extremely rare, and I don't have it. For this, I would only take your hand. You would feel a sense of my presence, no more. Once there, I will guide you to whatever hearth-witch magic you have. Once you know the path, you will be able to call it up whenever you wish. Though practice will help, of course."

"Very well." Cynthia was instinctively wary, but Lily inspired trust. She extended her hand.

The older woman's clasp was gentle and secure. "Close your eyes and relax," she said softly, her mind an unthreatening warmth that slowly grew in Cynthia's awareness. "Different people see their power in different images. Accept what your mind offers."

Cynthia nodded, relaxing under the touch of the older woman's words and power.

"Down and down and down and down," Lily murmured. "Travel to the deepest center of your power."

Cynthia closed her eyes, feeling as if she were sinking into a feather bed. And—she was not alone. Lily wasn't intrusive, simply there the way Cynthia's mother had been when Cynthia was little.

She felt a curious duality. Part of her was aware that she was sitting by the fire and holding hands in the real world. But in her mind, the two of them were sinking into a mysterious, shifting sphere of magical power.

They passed dark places she didn't want to explore, but also veins of light. She recognized a swirling torrent of weather power as Lily guided her into darker, deeper passages.

Down and down and *down* until they reached a dark chamber. In the center was a dancing flame of welcoming warmth. Voice sounding very distant, Lily said, "Reach into your power, Lady Cynthia. It won't hurt you."

Hesitantly Cynthia obeyed, stretching one hand toward the fire. Even when she warily touched flames, they didn't burn. Instead welcome heat rushed through every fiber of her body, warming places that had been cold so long she'd forgotten they existed. Laughing with delight, she lunged both hands into the magical flames. "I like this!"

Lily laughed with her. "Take your time. Play with the power. Become one with it so you'll always be able to draw this warmth into yourself and your surroundings."

Cynthia obeyed, pouring flame from one hand to another, tossing blazing balls up and catching them again. She understood now why Lily said hearth witchery was so ancient. Fire was the power that sustained life, and a hearth witch could bend that power to her will.

She grew the magic into a bonfire and dived into it like a playful otter. Again and again she danced through the light until she heard Lily say, "Ready to return?"

Cynthia nodded, withdrawing from the magic with reluctance.

"Float up like a bubble," Lily murmured.

Cynthia rose through the depths toward Lily's voice. As she did, she realized that a silver thread now connected her to the ancient hearth magic. It was part of her now and could be summoned at need. She emerged seamlessly in the Rainford kitchen.

When she opened her eyes, Lily released her hand. "How do you feel?"

"Splendid," Cynthia said, surprised. "As if I had a good night's sleep, but I was awake. At least, I think I was."

"You were in a light trance, not asleep. That let you see the world in different ways." Lily grinned impishly, looking too young to have two well-grown offspring. "Now to see what you can do with your power. Mrs. Brewster, do you need any water heated?"

"That would be right handy for the washing up." The cook brought over a sizable pot of cool water and set it on the hearth in front of Cynthia.

"Put your hand in and see if you can warm it up," Lily ordered.

Cynthia dipped her hand into the pot, then visualized heat from that deep power flowing into the water. . . .

With a small shriek, she yanked her hand back as the water began boiling around her. She rubbed at her reddened fingers. "I could have burned my hand off!"

"A few burns are part of the learning process." Lily regarded the steaming water thoughtfully. "You certainly mastered heat faster than any hearth witch I've ever taught. There is much more to learn, of course, but that's enough for one day."

Cynthia flicked her fingers at the fire, imagining the flames leaping higher. They increased in size a little, but nothing like what Lily Rainford had done. "This is a really useful power. Why do mages usually speak of hearth witchery so dismissively?"

"Because it's usually women's magic, and what women do is never taken so seriously," Lily said dryly.

Sadly true. If Cynthia had been born male, she would be a marquess like Allarde and she might have been able to escape Lackland. "Tell me more about the different forms of hearth witchery. Can I heat large amounts of air? Or the water in a hip bath?"

"Perhaps. It will take time and practice to learn the extent of your ability." Lily smiled reminiscently. "When I was first married, I would heat a small pond in the woods so my husband and I could swim by moonlight."

"Is Jack like his father?" Cynthia asked hesitantly.

"Very." Lily gave a small shake of her head and returned to her teaching. "To heat air, imagine walls of invisible energy around what you want to heat. Then fill the area inside with warmth."

Cynthia visualized a sphere a foot in width on her lap. When it was clear in her mind, she filled the interior with heat. Too hot for comfort! She hastily cooled it down to a more comfortable temperature. "I never have to have cold feet again! You do this with your house, don't you?"

Lily nodded. "When I first came here as a bride, I created an energy domain the size and shape of Swallow Grange. Within, I can adjust the temperature as I wish. Warm in winter, cool in the heat of summer. I never have to think about it because it became an automatic process that runs even when I'm sleeping."

Cynthia pursed her lips. "I wonder if I can do that with my room at the school?"

"It will take far more power there because of the suppression spell," Lily warned. "Experiment. You probably can't warm the whole room without using more energy than you can afford, but you should be able to warm your bed."

A cat appeared at Cynthia's feet. Naturally it was an ugly cat, a battle-scarred ginger tom with half his tail missing. The cat gave her a fixed stare before abruptly leaping onto Cynthia's lap in the middle of the ball of warmth.

She stiffened, tempted to shove the ugly thing off her lap, but it had large, strong claws. Dogs were all very well, but she'd never touched a cat in her life.

Lily laughed. "Cats are rather magical, I think. They often come when Rachel or I create warm spots. Caesar here is the ruler of all the Swallow Grange cats and gets first choice of all the best places."

Hoping he'd go away, Cynthia released the ball of warmth. It vanished like a small puff of warm wind. Caesar, alas, remained. Warily she stroked his neck and back.

The cat began to purr with rumbling intensity. The thick orange fur was very soft and pleasant to touch. She scratched his neck lightly. He purred even louder.

"Caesar likes you. He's a very good lap warmer, and you won't have to use any of your magic." Lily studied Cynthia. "When we were seeking your hearth magic, I sensed that you also have an automatic process running like the one I use on this house. I couldn't determine the nature. Perhaps something to do with your appearance?"

The faint lift in her voice made it a question. Cynthia felt the blood drain from her face. She stood so abruptly that Caesar had to jump for the floor. He gave her an irritated glance, then stalked off. "Jack said something about having luncheon here? I'm very hungry after all that magic."

"Sorry, I should have realized that you'd be ravenous after burning so much energy," Lily said apologetically. "I'll get you some bread and cheese. Would you like oxtail soup as well? That's good for rebuilding strength."

Heavy magical use did create a fierce appetite. But even more than food, Cynthia wanted to escape the topic of automatic magical processes and appearance.

CHAPTER 14

By the time Cynthia and Jack started back to the abbey along the cliffs, the storm was blowing in from the sea in short, fierce gusts. No rain fell on them, but power danced along her skin, speaking to her in the language of wind and rain.

"I love these winter gales," Jack said as he gazed out over the channel. "So much weather energy to enjoy."

Cynthia glanced at the clouds racing overhead. "You're keeping the rain away from us, aren't you?"

"It would be a pity to ruin that pretty riding habit of yours," he explained.

Cynthia smoothed a hand over the heavy blue fabric of her skirt. "Your mother said that she'd teach me the hearth-witch tricks of cleaning fabrics later, but for now, it's easier to prevent damage in the first place."

"She told me that you're the most powerful student she's ever had for hearth magic. Coming from my mum, that's high praise."

"She's a good teacher." Cynthia would have liked to say more, such as the fact that Lily Rainford was also a good woman and lovely to be around, but the words seemed too sentimental, so she held her tongue. "The waves are really crashing down there."

Jack grinned. "Perfect for a new trick that I've learned. Would you like to see it?"

"Weather magic?" Cynthia asked with interest. She'd learned a great deal from Jack during their Dunkirk days, and was ready to learn more.

He nodded. "We should dismount for this. We can tether the horses in that stone shed on the headland so they won't get chilled."

Cynthia nodded, in no hurry to get back to the school. Jack was good company today. Her friend, no more and no less. Just the way she liked him.

The shed was open on one side, but the sturdy stone walls provided protection for the horses, who were less enthusiastic about the stormy weather than the weather mages. Catching up her skirts so they wouldn't trail on the ground, Cynthia followed Jack out onto the headland.

Pitching his voice above the wind, he said, "If you hadn't tied the strings tightly, your bonnet would be halfway to Dover!"

She grinned back. "Show me your newest trick, weather mage. I'm not easy to impress."

"I've noticed!" They halted above a small cove. The famous white cliffs of the Kentish coast were only medium high here, but the headland still loomed well above the clashing waves.

Jack gestured at a path that slanted down to a narrow beach. "In summer, this is a good place to swim and fish. I keep a small boat in a cave. But today, weather magic."

Cynthia waited with anticipation. Was Jack going to part the clouds and surround them with sunshine? That wasn't really new and exciting, but under these conditions, it would be a major challenge. This smashing gale had Arctic power behind it.

Jack extended a hand toward the sea, his brow furrowed with concentration. "Watch this."

Cynthia watched. To her amazement, after Jack had concentrated for several minutes, the water at the mouth of the cove began to rise in a column while a tendril of cloud spun down from overhead.

"A waterspout!" she exclaimed as the top of the column rose to the height of their headland. "I've only heard of them. You're drawing the energy from the storm?"

He nodded, his brow furrowed with effort. "It gets easier with practice, but a lot of power is required. Try it."

She concentrated on the churning waves. *Draw the waves up, pull energy from the wind, from the clouds. Raise the sea. . . .*

Slowly, a smaller column wavered out of the water not far from Jack's. Though not as tall as his, she thought it quite decent for a first attempt.

"Well done, Cynthia!" Jack exclaimed, forgetting her title in his enthusiasm. "Can we run them together and make an even bigger waterspout?"

"We can try." Cynthia frowned as she moved her column of water sideways toward Jack's. This was tiring work.

The columns came together. Instead of making a larger column, both collapsed into huge roiling waves. Jack laughed. "Better luck next time. That's enough for one day. I need to get you back to the abbey."

Cynthia was about to turn away when something caught her attention in the churning gray seas. She narrowed her eyes to see better. "Dear God, Jack! Is that a boat out there?"

He followed her gaze. His gasp of horror matched hers. "A sailboat! It must have been caught up in the waterspouts and crashed on the rocks outside the cove."

Cynthia squinted through the gray storm light as she tried to see supper so you can meet Bouchard and his children. You must be hungry after using so much magic."

He was right, she was ravenous. But the thought of going out where everyone could see her made Cynthia shudder. "No. Have someone bring some food in."

"You'll have to come out sooner or later," Jack pointed out. "So do it now and get it over with. Food might improve your temper." He slid a hand under her back and lifted her into a sitting position.

"No!" Cynthia twisted around with a wild swing of her left hand. Her palm smacked Jack hard on his cheek.

He rocked back, the imprint of her hand white against his face. They stared at each other.

Jack stood, his lip curling, and stalked from the room. His wide shoulders were rigid as he slammed the door behind him.

Cynthia collapsed back into the pillows and sobbed. Could she possibly make things any worse? Even Jack, who was always good-natured and tolerant, despised her.

The prospect of returning to the abbey and being mocked for her scarred, ugly face made her feel ill. She wanted to run away, but how? She had no money or other resources. Without her magic, she couldn't sell her services as a weather mage.

It would be so much easier to walk into the sea. Then everyone would be sorry!

She didn't hear the door open, but Lily Rainford's soft voice cut through her misery. "Sit up, Lady Cynthia. It's time you ate something."

Cynthia wanted to sink through the floor and vanish. Since that wasn't possible, she rolled over and sat up against the pillows, wiping at her tears with both hands. She must look a fright, with a reddened nose and tear tracks as well as her scars and ugliness.

Looking as imperturbable as always, Lily carried a tray with short legs. She set it over Cynthia's lap. "Eat something before you do someone a serious injury."

Jack's face froze with shock. "You poor mage-born aristocrat! Did your father say that?"

She nodded, the memory of that scene seared into her mind.

Jack pushed her fingers away and gently traced the thin line that curved from her cheekbone back toward her ear. "He did this?"

She bit her lip. "When my father discovered I was a mageling, he struck me. The scar is where his signet ring sliced my face."

Jack swore under his breath. "I wish I'd been there to teach him a lesson! I don't care if he is a duke, the man is a disgrace."

Cynthia looked up with a glare. "Don't you dare insult my father!"

"Any man who beats his young daughter because of what she is deserves more than insults!" Jack retorted. "Here you're appreciated. The Comte du Bouchard can't wait to thank you for your part in rescuing him and his children."

Attention caught, Cynthia said, "The Frenchman is a count?"

"He has a castle southeast of Calais. Bouchard is a decent fellow, for an aristocrat."

"What on earth was he doing on the English Channel at this season?"

"Running for his life. He learned that he was about to be arrested for treason against the state, and his children with him," Jack explained. "Rather than stay there for Madame Guillotine, he decided to take his chances on the sea since he's a good sailor."

Cynthia remembered the canvas bag the man had thrown into Jack's rowboat. "So he packed the family jewels and as much gold as he could lay his hands on and ran for his life. What about his wife? Was she lost before we could reach them?"

"No, she died not long after Marie-Annette was born." Jack looked wistful. "I'd love to see Castle Bouchard. His son, Philippe, says it's very old with towers and a moat and secret tunnels and hidden rooms to play in."

"If you want secret tunnels, Lackland Abbey has them," Cynthia pointed out.

"That's true," he said, brightening. "Come out and join us for

There was some satisfaction in that, but not enough to lift her anguish. "My magic is gone," she said dully. "I burned it out."

"No wonder you're in a mood," he said. "But it's only burned out, not gone. Remember how Polly Rainford burned out her weather magic on the other side of the mirror? She not only recovered all her power, but Nick says she's stronger than ever. The same will happen with you. It will just take some time."

"Too long," she whispered. "Now everyone will know how ugly I am."

"You're not ugly." He rolled her over so that she was looking up at him. She screwed her eyes shut so she couldn't see his pity and revulsion, and her left hand rose reflexively to cover her scarred left cheek.

"My mother says you must be a powerful illusion talent." There was admiration in his voice. "Amazing that you've been able to alter your appearance for years even under the Lackland Abbey suppression spell."

She began to sob uncontrollably. Jack's arms came around her and he patted her back and made comforting noises. She gave a brief thought to the shocking impropriety of this. To be in the arms of a young man, and in a bedroom, no less!

If they were part of polite society, they'd have to marry. More likely, given the difference in their stations, Jack would be horsewhipped or worse for his behavior.

But polite society was forever closed to her, and her magic was far more disgraceful than clinging to a commoner. A commoner whose kindness was soothing some of her misery. "I thought . . . that if I was perfect and beautiful, my father might not send me away," she faltered. "But he did."

Even more, she'd wanted the duke to love her. She'd failed utterly in that.

"You are beautiful," Jack said. "Not perfect, but beautiful. And far more interesting than when you were only perfect."

"Liar!" she said bitterly. "I'm an ugly slut who should be dead like my revolting mageling mother."

she'd prayed frantically to an unresponsive God to make her different, *normal*. Now there was only emptiness where her power had been a constant pulsating awareness. Instead of being glad, she felt as if a limb had been chopped off.

"Finally you're awake! Would you like some tea or maybe some soup?"

It was Jack's voice, so she must be at Swallow Grange. Memories rushed in of the storm, the shattered boat, their attempt at rescue.

Jack was lounging in a chair by the bed. He looked tired and thinner, which wasn't surprising given how much magic and physical strength he'd burned in their desperate rescue attempt. He had his usual cheerful smile, though.

Cynthia was about to ask if the French family had survived when horrified realization struck. With her magic gone, *everyone could see what she really looked like*!

She gave a small shriek and rolled away from Jack to bury her face in the pillows. She wished she were *dead*.

The bed creaked as Jack sat on the mattress and laid a warm hand on her shoulder. "You're a real heroine, Cynthia. If I'd been alone when I saw the boat wreck, I'd have gone haring off to the rescue in my rowboat and drowned."

She shook off his hand, not lifting her head. "And good riddance!"

He chuckled, unoffended. "Without your power, we never would have succeeded. Adding your weather magic to mine made it possible for me to row out to the wreck, and your hearth magic kept us all from dying of the cold and wet. If you hadn't been able to generate so much warmth and hold it so long . . ." He stopped, not wanting to say more.

Perhaps she was a heroine, but an ugly, scarred, repulsive one. Face still in the pillow, she asked dully, "The little girl. She's all right?"

"She is indeed. It's possible that her father and brother would have survived without your warming them up, but Marie-Annette wouldn't have made it," he said seriously. "You kept her alive long enough for us to call in the village healer."

CHAPTER 15

She was drowning, drowning in the cold gray sea . . . cold and lost and alone forever. . . .

No. Cynthia's mind cleared and she realized she was cradled softly in a feather bed with warm covers over her. Not at Lackland, this bed was far more comfortable. Where was she and how did she get here?

She and Jack had been riding back to the abbey after the lesson with Lily Rainford. Something had happened. A boat ride? In the storm?

Her attempt to recall was interrupted by the realization that there was something wrong with her. Not a physical injury. More like something missing, like a lost tooth.

Dear God, her magic was gone! *Her magic was gone!* Her eyes shot open in horror. She was in a pleasant bedroom, the sky was dark outside, and *she had no magic!*

When she first realized she was cursed with magical abilities, death. Cynthia wrapped the little girl in her arms, pouring waves of warmth into the limp body.

Jack said, "Tell him he has to get here on his own, we can't lift him over!"

Of course Jack wouldn't speak French. Cynthia called over the wind, "Find the strength to cross over, *monsieur*. Your children need you."

That cut through his stupor. With his free hand he reached into the bow of the sailboat, the only part that was still intact, and pulled out a heavy canvas bag. He managed to throw it in the stern of the rowboat. After mustering the last of his strength, he lurched forward so half his body was over the gunwale while Cynthia leaned backward to keep them from tipping over.

Slowly, painfully, the man pulled himself into the boat. He tumbled to the bottom, barely avoiding his son.

Jack instantly pulled away from the rock, turning the bow back toward shore. He looked on the verge of collapse from fighting the storm. "Put your power into warming these people, Cynthia! If you don't, they may not last long enough to get to shore."

"Very noble of you," she snapped, "but you need warmth and weather help as well. I can handle all of it as long as necessary."

She was lying, she was already scraping the bottom of her magical reserves. Desperately she tried to balance all the demands on her magic, helping Jack keep the water smooth, encasing them all in a bubble of warmth, and most of all, warming the child she held in her arms, who was as white and still as a wax doll.

She was a pretty little thing, blond even with the water darkening her hair. Cynthia thought she saw a pulse in the delicate throat, but perhaps she was fooling herself.

Survive, ma petite, she thought with the last dregs of awareness. *You are too young to leave.*

She could maintain warmth and weather magic as long as necessary. She was a duke's daughter, she was strong enough for anything,

She could *do* this. . . .

Jack bolted past Cynthia and ran to a small opening in the cliff a yard or so above the dense sand. She didn't notice the hole until he reached inside to drag out a small rowboat.

The rowboat smacked onto the beach, sending wet sand flying. It looked very small to be braving such stormy seas. Jack dragged the boat to the water's edge and set the oars into the locks.

Guessing he might try to take off without her, Cynthia caught up with him. "Can I climb in now?"

"Yes," he said shortly, realizing he couldn't escape her. "Concentrate on smoothing the water where we're going in."

She obeyed, clutching the side of the boat. The gunwales, she thought the edges were called. Strictly speaking, weather magic wasn't power over water, but in a storm, calming the air could be extended to calming the waves. She focused all her power on the area around the boat.

After a brief struggle with the elements, she managed to create a zone of still air and still water that allowed Jack to launch the boat. Though not before a wave splashed over her. Every inch of her beautiful habit was saturated and the dashing shako bonnet was torn from her head and lost in the water.

The sea was icy cold, chilling her to the bone. Since the outfit was already ruined, she used her numb fingers to rip the lower section of her skirt away so she could move more freely. There would also be less heavy fabric to pull her down if she fell into the water. Though she'd probably drown anyhow since she couldn't swim.

She was shivering in the bitter wind when Jack barked, "Use your hearth-witch magic!"

Exasperated that she hadn't thought of that, Cynthia created a zone of warmth around her. It was tricky to operate that in addition to her weather magic, but the blessed warmth kept her from freezing. Hoping she could continue to wield both magics at once, she extended the warm field around Jack.

"Thanks!" he said as he pulled on the oars. "We might survive after all!"

how much damage the small boat had sustained. It was jammed onto a jutting rock with waves battering the hull. Dark shapes clung to the wreckage as the sea tried to tear them away.

Feeling sick, she said, "There are at least three people in the wreckage. Jack, two of them are children!"

"The boat might have made it to the beach if we hadn't been playing with the water." He swore under his breath. "I'll have to go after them."

Cynthia stared at the waves. "Can you control the water enough to row out there without getting wrecked? It must be freezing! You'll be drenched and unable to row after the first wave goes over you."

"I have to try," he said grimly. "I can't let them die because I wanted to show off for you." He headed toward the path that led down to the beach.

He was trying to impress her? Not sure whether to be pleased or alarmed, Cynthia raced after him. "I'm going with you! Together, we have a better chance of controlling the waves and getting out there and back safely."

He stopped in his tracks and glared at her. "*No!* I forbid it! I'm not going to have your life on my conscience."

She glared back. "You do *not* tell a daughter of the Duke of Branston what to do!" she snapped. "I'm going with you, and that's final. We have a much better chance together."

He hesitated, his expression torn. "A better chance. But still not a good one."

"Stop arguing, you stupid boy!" Catching up her skirts, she darted down the path. "If we don't act now, it will be too late!"

She could feel anger rolling off him, but he stopped arguing and followed. Luckily the path was fairly wide, or they might have been blown off. Cynthia clutched her skirts, not caring that Jack could see her ankles and more. She didn't much like children, but they deserved a chance to grow up.

The beach was narrow with waves pounding only a few feet away.

Cynthia studied the tray. "There's enough food here for three people."

"You'll probably eat all of it." Lily sat in the chair her son had vacated. "Jack ate twice this much when he arrived home."

Cynthia selected a meat pie and took a huge bite. The beef and onion filling was the most delicious thing she'd ever tasted in her life. She gobbled the pie down like a hungry puppy, flakes of pastry crumbling onto the tray.

She washed the meat pie down with a swallow of tea and consumed a chunk of cheese before she was restored enough to speak. "How did Jack manage to return here for help? He must have been on the edge of collapse by the time he reached shore."

"He and Rachel often swam and fished in that cove, so when he sent out a mental cry for help, she sensed where to go and what to do." Lily poured more tea for Cynthia. "She collected several men and a wagon. They reached the cove just after Jack got the boat to shore. You were unconscious, so Rachel took over the job of warming everyone."

Cynthia dug into the sliced beef. "Jack said the local healer was summoned."

"Yes. We had to pry Marie-Annette out of your arms. You saved her life, Lady Cynthia."

"She's so little! I'm glad she's all right." Cynthia kept her gaze on the food. "I didn't mean to slap Jack," she said, her voice small. "He was trying to make me get up and join everyone else. I . . . I lashed out at the world, and hit him by accident."

"Jack is not always tactful." Lily's voice was smooth but implacable. "He's right, though. Eventually you'll have to face the world."

Feeling sick, Cynthia said, "I'd rather stay in this room forever."

"I know how you feel, Lady Cynthia. Though things look bleak now, they will get better," Lily said quietly. "I promise you that."

Cynthia blinked back tears. "How can you know what I feel? Commoners *like* magic. You weren't taught to hate yourself for what you are. I've used my rank and magic to protect myself. Now my magic is gone and since my father disowned me, the rank is as false as my beauty. I'm ugly and friendless and alone and"—she gulped, on the verge of complete breakdown—"and *afraid!*"

"Let's take those points one at a time," the older woman said calmly. "To begin with, properly speaking, I should be known as the Honorable Lily Rainford." Her smile was compassionate. "So I understand exactly how painful it is to be exiled from everything and everyone I'd ever known."

Cynthia's jaw dropped. Jack's mother was of noble birth.

Cynthia was going to have to adjust her thinking.

CHAPTER 16

Cynthia studied Lily Rainford with hungry eyes. She'd known that Lily had been an Irregular, but assumed that she was from the village. Instead, Lily really did know the horror of being raised to despise magic and mages only to discover the evil within herself. "How did you get from there to here?" She waved her hand, indicating Swallow Grange and the prosperous, happy life led by its mistress.

"I started out fighting and swearing that I'd be cured and home in no time. In other words, I was much like every other student in the abbey." Lily made a face. "Though it was a difficult passage, slowly I realized that being a mageling didn't make me despicable. And that if I became more flexible, my life would run much more easily."

"How did you manage to learn that?"

"One step at a time, with frequent backsliding. Changing my view of the world wasn't easy, but not changing would have been much worse."

Cynthia suspected that there was a not too subtle lesson in Lily's words. Flexibility had never been one of Cynthia's strengths.

Lily continued. "Secondly, you do have friends despite your prickliness. Among the Irregulars, you are respected for your abilities and the courage you displayed on the other side of the mirror."

Cynthia laid down her fork, appetite gone. "I may be respected, but how many of them actually like me?"

"The ones who see beyond your anger do," Lily said gently. "Jack likes you."

Cynthia winced as she remembered her hand connecting with his cheek. "Probably not anymore."

"You could try apologizing. It's amazing how effective it is to say 'I'm sorry' if you mean it."

Cynthia began to shred a bread roll with tense fingers. She had been raised to believe that the daughter of a duke never apologized. But maybe a disowned duke's daughter should learn how. "I've always been able to get away with many things because I looked beautiful. Now I'm ugly. It will take time to recover enough magic to look beautiful again, and by then, everyone will know the beauty is only an illusion."

"Which brings me to the third point." Lily rose and lifted a hand mirror from the dressing table. Holding it in front of Cynthia, she said, "Look at yourself."

When Cynthia tried to turn away, Lily said sharply, "Don't! When is the last time you really looked at yourself without using your illusion magic?"

Reluctantly Cynthia forced herself to stare at her image. Her fingers went to the disfiguring scar she'd been hiding for years. "I'm ugly! My hair is dull, my face is scarred, my complexion is bad. *Ugly!*"

"Your view of yourself is inaccurate, Cynthia." Having revealed her own rank, Lily had dropped Cynthia's title. "You don't look very different now from when you had the illusion spell in place. Your features haven't changed, nor the shape of your face. Your hair isn't quite as bright a gold, but it's still a lovely thick blond. Though your complexion is no longer perfect, it's very good. Your figure hasn't changed at all, and believe me, men notice figures even more than faces."

Cynthia stared at the mirror and tried to see what Lily was describing. "Even if what you say is true, my face is still scarred."

"Yes, it is," Lily said calmly. "All students who are sent to Lackland are scarred in some way. You are not the only one whose scars are visible. But your scar is much less disfiguring than you think. It emphasizes your high cheekbones, rather like the face patches women wore in my grandmother's time to call attention to good features."

Cynthia examined the scar, trying to see it as Lily did. She had done her best not to look ever since the original injury. It—wasn't as bad as she remembered. The line was thin and not ragged, and it had faded some. Though her face was still scarred, perhaps she wasn't as ugly as she believed. "What can you do for fear?"

"You're the daughter of a duke. Your ancestors were warriors," Lily replied. "When you're unsure of your welcome, hold your head high and remember that it doesn't matter what others think."

"But I'm no longer a duke's daughter," Cynthia said bitterly.

"Though he may have legally disowned you, he can't take the warrior blood from your veins. You still have the heritage if not the title," Lily said firmly. "And though he has behaved badly, he has enough family pride to pay Lackland Abbey's fees."

"The only family pride he feels is for the children of his second wife." Cynthia's mouth twisted. "They are all safely nonmagical. He has obliterated every trace of me and my mother. The fees and all my other expenses are paid out of the money left to me by my mother's aunt. If I died, the duke wouldn't spend a shilling for candles." Cynthia tried to keep her voice even, but she couldn't conceal the pain.

"The man's a fool," Lily said tartly. "But you aren't. You're a strong, brave young woman who is beautiful without being perfect. You have the potential to build a full, satisfying life, or to wallow in anger and bitterness. Neither path is easy, but the first is far more enjoyable. It's up to you how you use your gifts."

The older woman got to her feet, catching Cynthia's gaze with her own. "You can hide here for a little while longer if you wish. Or you can come and join the rest of us. The choice is yours."

Quietly she left the room.

Cynthia stared blindly at the remnants of the food. Rain still lashed the windows though the worst of the storm had passed. Laughter sounded downstairs, where Lily and her family and guests were enjoying themselves.

You have the potential to build a full, satisfying life, or to wallow in anger and bitterness. Anger wasn't doing her much good. But the thought of going downstairs without the protection of her illusion magic made her want to crawl under the bed and never come out.

If she was going to be miserable, she might as well be miserable where there was food, because, blast it, even after consuming almost everything on the tray, she was still hungry. Setting the tray aside, she slid from the bed, shivering a little. The house benefited from Lily's hearth-witch abilities, but Cynthia wore only a shift.

She wondered who had undressed her. She had a brief, shocking image of Jack's hands touching her, followed by a rush of heat. She wasn't sure if it was outrage, or . . . something else.

She reminded herself that Lily would not have allowed her son to undress an unconscious guest. Besides, Jack would have been too exhausted to care.

Her poor ruined riding habit had vanished, but in the clothespress, she found a lightweight corset, slippers, and a simple blue wool dress. Probably the garments were Rachel's, since the two of them were close to the same height.

Her hair was still somewhat damp and it fell around her shoulders in unruly waves, so she brushed the tangles out. There was a blue ribbon on the dressing table, clearly chosen to go with the gown, so she tied her hair back.

Then she forced herself to study her image in the narrow mirror set in the clothespress door. She was shocked to see that she looked quite presentable. Not beautiful and certainly not perfect, but the gown was a becoming shade of blue and the simple style suited her.

In fact, the image in the mirror wasn't too different from what she was used to. Lily had been right. Her hair was still blond, her complexion was good, and her figure had never required illusion magic. There was still the ugly scar, but it wasn't as horribly obvious as she'd always believed.

After drawing a deep breath, she left the safety of the bedroom and headed downstairs. Following the laughter led her to the dining room. The supper was informal with the Rainfords and the French family gathered around the table.

Absolute silence fell when Cynthia entered the room. For a horrified instant she felt hideous and she almost bolted.

Then the Comte du Bouchard rose swiftly. He was lean and dark-haired, with tired brown eyes.

He bowed deeply to her. "My Lady Cynthia," he said in halting English. "Words cannot express the depths of my gratitude. I am grateful you have taken no harm from your heroic endeavors on behalf of me and my family." He smiled a little. "You are as beautiful as you are brave."

She studied his face. He didn't have the dazzled look she often saw in men's eyes, but he did think she was attractive. He wasn't repulsed by her scarred face! Relieved, she said, "I'm glad I could help."

Bouchard's children slipped from their chairs and approached Cynthia. His son, Philippe, was perhaps ten. Dark-haired and dark-eyed, he looked very like his father. He even bowed exactly the same way as he murmured thanks in French.

The little girl's fair hair must have come from her late mother. Cynthia wasn't good at guessing children's ages. Three, perhaps? Four? Adorably earnest, Marie-Annette curtsied. "*Merci,* milady," she said in a sweet voice.

Cynthia smiled, her mood lifting. For all her flaws, this was one job she'd done well. "Without Jack, I could have done nothing." She risked a glance at him. He was sitting at the end of the table opposite his mother, his expression wary.

Turning to him, Cynthia said baldly, "I'm sorry, Jack. I didn't mean to . . . do what I did. It was an accident."

His expression eased. "I should have known better than to try to coax a wildcat out before she was ready." He got to his feet. "I'll get another chair. I'll bet you're still hungry. I'm going to be eating for the next week to make up for all the energy I burned."

"I'm glad I'm not the only one!" Cynthia moved around the table to the new place setting that was being laid next to Jack. What she had thought impossible was turning out to be easy.

Lackland Abbey would be harder. Much, much harder. But she'd worry about that later. For tonight, at least, she was among friends.

Friends who didn't seem to think she was ugly.

CHAPTER 17

Lackland Abbey was still almost deserted when Tory returned after a tiring winter journey. She'd left Layton Place sooner than planned because it was hard to be cheerful when her heart was bleeding. The heaviness of the suppression spell suited her mood.

It was mid-evening so the matron on duty had given Tory a lantern to light her way. She blinked when she reached her room and found a sign on the door. At the top was a large black "X." Underneath in Cynthia's handwriting it said,

Plague Spot!
Go away!
Leave food trays on floor.

A plundered tray sat beside the door. Tory wondered if Cynthia was unwell, or just wanted to avoid the company of the other girls. She'd been angry when Tory left, and might be angry still.

Cautiously Tory opened the door and stepped inside. She was unsurprised to see that her roommate's possessions had expanded onto Tory's bed and desk.

Setting her canvas carrying bag on her desk, she glanced around the room. "Cynthia, are you here? Have you been ill?"

"Go away!" Cynthia was a lump in her bed and a brusque voice.

Ah, yes, home again. Tory grinned and said in her most irritatingly cheerful voice, "You can't throw me out. I live here."

The lump in the bed shifted. "Tory?"

"Yes, and I've brought provisions back from my brother's house." Tory removed her outer garments and hung them in her clothespress. "Would you like some elderberry wine and cakes?"

Still buried completely, Cynthia asked, "How was the wedding?"

"Really lovely." It had been, too. Tory had been simultaneously glad to be present even though she sat quietly to one side, and miserable at the contrast between her own situation and the radiant happiness of Sarah and Lord Roger. "I think my sister and her husband will suit very well. I assume things were quiet here?"

"Not entirely." After a long silence, Cynthia said, "Your mother's pudding was well received at the Rainfords' Christmas dinner."

"I'm glad. Were you there, too, or did the pudding attend on its own?"

"I was there." Cynthia sighed heavily, then pushed the covers away. "I suppose I can't hide from you if you're going to insist on staying here."

"Well, it's my room as well as yours," Tory pointed out.

"If you laugh at me, I'll never forgive you!"

Cynthia sat up and swung her legs over the edge of the bed, her expression wary. Her blond hair was in a long braid and she wore a warm bathrobe over her shift, but there was nothing to inspire laughter in her appearance. Except . . .

Tory frowned. "Did you have an accident? Your cheek looks scratched."

"It's . . . it's complicated." Cynthia drew a shaky breath, looking on the verge of tears. "I have to tell someone, so I suppose it will have to be you."

Cynthia was as gracious as always, Tory thought dryly as she dug into her bag for the elderberry wine and the box of hazelnut shortbread. She had two glasses in her clothespress, so she poured them each some wine.

Crossing the room to give a glass to Cynthia, she said, "Speak and I shall listen, and not tell anyone else if you don't want me to."

This close, she saw that the line on her roommate's cheek was not a scratch, but a long-healed scar. Confused, she looked harder, and realized that Cynthia's appearance was subtly different. Not quite believing what she was seeing, she asked, "Have you been using illusion magic and now you've stopped?"

"Is it that obvious?" Cynthia wailed as she broke into tears.

Tory hastily took the glass of wine from the other girl's hand, then sat in the chair by Cynthia's bed. "It's not obvious, but that scar isn't new. I just remembered that when we returned through the mirror, for a moment it seemed as if your features were melting." She shivered. "It was very strange, but so quick I thought I must have imagined it."

"You didn't." Cynthia wrapped her blankets around herself and began a disjointed account of her holiday. "I've been using illusion magic constantly ever since . . . ever since I got this scar. Going through the mirror was so draining that for a moment I couldn't maintain my appearance."

As Cynthia continued, Tory listened quietly, not wanting to interrupt the flow of words. So the other girls had been dreadful, Jack Rainford had dragged Cynthia to Swallow Grange, she'd turned out to be a powerful hearth witch—Tory felt a pang of envy—Cynthia and Jack had rescued a French refugee family from drowning, and in the process Cynthia had burned out her power.

"I've been hoping that my magic would recover enough so that I could disguise my face before classes start again," Cynthia finished brokenly. "But it hasn't. It might *never* come back!"

"I've never heard of magic burning out permanently." Tory handed her roommate the elderberry wine and set the box of hazelnut shortbread on Cynthia's desk where they could both reach it. "According to Nick, it was a fortnight or so before Polly Rainford really began to recover. You've only had a few days."

"That's another thing. Nick hasn't sent a message in weeks." Cynthia helped herself to two pieces of shortbread. "Jack is getting really worried."

Tory bit her lip, concerned. "There could be any number of reasons."

"None of them good," Cynthia said gloomily. She took two more pieces of shortbread. "I've been hiding out here since I returned from Swallow Grange. Since I put the sign on the door the maids leave food outside, but it's never enough."

"You'll have to come out when classes start," Tory warned.

"Tell everyone I'm too sick!"

"If you don't emerge, eventually a teacher will come looking." Tory replenished their wine. "They'll wonder if I murdered you."

Cynthia gave a rusty crack of laughter. "The other girls would think you were justified if you did." Her brief levity vanished. "I'm praying that I'll be able to hide until I have enough magic to cover up at least the scar." Her hand went to her left cheek.

"Maybe I can help," Tory suggested. "I couldn't manage a full illusion spell here in the abbey before, but I might be able to conceal the scar until you can do it yourself."

Cynthia's face brightened. "That would be wonderful! I can't bear to have everyone see this ugly scar."

"It's not that noticeable, but I'm sure it feels horribly visible." Tory leaned forward and touched the scar. "If I can't do this, perhaps Elspeth can. She was planning to return tomorrow and she's better with illusions."

"She would probably tell me that humiliation is good for my character," Cynthia said tartly.

Tory smiled, then concentrated on summoning her magic to create the illusion of smooth, unmarred skin. To her regret, she had to use all the power available to her under the abbey suppression spell. Dropping the hearth-witch magic left her shivering with cold, but she was successful.

"There." She sat back, pleased with her effort. "That should hold you until you can conceal it on your own. The other changes in your appearance are too subtle to really be noticed." Privately she admitted to herself that she'd always found Cynthia's perfect appearance irritating. She was still intimidatingly pretty, but she looked more real.

Cynthia rose and carefully studied her appearance in her clothespress mirror. Touching her cheek, she said, "I can feel the scar, but as long as no one can see it, I'm all right. Thank you! I am so sick of being in this room."

Tory frowned thoughtfully. "A thought has occurred to me. Traveling through the mirror has been hardest for you."

"It almost killed me!" Cynthia shuddered. "Never again."

"I hope none of us do," Tory agreed, though she didn't know if they'd be that lucky. "I wonder if you had so much trouble going through the mirror because you were using your illusion magic. That might have interfered with the mirror magic."

Cynthia shrugged. "Perhaps, but there's no way to be sure since I'm certainly not going to travel through time again. I'll settle for passing through the refectory without having other girls sneer at me."

"I'll enjoy getting back to most of my classes," Tory said. "Except Miss Macklin, of course."

"Of course." Cynthia sat on her bed and took two more pieces of shortbread before Tory prudently closed the box and moved it out of reach. "I look forward to study sessions in the Labyrinth. You must be pining to see Allarde."

Tory winced at the unexpected mention of his name.

Cynthia frowned. "What's wrong? Surely Allarde didn't send a letter to your brother's house to end things between you! The lad is mad for you."

Tory squeezed her eyes shut, fighting tears. "His family seat is only a few miles from my brother's estate so we saw each other over the holiday. We rode over to Kemperton. When I saw how strongly he is connected to that land and realized that he'd be disowned if we stayed together, I told him we could no longer be together."

"Oh, Tory!" Cynthia stared at her. "How miserable for you. For both of you." She frowned. "Don't you ever get tired of being noble and self-sacrificing?"

"Cynthia, *don't!*" Feeling shattered, Tory kicked off her shoes and dived into her bed fully dressed. She pulled the covers over her head and buried her face in her pillow, completely understanding Cynthia's desire to hide from the world. Sharing her room with Molly, Tory hadn't allowed her grief to run free, which made this disintegration even worse.

Her bed sagged under Cynthia's weight. If her roommate tried to pull the covers off, Tory would scratch out her eyes.

Instead, Cynthia pushed a handkerchief under the blankets near Tory's hand. In a surprisingly gentle voice, she said, "I'm really sorry. Not only that it's over, but that he isn't even available for me." She patted the blanket in the vicinity of Tory's shoulder. "One thing every student at Lackland learns early is that no matter how dark things seem, they will get better."

The mattress creaked again as Cynthia moved away. Probably to finish off the box of shortbread. But as Tory wiped her nose with the handkerchief, she felt a little comforted.

It will get better.

Tory was so paralyzed by the thought of seeing Allarde again that she could barely force herself to return to the Labyrinth for their first post-holiday meeting. But she needed to see her friends.

She was so tense that a rabbit would have made her fall into hysterics, but Allarde made it easy for her. He didn't come to the session. Nor to the one two days later. Tory began to worry. He needed the group as much as she did, and she hated that she might have driven him away.

He came to the third session, arriving late and slipping in quietly. She didn't realize he was there until it was time for the closing circle and she felt his energy when everyone joined hands. She flinched at the familiar warmth, and hoped that no one noticed her reaction. After the circle he didn't stay for the eating and socializing that followed each session.

He arrived on time for the fourth session, but quietly kept his distance from Tory. She had to admire how well he did it. She no longer flinched when she looked at him. She doubted that he did any flinching. His handsome face was entirely calm and contained and detached.

The other Irregulars noticed, of course. Several girls made attempts to catch Allarde's attention. Tory was profoundly grateful that he had no interest in them. Apparently he'd learned his lesson and would now avoid mage-born girls.

She told herself that perhaps, in time, they could be in the same room without her being intensely aware of him at every moment.

She told herself that again and again—and knew that she lied.

CHAPTER 18

Tory and Allarde were doing a fine job of mutual avoidance—until a Labyrinth session a month after Christmas. In the good-natured swirl of departing Irregulars, she turned and almost ran into him.

He was a mere yard away, so close she could feel the warmth of his body. She wanted to step into his arms.

Allarde froze, as shocked as Tory. Though his expression didn't change, his gray eyes were full of pain.

Tory ran.

Not quite literally, but she gave Allarde a bare nod before spinning away and taking refuge in the nearest tunnel leading out of the Labyrinth. She stopped when she was out of sight and leaned against a wall, heart pounding. Broken hearts were supposed to get better. Hers wasn't cooperating.

She closed her eyes and tried to think of something beside Allarde. Cynthia was a good topic. In the weeks that had passed since the end of the holidays, Cynthia had recovered enough power to disguise her scarred cheek herself.

Tory was grateful for that. The winds off the English Channel were freezing, and she needed what hearth witchery she had to stay warm in the viciously drafty corridors.

There was no more talk of changing roommates. Tory and Cynthia were getting along well, perhaps because they knew each other's secrets.

There was still no word from Nick Rainford in 1940.

Despite settling back into the school routine, Tory had felt restless, as if something was about to happen. She wasn't sure what. A message from Nick? Invasion by Napoleon's army? She would reach her breaking point and shatter into small pieces?

With a sigh, she opened her eyes. This particular tunnel led to Merlin's mirror, which she hadn't visited since before Christmas. Of all the Irregulars, she had the strongest affinity for the mirror. Even several turns of tunnel away, she could feel the deep thrum of its energy.

Should she check the mirror to see if a message had arrived from Nick Rainford? He was the first person Tory had met when she accidentally fell through the mirror and was terrified by the strange new world she found herself in. She would always be grateful for his taking her home to his family, and becoming her friend.

But Jack checked the mirror regularly, and Allarde and Elspeth probably did the same. A message stone was unlikely to lie unnoticed for long, so there was no need for Tory to look. She was upset enough already without subjecting herself to the mirror.

She was heading back to the hall when she felt a twang in that deep energy. Something had happened at the portal.

Hoping it was a message from Nick, she swiftly made her way to the mirror, mage light in hand. She rounded into the corridor where the mirror blazed invisibly. To her shock, a motionless body lay on the chalk floor below.

The blond hair looked like Jack Rainford. Had he come looking for a message from Nick and fallen?

Not Jack, *Nick*! She ran the remaining distance and dropped on her knees beside the limp body. Tossing her mage light up to hover over her head, she gently rolled Nick onto his back. He was breathing, thank heaven, but his hand was icy cold when she clasped it.

She rubbed his hand between hers, surprised at the calluses and scars he'd acquired. He had been doing heavy labor recently.

"Tory?" His eyes fluttered open. "Thank God I'm in the right place!"

She frowned as she helped him sit up. "Nick, what happened? We've all been worried because we hadn't heard from you. Are Polly and your mother all right?"

"They're fine." Nick tried to stand and lurched so badly that Tory was barely able to keep him from falling. Once he was steady, they began walking back toward the hall, Nick leaning heavily on her.

"And your father and brother?" She'd never met his brother, Joe, who had been training as an RAF pilot, but Nick's father, Tom Rainford, had led her to the greatest adventure of her life.

"They're also well," he assured her. "But the tunnel to the mirror collapsed when bombs landed on the abbey ruins. Rather than try to clear it, I mapped the surrounding tunnels and found the shortest way to reach the mirror. It took time, though."

"I can imagine!" Tory exclaimed. "A good thing chalk is soft."

"Not soft enough." He held out one callused hand. "When I finally broke through to the mirror, I found a whole pile of stones with messages."

"Why didn't you send us a message immediately?"

"It's complicated," he said with a sigh. "Are the other members of the weather brigade in the hall? Easier to talk to everyone at once since I need advice."

"Advice is easy," she said warily. "Going through the mirror to help would be a very different matter."

"Believe me, I know! It's not something I would ask of anyone else."

"You did once before." She glanced at his face, thinking he'd aged in the last months. He and Jack, his distant relative, were about the same age, but Jack always seemed older. Perhaps having lost his father young had matured him. Now Nick looked older than Jack. A lot older. "You'd ask again if you thought it necessary."

"You're probably right," he said with rueful humor. "Things are bad, Tory. Evacuating so many soldiers from Dunkirk made it possible for Britain to keep fighting, but now the Nazis are trying to bomb us into surrender. Since Lackland is right on the southeast coast, we have fighter planes and bombers flying overhead all the time. I've seen more dogfights between the RAF and the Germans than I can count." He swallowed. "Sometimes the pilots manage to bail out in time, but not always."

It sounded dreadful. "You said your brother is all right?"

Nick's face eased. "Joe has had some close escapes, but he's never been injured. Mum gave him the sixpence you infused with protective magic, and it's working."

Privately Tory hadn't much faith in the coins she'd charged with magic before returning from her first trip through the mirror. She'd given them to Nick and Polly and their mother mostly as a token of her gratitude. Perhaps believing in luck helped create luck. "Given the magical talent in your family, Joe may have some special abilities that are helping him stay safe."

"I surely hope so." They were nearing the main hall, so Nick straightened, removing his arm from around Tory's shoulders. "Better not to show up draped over you. Allarde might not like it."

The usual pain stabbed through Tory. She managed a brittle smile. "No need. We are no longer together."

Nick stopped and stared at her. "How is that possible? Even I could see the energy bond between you."

"It's complicated. Don't worry, there was no horrid fight. It's just . . . better this way." Tory was relieved to enter the main hall so she needn't say more.

Most of the Irregulars had left for home. Usually the two teachers and the student prefects were the last to leave, but tonight Miss

Wheaton and Mr. Stephens had left earlier than usual. They were in love with each other, and Tory guessed they had wanted some private time.

Unfortunately, Allarde was the prefect for the boys' school, so he was still present, along with Elspeth, Cynthia, and Jack and Rachel Rainford. To her surprise, Tory noticed an energy bond between Cynthia and Jack. Was there something going on there? They squabbled all the time.

Now that Tory thought about it, Cynthia had been avoiding Jack since the spring school term began. Something interesting must have happened during the holidays. Given Cynthia's snobbishness, it would be delicious if she couldn't resist Jack's considerable charm.

Tory's companion was recognized immediately. "Nick!" Jack was the first to leap up. He reached Nick and pounded him on his shoulder. "Where the devil have you been?"

Nick gave a tired smile. "Sorry to have worried you."

"The mirror passage was as ghastly as usual, I see." Elspeth took Nick's hand so she could send him healing energy. "A message stone would have been easier than coming in person."

"I presume you had your reasons." Allarde studied Nick narrowly. "You want us to go through the mirror with you."

"That is *not* going to happen!" Cynthia exclaimed.

Elspeth arched her brows. "You'd better explain yourself quickly, Nick, or we'll all perish of curiosity."

"Mustn't have that." Nick sank into the nearest worn sofa. The Irregulars had become skilled at taking care of someone suffering from mirror shock. While Nick repeated what he'd told Tory, he was efficiently swathed in a blanket and fed cups of steaming tea and all the currant cakes left from the evening's social session.

As Nick paused to eat his fifth currant cake, Jack asked impatiently, "I'm glad you were able to clear your way to the mirror. Are you ready to tell us what brought you back in person rather than tossing a rock through?"

Nick swallowed the last bite of cake. "I wanted Tory's advice. The old accounts say that Merlin or whoever made the mirrors created seven. Maybe that's just poetry, but there is more than one. When I've made the passage, I've sensed that there were other portals besides this one. If I've sensed that, surely Tory has, too, since she has the strongest mirror magic."

"I have," she replied. "But only very dimly. I don't know where or when the other portals go."

"I've felt them, too." Frowning, Elspeth brushed back her silvery blond hair. "If I had to guess, I'd say the portals go to different locations, and for someone gifted in mirror magic, each portal could be used to reach different times."

Nick leaned forward eagerly. "Might one of the portals be in northern France?"

"It's possible," Tory admitted as she recalled her ancient British history. "The creator of the mirrors would likely place them in territories his people traveled to regularly. That would include Great Britain, Ireland, northern France, and the Low Countries. I've no desire to explore those other portals, though!"

"That's exactly what I need to do," Nick said flatly. "Explore the mirrors to see if I can find a secret way into northern France."

The room was utterly silent until Jack asked incredulously, "Why would you want to do a mad thing like that? Didn't you tell us the Nazis have occupied France?"

"Which is why I have to find my way in secretly," Nick replied. "There's a man there who needs rescuing, a scientist named Daniel Weiss. Apparently his work could be vital to the war effort."

"Then why isn't the government doing the rescuing?" Allarde asked. "Why do you need to be involved? Surely your father wouldn't ask his sixteen-year-old to do something so dangerous! He probably hasn't recovered yet from seeing you at Dunkirk."

"He hasn't." Nick ran tense fingers through his unruly blond hair. "I'd better go back a bit. I told you my father had gathered some very useful information about the Germans when he and his men retreated to Dunkirk. Because of that, he was recruited by some mysterious intelligence agency. He's based outside of London and manages to get home for a couple of days every few weeks."

"Which is nice for you all, but . . . ?" Jack prompted.

"The most recent of those weekends, Dad received a visitor, a research scientist from Oxford called Florey. This fellow had already asked for official help in getting Dr. Weiss out of France. When he was told that wasn't possible, he came to plead his case directly with Dad since they have some mutual friend and Florey is desperate."

"And just how did you happen to hear this very interesting conversation?" Cynthia asked tartly.

Nick smiled, unabashed. "It was a warm night, so I decided to enjoy the fresh air under the open window of my father's study."

"Why did Florey think Weiss should get special treatment when everyone in France is under the control of the Nazis?" Allarde asked.

"Dr. Florey leads a team of scientists for some really important research, and he thinks Dr. Weiss can help them succeed. Plus, Dr. Weiss is Jewish and Hitler hates Jews. When he became chancellor of Germany, persecution and restrictions on Jews increased horribly. The same thing is happening in the countries he's conquered, so Dr. Florey is worried about Weiss's safety as well as needing his help."

Tory frowned. "Why does Hitler hate Jews so much?"

"I don't know," Nick said. "But two years ago there was a giant riot across Germany and Austria. It lasted for days and Jewish homes and businesses were smashed and destroyed. A lot of people died, more were injured. It's called Kristallnacht because the streets in Jewish neighborhoods were filled with broken glass."

Everyone gasped. Tory didn't have to know any Jews personally to be appalled. "How can Hitler treat his own citizens so horribly?"

"Because he's evil," Nick said flatly.

"And because he needs scapegoats," Allarde said soberly. "Someone to blame for all the ills of society. When people are unhappy about their lives, tell them that a group that's a little different is the cause of their problems, and they'll follow a tyrant into hatred. The history of war is all about *us* against *them*."

Painfully aware of how right he was, Tory asked, "What kind of work does Dr. Weiss do that's so valuable to this Dr. Florey?"

"This research team is trying to perfect a drug that can save people from dying of blood poisoning or infections like pneumonia," Nick said, his voice sober.

This time the silence was awed. "Is that really true?" Elspeth asked in a hushed voice. "Mage healers like me spend most of our time trying to stop inflammation from spreading and killing patients. A medicine like that would change the world."

"I hope so." Nick shook his head, remembering. "A classmate of mine scratched his knee playing cricket. It was hardly anything, but blood poisoning set in and he died."

Tory guessed all of them knew of such cases. Inflammation was always the great fear after an injury. "If Dr. Weiss can help create such a medicine, I see why he needs to be rescued, but why won't the government do it?"

"After hearing him out, Dad said that he knew of Dr. Weiss's research and agreed that it has great potential, but there is simply no way to get him out of France. The Germans have locked him up in a castle near Calais, and it's surrounded by troops. Dr. Weiss has been given a laboratory and assistants because the Nazis want his work, too."

"If the military intelligence lads can't get Weiss out, it's unlikely anyone else can," Jack pointed out.

"From what I've heard . . ." Nick said.

"Under windows?" Cynthia asked acidly.

"Sometimes." Nick gave her a quelling look which had no effect on her whatsoever. "British intelligence is sending agents into France and building a network with Frenchmen working against the Nazis, but that takes time. There aren't enough resources to rescue a man who is heavily guarded. But I can try. And I will."

Tory bit her lip. "It sounds as if Jews all across Europe are being threatened. Is it worth risking your life for a man you don't even know?"

Nick slouched back in the sofa with a tired sigh. "This is where it gets hard to explain. The night after I overheard Dr. Florey talking, I had a dream. The most vivid of my life. I was at the funeral of a member of my family, but I didn't know which one. All I knew was the death could have been prevented if Dr. Florey's medicine was available."

Tory felt a chill. His sister, Polly, might die? Or his mother or father? After Dunkirk, she felt almost as if they were her family, too. "Did it feel like a true dream? Or might it have been your fears for your family since you heard the subject talked about?"

"I wish it was just fear," he said, his voice bleak. "But this was different from anything else I've experienced. I fear it's true, and not too far in the future. If I had to guess, I'd say it was Joe who died. Flying a fighter plane is about as dangerous as life can get. But I don't really know. It could be anyone in the family."

"The only way to know if it's a true dream is if it happens," Cynthia pointed out. "You could throw your life away for a total stranger."

"Don't underestimate me, Cynthia. I might succeed," Nick retorted. "This is something I *have* to do. For all the reasons I know, and maybe some I don't know."

"Nick is right," Elspeth said unexpectedly. "Dr. Florey's team is on the edge of something great, and Dr. Weiss could make the difference. I'll help you, Nick."

As everyone stared at Elspeth, Nick said, "That's wonderful of you, Elspeth, but I don't want to risk anyone else's life. If there's a mirror portal that will drop me close to where Dr. Weiss is being held, I'll find him, then figure out a way to break him free and take him back to England through the mirror."

"Are you sure you can find him?" Jack said dubiously.

"My finder talent has been getting stronger and stronger since Dunkirk," Nick replied. "I truly believe I can locate Dr. Weiss if I can reach the general area."

"How good is your French?" Tory asked. "Good enough for you to move about without being recognized as English?"

Speaking in French, Nick said, "I've studied the language for two years. I think I can manage well enough."

"Your accent is terrible," Tory said bluntly. "You'll be coming through the portal to an unknown location. After you learn where you are, you'll have to travel to a strange place to free a heavily guarded man. If you manage to get him out, you then have to get him back to the local mirror and home to England. Someone so obviously English will never be able to do that."

"My French will have to do." Nick made a face. "I hated studying the language. It never occurred to me that French might be useful someday."

"More than useful. Vital," Allarde said, his expression thoughtful. "Luckily, most of us at Lackland Abbey were raised with French governesses and tutors. My French is excellent, so I'd better go with you."

CHAPTER 19

Tory gasped at Allarde's calm statement that he'd go with Nick into a war zone. Was he trying to get himself killed? If so, could it be because of her? The thought was unbearable.

He continued slowly, his awareness turned inward, "I have some foreteller ability, and I have a powerful feeling this is something that should be done."

Biting back her instinctive protest in favor of logic, Tory said, "Surely you need some kind of plan. At this point, we don't know whether there's a mirror close enough to Dr. Weiss to be of use. Even if there is, are you sure you could reach it? It would be a jump in time and also place. A strange place you've never been before. Even though my mirror magic is the strongest, I don't know if I could do this."

Nick's jaw set stubbornly. "I'm probably next to you in strength of mirror magic, and I'm determined. That will have to be enough."

Cynthia said with exasperation, "Can't we just crack his head against the wall until he gets over this mad idea?"

"Tempting," Jack said, "but since this is a good cause, I'll go with you, Nick."

"You *are* mad!" Cynthia exclaimed, her expression horrified. "Is this why we have war? Because men are so keen on getting themselves killed?"

"There may be something to that," Jack said cheerfully. "One of my reasons for volunteering is to make sure Nick comes back safely. But another is that I missed the fun during the evacuation. I was sitting safe in England working the weather while the rest of you got to be heroic."

Tory shuddered as she thought of the destruction and fear that sometimes woke her up at night. "If you think what we did was fun, you really are mad!"

Jack sobered. "I shouldn't have been flippant. It bothers me that you and Polly went to war and I didn't. This feels like a chance to do something important, and maybe help Nick survive to do something equally stupid later."

"Thanks, cuz," Nick said wryly.

"I was glad to sit safely in England and work the weather." Cynthia's glare at Jack could have scorched paint. "It didn't leave me with the slightest desire to undertake a dimwitted, suicidal mission to France."

"That's because you're a girl," Jack explained.

A pillow whirled off the sofa and smacked him in the face. His muffled "Hey!" was drowned out by Cynthia's tart, "You're lucky I didn't have a rock to throw!"

Jack laughed as he tossed the pillow back on the sofa. "I see it's dangerous to tease girls who are mages."

"Let's get him, girls!" Cynthia purred. "The three of us can hang Jack from the ceiling if we work together."

"Tory's right, we need a plan," Nick said hastily. "I have a map of France, but it doesn't show Castle Bouchard. All I know is that it's south and east of Calais."

"Castle Bouchard?" Jack said, startled. "Over the holiday, Cynthia and I rescued the Comte du Bouchard and his children. He was fleeing arrest and likely execution by Napoleon's government. The castle is built on a huge outcropping of sheer rock with a small lake around half the base. The count said that he and his children escaped through a secret tunnel. But much might have changed between now and your time."

"But maybe it hasn't!" Nick leaned forward excitedly. "This sounds like fate, Jack. I need to talk to the count. Get him to draw maps. If there's a mirror portal nearby, we might be able to get in and out quickly and safely."

"You don't even know if there's a mirror in that area," Tory pointed out. "Plus, I think you'll have to go in two jumps. First back to your time, and you'll have to search for other portals during the passage, which isn't easy. If there *is* another portal where you want it, you'll probably have to jump there from Lackland. I think you could, but we really don't know if it's possible to jump from place to place in the same time."

Nick's jaw set stubbornly. "I'll experiment on my own so no one else will be at risk until I'm sure of where to go."

He would do it, too, the fool. And maybe kill himself in the process. Tory's brow furrowed as she thought about alternatives. "It might be possible to map the portals without going through the mirror. The energy always calls to me when I'm near. Usually I resist it, but if you and I combine our mirror and finder magic, we might be able to locate the portals from outside. Do you want to try?"

"Of course." Nick was still gray with exhaustion, but he gamely got to his feet. "As long as I don't have to go through again!"

He and Tory led the way to the mirror with the others trailing behind. "I wonder about the minimum time between trips," Elspeth mused. "It takes time to recover, but how much? Twelve hours? Twenty-four? More?"

Tory thought. "Nick made two trips about twenty-four hours

apart when he came back to ask for weather magery. How bad was the second trip, Nick?"

"No worse than the first, but that's not saying much," he said tersely.

"I've been wondering if healing energy could make passage through the mirror easier," Elspeth explained. "I don't know quite how to apply it, though."

"Practice on me!" Nick said. "I'll try anything that might make the trip less awful."

They reached the mirror corridor. The mirror wasn't visible, but Tory could feel the blaze of its energy. "Take my hand as we go nearer, Nick. I'll try to open my mind to the energy without being swept into it. Use your finder ability to see if you can sense other portals. And if so, where they might be."

He nodded and took her hand. "Are you sure we won't go through the mirror?"

"No." She suspected her palm was damp. The tightness of Nick's grip showed that he was also nervous. "But what's the worst that can happen? We go through the mirror again and feel as if we've been chopped into small pieces and reassembled. The usual mirror passage."

"You are so comforting," Nick muttered, but he managed a smile.

Hand in hand, they approached Merlin's mirror. Tory sensed tension from the other Irregulars, Allarde in particular. The heightened magic of the Labyrinth made it easy to read him even when he was behind her. The bond between them might have been damaged, but it wasn't fully destroyed.

Tory stopped a yard or so short of the mirror, which was currently invisible. The silvery surface only appeared to normal eyes when the portal was open and ready to transport someone to another time. Then it turned black as the abyss.

"Close your eyes and share your energy with mine, Nick," she ordered. "When our energies are blended, I'll reach into the mirror magic and you can search for other portals."

"It's a good theory." Nick's voice was steady despite his fatigue. His energy flowed out to hers, sinking in until their powers were joined. Together they were much more powerful and had a wider range of abilities.

Tory closed her eyes and the mirror's power blazed through every corner of her mind. Could such magic have been created by one person, even the legendary Merlin? Or had it been the product of many powerful mages working together?

The mirror *laughed* at her! Never before had she deliberately chosen to explore the mirror's energy. Her first passage had been by accident. The other times she'd been anxious and concerned only with reaching her destination safely.

Now that she was consciously reaching out to the mirror, she experienced it as a kind of living entity that blazed through time and space. Not alive like a human, but she would swear that the ancient magic sensed her presence. It rather approved of her, like a powerful old uncle amused by a small girl child who was ignorant but had potential.

Cautiously she explored the dimensions of the mirror's power, Nick shadowing her awareness. She realized that there weren't multiple mirrors. Instead, one enormous conduit of power was anchored to several physical locations in her world. The energy ran centuries into the past and disappeared into the dim future.

As she immersed herself in the mirror energy, Nick extended his finder talent toward the places where it was anchored. Tory could sense the anchors, but couldn't connect them with a mental map.

Nick could. She let him set the lead as he located portals one by one. He started with his home time in the Lackland mirror. There was another to the north. Scotland? Another to the south. France? No, Nick rejected that and moved on.

There! She felt his excitement kindle as he discovered the portal he'd been seeking. Northern France, as Nick had hoped.

The mirror blazed with consuming fire. Dear God, Nick's excitement and desire to rescue his stranger had triggered it and they were being drawn through!

A hard hand clamped on her arm and then she was in the maelstrom, torn to pieces, disintegrating. . . .

Her last conscious thought was *Damn you, Nick Rainford!*

Cynthia gasped and retreated involuntarily as the mirror blazed silver, then turned night-black and sucked in Tory and Nick. Allarde, too. He'd leaped forward to catch Tory's arm as the mirror came to life. Instead of saving her, he'd vanished into the portal with them.

"Nick is a damned fool for going through!" Jack swore, his hands knotting into fists. "He shouldn't have taken Tory. She hated the idea of another mirror passage!"

"I doubt it was deliberate." Elspeth's hand was pressed to her chest and she didn't look as imperturbable as usual. "The mirror energy was so intense that it might have only needed a thought to trigger it."

"Allarde should stop being so blasted heroic!" Cynthia snapped, her fear turning to anger. "Now he's gone, too. But I suppose it's another lesson in mirror magic. Anyone touching the wizard who opens the portal is going for a ride."

"I wonder where they are," Jack said. "And when. If there are several mirror portals, they could be anywhere."

"Let's wait and see if they return soon," Elspeth suggested. "Or at least send us a message." Looking tired, she slid gracefully down the wall to sit while she waited.

Cynthia had always hated the mirror, and now she hated it more. "What if they can't find their way back? Do we have to try to follow them?"

"Not if there's no clue where they are," Jack said. "Whoever built the mirrors probably placed them in concealed locations like the Labyrinth. Even if they end up in some strange place, they should be safe enough until they can return home. They're all clever, powerful mages."

"I hope you're right." Cynthia stared at the energy-charged space that held the mirror, wishing there was something she could do. But her trips through the mirror had half killed her, so she wasn't qualified to help.

Jack wrapped an arm around Cynthia's shoulders, snugging her close to his side. "If you want to fill the time while we wait, you can fight with me. You always seem to enjoy that."

For an instant Cynthia leaned against him, grateful for his warm strength. Then she jerked away, not wanting to give him the wrong idea. "At least you weren't stupid enough to go through the mirror, too. I half expected you to follow the others."

His lips twitched. "I may be stupid, but I'm not that stupid."

As the minutes dragged, Cynthia paced the end of the corridor, keeping her distance from the mirror. How long should they wait? Not that there was any point in returning to her empty room. She'd never be able to sleep.

The mirror flared and a stone appeared, dropping to the floor and rolling close to Elspeth. She caught it up and swiftly scanned the paper tied around it. "It's from Allarde. He says they're safe, but not sure of when and where they are. They'll probably have to wait a day or two before Nick recovers enough for another passage. Tory thinks she can bring them back here safely."

"Thank heaven!" Cynthia pursed her lips. "But we'll have to make sure the school authorities won't wonder where Tory and Allarde are. I can say that Tory has caught the same cold I had. Since I'm over it, I can take her food. I'll ask Miss Wheaton to verify that Tory is unwell but not seriously ill."

"Allarde will have to be declared ill also." Elspeth frowned. "We'll have to get word to Mr. Stephens in the morning. He can talk to Allarde's roommate, Halliwell. But we won't be able to maintain the pretense for very long."

"It was easier for me during the holidays when almost no one was here," Cynthia agreed. "There will be another meeting of the Irregulars in two nights. If we haven't heard anything from them by then, we can take action."

What sort of action, she had no idea.

CHAPTER 20

Tory landed on an unfamiliar stony floor in total darkness. Not the chalk tunnels of Lackland. She groaned as she pushed herself to a sitting position and wondered where and when she was.

"Tory, are you here?" It was Allarde's voice, tense with concern.

"Justin?" she asked in disbelief.

She created a wavery mage light that showed that he had also come through the mirror and landed about a yard away. He was leaning on one arm and looking around. When he saw Tory, he scooped her onto his lap, crushing her close. "Thank God you're all right! What just happened?"

She clung to his familiar strong, lean body. This was not the time to remember that they were no longer a couple. His warm embrace was the surest thing in a scrambled world. "Nick found the portal he was looking for, and his excitement triggered the mirror so we were drawn through," she explained. "How did you get here?"

"When I saw the mirror shimmer into sight, I grabbed your arm to pull you back," he said ruefully. "Instead, I was yanked through with you."

She made herself pull away, wishing he hadn't tried to catch her. Knowing that he could never be less than protective. Glad he was here. In his eyes, she saw a similar jumble of feelings as he released her.

"Where is Nick?" She looked around and saw irregular stone walls with moisture dripping in several places. They were in a natural cave whose floor had been smoothed for safe walking. A faint draft suggested that there was an exit not far away.

At the edge of the ring of mage light, Nick was sprawled on the ground, his face as pale as death. "Nick!"

She pulled away from Allarde and crawled over to Nick. His skin was cold and clammy, but she felt a pulse in his throat. "He's alive," she said. "But taking a second trip through the mirror so soon has been a tremendous strain."

Allarde straightened Nick out so he was lying on his back. "Can you manage some hearth witchery to warm him?"

"I'll see if I have any power left." She took Nick's hand and concentrated on warming him. It took most of her available energy, but she managed to channel heat into him and also warm a bubble of air around her and Allarde. Nick regained color and his breathing grew stronger, though he didn't awaken.

"The warmth feels good." Allarde rolled up his coat and tucked it under Nick's head. "Do you have any idea where we are? And when?"

"My best guess would be northern France in 1940 since Nick became excited when he found the portal. But I don't really know," she admitted. "We could be at that portal in our time, or a different portal altogether."

"Can you take us back where we came from?"

She closed her eyes and tried to recall every detail of the passage that had brought them here. "I think so, but we can't go through the mirror again until Nick has had time to recover. He might not be able to survive a third passage so soon. We should wait at least a couple of days, I think."

"I agree, but we should send a message back. Do you think you can reach Lackland at the right time?"

She reached deep and managed to summon the dregs of her power. "Perhaps. It's worth trying so everyone doesn't worry."

Allarde pulled a pencil and piece of paper from an inside pocket. After neatly printing a short message, he produced a piece of thin cord from another inside pocket and tied the message to an apple-sized rock. "I said that we're all right, but we won't return right away because we need recovery time."

Wearily Tory got to her feet. "Are you always equipped to send mirror messages?"

His eyes twinkled. "Yes."

Tory weighed the rock in her hand. The mirror wasn't visible, but its fierce energy blazed only a few yards away. She carefully touched the mirror with her own magic, then concentrated on the time and place she'd just left.

When she felt that the correct route was clear in her mind, she tossed the stone. The mirror flared silver for an instant, then turned night-black as it swallowed the stone. "With luck, that will reassure everyone."

Turning, she continued, "I'd like to get farther away from the mirror energy. It's not comfortable to be so close. Can we can move Nick if we work together?"

Allarde nodded. "First let me do some exploring." He created a mage light. "I'll only be gone for a few minutes."

Tory suppressed the craven impulse to beg him not to go. "I suppose it's too much to hope that you'll find food in your explorations. I'm starving."

"Going through the mirror certainly gives one an appetite," he said ruefully. "Once we have an idea where and when we are, I'll go foraging."

As he set off in the opposite direction from the mirror, Tory curled up by Nick, resting a hand on his shoulder to maintain warmth. She tried not to think how good it had felt to have Allarde's arms around her again.

She failed.

Allarde returned after a few minutes. "The cave curves and splits into several tunnels before it opens up on a wooded hillside. There are some tight places and they're all bespelled to keep people from seeing this branch of the cave. The outside opening is also spelled. Some powerful mages have done their best to make sure no one finds this mirror by accident."

"Any signs that animals use the cave as a den?"

"The spells seem to keep them away." Allarde studied Nick, who was breathing well but still unconscious. "If I take his arms and you take his feet, we can move him farther from the mirror."

Tory took hold of Nick's ankles while Allarde grasped under his arms, taking most of the weight. Even so, Nick was heavy. They moved cautiously toward the entrance to the cave, doing their best not to bang their sleeping burden into a wall.

After a slow ten minutes, they reached a decent-sized chamber with a noticeable breeze. Lowering Nick gently, Allarde said, "The entrance is just around the bend in that passage, so this room will make a good headquarters."

After they settled Nick on the floor, Tory studied his energy field. "He's close to waking up." She moved to the entrance of the cave. The night was pleasantly cool. That would fit with early autumn, which was the time Nick had left from. The woods were too thick to see any distance. There were no signs of human habitation.

When Allarde joined her, she said, "There's no way to tell what year we're in."

"1804 or 1940 seem most likely since we have connections to both years. But we could have landed in a completely different time period."

"That is *not* an encouraging thought!"

"Wait." He caught his breath. "Can you hear that?"

There was a distant mechanical hum. It was growing louder. Louder. *Louder.* She guessed, "Airplanes?"

"Yes." He listened for a long minute. "German bombers. It's likely that we landed in autumn 1940, Nick's departure time."

Tory felt chilled. "We're back in a war zone."

"I'm sorry you're here," Allarde said quietly. "You didn't want to come."

She gave a twisted smile. "Life doesn't always give us what we want."

"I'll go on a scouting expedition. With luck, I'll find a village and information about where we are. And food."

"Can you find your way back here in the dark?" she asked. "We could be many miles from anywhere."

"My sense of direction is good, and I speak German as well as French. I should be able to manage," he said reassuringly.

"I didn't realize you spoke German. That could be useful."

"The royal court still has many ties to Hanover and the other German states, so my father thought I should be able speak the language," Allarde explained. "Time to venture out. I'll aim to be back before dawn."

"Whenever that is." Tory rubbed her arms, feeling the chill. "Be careful. This is much more dangerous than my first trip through the mirror. At least I was in England. If this is Nazi-occupied France, it's very dangerous out there."

He gave a ghost of a smile. "My foretelling ability is minor, but it usually warns me if I'm in danger. I don't feel any at the moment. I have my stealth stone, so it's likely no one will even notice me."

"Your danger instinct must have been overworked at Dunkirk," she said, trying to make her voice light.

"It burned like a Guy Fawkes bonfire. But not this time." He disappeared into the woods within half a dozen steps. The German bombers were overhead now, dozens of engines flooding the sky with throbbing menace.

Chilled in a way hearth magic couldn't touch, she returned to the cave. Nick was shifting restlessly, so she sat beside him and took his hand. "Nick, can you hear me?"

"Tory?" His voice was rusty with uncertainty. "I made it to your time?"

"Yes, and then you hauled Allarde and me back through the mirror," she said wryly. "How are you feeling?"

"Like I was flattened by a convoy of lorries." His gaze moved around the unfamiliar surroundings. "Where the devil are we?"

"We don't know. Allarde has gone in search of information and provisions. Since German bombers just flew over, we might be in France as you hoped to be."

He groaned. "It's coming back to me. Lord, this is my fault, isn't it? You and I were trying to map the mirror portals to see if there was one in northern France. When I found one I just knew was right, *Wham!* The portal pulled us through before I knew what was happening." His brow furrowed. "But how did Allarde get here?"

"When he saw that the portal was opening, he tried to pull me back. Instead he was dragged through with us."

"He must want to thrash me," Nick muttered.

"I'm the one who wants to thrash you," she said tartly. "Allarde and Jack volunteered to come through the mirror. I wanted never to travel through it again."

He sighed. "I'm really sorry, Tory. I didn't want to risk anyone else in this mad quest of mine. It's a beastly return after all you've done for me."

She studied his tired face. "If Dr. Weiss can help create a medicine that does what you said, this is worth it."

"You can go home right now," he said earnestly. "I'll be all right."

"It's too late. I'm part of this mad scheme now." Unfortunately.

As Nick closed his eyes with exhaustion, Tory made a fervent mental wish that they would be able to rescue Dr. Weiss and get away safely and soon. But one didn't have to be a foreteller to know that they wouldn't be that lucky.

CHAPTER 21

Since Tory and Nick were exhausted from the mirror passage, they dozed off while waiting for Allarde to return. Tory set the hearth-witch spell to keep them warm.

Even though resting against the wall wasn't comfortable, she felt stronger when she came awake. Quietly she asked, "How are you doing?"

"Better." Nick covered a yawn. "Still night, I see."

"Dawn can't be too far off." Tory stretched her stiff muscles. "I hope Allarde finds some food. I'm ready to go outside and gnaw on a tree. You must be even hungrier since you went through the mirror twice within an hour."

"Ravenous, but you Irregulars fed me well after the first mirror passage." Nick sat up against the opposite wall and dug into a jacket pocket. "I was so tired that I didn't remember earlier that I'd brought some food to help me recover." He pulled out a small crinkly bag. "Want some chocolate digestive biscuits?"

"Nick!" She grabbed the packet and ripped it open. "I may forgive you for bringing me here after all. How many of these do you want?"

"I think I packed six, so two for me."

After checking the number of biscuits, she gave a pair to Nick, and put two aside for Allarde. She ate her own two slowly, nipping off small bits to savor the taste and make them last longer. The flat, chocolate iced cakes were one of the unexpected pleasures she'd discovered in 1940. "You'd better put Allarde's share away," she said as she licked the last crumbs from her fingertips. "I'm not sure I trust myself around them."

"I don't, either." Nick put the diminished packet back in his pocket. "I should have brought more food."

Wanting distraction from the remaining biscuits, not to mention the fact that Allarde was off exploring an occupied country where his clothing would get him noticed and his Englishness could get him shot, she said, "Tell me more about what has been happening with the war since we left in June. Not well, from what you said."

"Hitler has eaten up more small countries," Nick said, looking older than his years. "He's trying to bomb Britain back to the Stone Age, and now Italy has declared war on us. Germany, Italy, and Japan have just signed a treaty declaring themselves to be the Axis powers, as if the world revolves around them."

"Japan?" Tory's brow furrowed as she tried to place the name. "Where is that? Near India?"

"Japan is a group of islands off China. They're ruthless and have a powerful military that they've used to conquer their neighbors. They're formidable allies for Germany and Italy."

Tory absorbed that. "Your war is getting bigger and bigger."

"Half the world is already fighting," Nick said grimly. "Everyone on the south coast can see daily dogfights between the RAF and the

Luftwaffe. Fishermen from Lackland have pulled RAF pilots out of the channel, and a German pilot was captured by a farmer with a pitchfork within two miles of our house."

"It sounds dreadful!" Tory bit her lip, ill with the knowledge that the war she'd seen at Dunkirk had moved to England. "So the RAF, the Royal Navy, and the English Channel are all that stand between Britain and being conquered?"

Nick nodded. "All that, but especially the RAF. It's a lot to ask of a handful of pilots. Casualties are horribly high."

And every time the Rainfords saw a dogfight, they'd wonder if their oldest son was up there risking his life. "You said your brother, Joe, was all right?"

"So far, but he's been shot down twice, once over the channel, once near London. He escaped both times with no serious injuries." After a silence, Nick continued, "He hasn't told my parents, but he did tell me so I wouldn't get any romantic notions about the RAF. If this war goes on for another couple of years, I'll be called up."

Tory smothered a horrified gasp. She hadn't recognized that Nick might be in uniform soon.

Seeing her expression, Nick said soothingly, "Don't look like that, Tory. It doesn't matter if I choose land, sea, or air. None are necessarily more dangerous than living in Lackland and maybe have an airplane or bomb fall on my head."

"I do not find that a cheering thought," she said tartly.

"I don't, either, but I don't have much choice. Nor would I stand on the sidelines while my friends are dying for England." His voice lightened. "Joe was home for a weekend leave a fortnight ago. He spent most of it sleeping and eating Mum's cooking, but he did say that the Nazis have bungled their air war. They started out by pounding on Fighter Command, which means all the RAF airfields and aircraft, especially along the southeast coast. They could have totally destroyed the RAF if they'd kept that up."

"I gather they've stopped, but why?" Tory asked.

"The Nazis bombed London," Nick said succinctly. "Maybe it

was a mistake since up till then, they'd attacked only fighters and airfields, not civilians. Churchill retaliated by sending bombers over Berlin. Hitler went berserk and now the Luftwaffe is concentrating on blasting London into smoking ruins. They've bombed the East End docks, St. Paul's Cathedral, even Buckingham Palace, where the royal family lives."

Tory caught her breath. She loved the splendid dome of St. Paul's and tried to visit whenever she visited London. The current church had been built in the 1600s. It was appalling to imagine it bombed to rubble. "So innocent people are dying in London, but the airfields and pilots are spared to keep on fighting."

"Exactly." His lips twisted. "How many more people will die of this insanity? Would it be better if we just surrendered?"

"No," she said instantly. "Everything I've heard from you and others in your time says that a world ruled by Hitler would be a dreadful place." Wanting to change the subject, she asked, "Have you tried using your finder talent to locate Dr. Weiss? Is he near here and now?"

"My wits have been so scrambled I didn't think to try. Let's see. . . ." He closed his eyes and focused on the man he wanted to find. After a long minute, his eyes popped open. "He's near here, Tory! I'd guess within two or three miles of this cave. I could walk right up to him, I'm sure of it!"

"If you could walk three miles at the moment," she said dryly.

Nick smiled, unabashed. "By tomorrow I should be able to. This may be easier than I thought, Tory. If I can break Dr. Weiss out of his captivity, I can bring him here and take him through the mirror to Lackland."

"A good plan, but the breaking him out of captivity part needs work," Allarde's voice said from the cave entrance.

Tory jumped to her feet, increasing the range of her mage light so she could see him clearly. Allarde wore shabby twentieth-century clothing and carried a large sack. "It looks like you were successful. Did you run into any trouble?"

"Nothing serious." He set the sack down. "Nick, you look much better."

"I am." Nick offered the bag with the remaining biscuits. "Healed by chocolate digestive biscuits. Here are two for you."

Allarde ripped open the small bag. "Your era has some definite advantages, Nick. I wonder if biscuit boxes could be thrown through a mirror like our message stones?"

"What a wonderful idea!" Tory exclaimed. "It should work." She was getting better at being near Allarde as a friend. Or at least she was reasonably sure she wouldn't throw herself into his arms and refuse to let go. "Tell us what happened. Nick's finder talent says Dr. Weiss is only a few miles away. Is he right?"

"Castle Bouchard is very near, so if your scientist is there, we've come to the right place and time." Allarde bit into his first biscuit, savoring the chocolate. "There's a village, St. Christophe, a mile or so from here. In the town center I saw a sign pointing toward the castle and saying three kilometers, which fits. On a side street I found a little shop that carries used clothing and such, so I acquired what we needed."

"How?" Nick asked. "Surely it wasn't unlocked. Did you break in?"

"That would be ungentlemanly," Allarde said with a glint of humor in his eyes. "So I magicked the lock. It was simple to move the internal bits so I could walk in. You should be able to do the same thing, Tory."

"It never occurred to me to try." Her eyes narrowed as she imagined how one might unlock a door. She gave a short nod. "But I will next time I have a chance."

"I have no talent for moving objects," Nick said regretfully. "A good thing you do. What did you find besides the undistinguished outfit you're wearing?"

"I assume your own clothing won't draw much notice here since we're in your time, but it might be good to cover up with an overcoat. This looks like something a young French farmer would wear."

He opened his sack, which turned out to be a ragged blanket tied at the corners, and extracted a dark garment.

Nick's nostrils flared as he shook out the coat. "Smells like a farm, all right. This should cover anything too English-looking in my appearance."

"Did you find something for me?" Tory asked.

Allarde dug deeper into his bag. "There was a schoolgirl's outfit, but it was much too large. Since you found trousers practical when Nick took us sailing, I decided to get you boys' clothing." He handed several folded garments to her. "I'm sorry they aren't as clean as you might like."

Tory examined her new outfit. The coat was drab but warm, and the hat would obscure her features. Though the trousers were shapeless and too long, they could be rolled at the ankles. Disgraceful though it was for a lady to don trousers, she'd found unexpected freedom wearing them on their trip to Dunkirk. "No one will give us a second glance. I'm just sorry it's necessary to steal."

"I don't like it, either, but we don't have much choice," Allarde agreed. "Since I had some coins with me, I left a gold guinea. The shop owner might be able to get some value from that." He produced two more tattered blankets. "These are worn, but better than trying to sleep on stone."

"You did well." Tory shook out the blanket he gave her. It was small and woven of coarse, ugly wool, but it would keep the drafts out.

"I have food, too. Bread, this block of cheese, and a bottle of white table wine." Allarde set a sizable slab of cheese and two skinny loaves of bread between them, along with a bottle. "I also picked some ripe pears from a tree on the way back."

"You can forage for me anytime, Allarde." Nick pulled out a folding penknife and began slicing the cheese. "You had a flawless mission."

"Not really," Allarde said wryly. "The owner lives above the food shop I entered. She heard me and came down holding a shotgun."

"Good heavens!" Tory exclaimed. "Did she raise the alarm?"

"I lifted my hands in the air and tried to look harmless while I explained that I merely needed to buy food. My French must have more of an English accent than I thought because she cut me off and said she didn't want to know more."

"She probably thought you were a British aviator." Nick cut a ragged piece of bread. "My brother said there are Frenchmen who secretly help downed pilots escape."

"That would explain it. She didn't say much, but she wrapped up the cheese and bread and gave me the wine and told me to leave quickly and quietly." Allarde put a piece of cheese on bread and bit in with pleasure. "She said something odd. That I must be careful not to be seen since there are no men in St. Christophe."

Nick frowned. "I've heard there are towns where the only males left are little boys and old men. All the men in between were shipped to Germany to do forced labor."

Tory sucked in her breath. "Are you sure your century is more civilized than ours, Nick?"

"No," he said bleakly. "But it reminds me why we need to keep fighting rather surrender to Hitler."

Allarde opened the wine bottle and took a sip. "A light table wine, but it goes rather well with the bread and cheese. Nick?"

Nick wiped the mouth and tasted. "Nice. This will make a dashing and romantic tale for our grandchildren." He passed the bottle to Tory.

"Assuming we live long enough to have grandchildren." She tried not to think how Allarde had drunk from the same bottle. They were comrades, not lovers, and this was just wine.

Nick reached for more bread and cheese. "A few pieces of this and I'll be ready to go find Dr. Weiss."

"We shouldn't travel by daylight," Allarde said. "Even this late, I had to avoid several German army trucks on the road. Better we rest through the day and head for Castle Bouchard when it's dark again."

"Will you be rested enough to return home by then, Tory?" Nick asked. "Or will you wait to see how our mission goes?"

"I'm going with you, of course," she said calmly. "I have no intention of sitting here in this cave and wondering if you two fools are dead or alive. I'm a mage, not a helpless schoolgirl."

Allarde looked appalled. "It's male nature to protect women and children."

"If you're saying that Tory needs protection, you'll be in trouble," Nick said with a grin. "I'll be glad to have her along. She's one of the most powerful mages in the Irregulars, and her talent for blending power from all of us could be useful. Having her increases our chance of success."

Allarde caught Tory's gaze, his gray eyes troubled. "I can't persuade you to the wiser course?"

"No, but you can give me one of those pears."

He gave her a pear and she polished it on her sleeve before sinking her teeth into it. The pear was ripe and sweet and juicy. "Lovely. This is the best picnic I've ever been on." She took another bite.

The best, and also the strangest. But she couldn't regret being near Allarde even if an impassable barrier remained between them.

CHAPTER 22

Tory and the others slept most of the day. She awoke to soft rain and early dusk. After eating again, they set off into the night. As the rain increased, she was grateful that Allarde had thought to acquire coats and hats for them. Though her hearth-witch magic kept her warm, the rain was still wet.

A pity they didn't have a weather mage to push the rain away. Hiking through unknown territory in darkness, mud, and rain was an adventure she could do without.

Nick led the way, never hesitating except when choosing the best way to detour around a farmhouse. They passed one farm close enough to set off a chorus of barking dogs, but there was no sign that humans noticed them. If the women and children were working the farms, they were probably too tired to wake easily.

After an interminable walk, Nick said in a low voice, "Dr. Weiss is very close. Just the other side of the hill, I think."

They headed up a hedged lane just wide enough for the three of them. Tory was tiring, though she'd rather drop in her tracks than admit that to her male companions.

They reached the hilltop and got their first sight of Castle Bouchard. "Dear God," Allarde whispered.

"No wonder your father said it was impossible to rescue Dr. Weiss," Tory said, stunned by the massive stone escarpment. The stone castle rose from the crest, well above their present height. A sheer cliff dropped to the small village below, while a lake glinted to the left of the escarpment.

The village was surely as old as the castle, but the weathered stone buildings had been transformed into a military camp surrounded by barbed wire and guards. A road snaked up and around the cliff, probably climbing to the castle by a less impossible route.

The perimeter fence was swept by searchlights and a guardhouse controlled the main gate. Other guards could be seen stolidly patrolling inside the compound. "It might be possible for us to get into the castle," Tory said doubtfully. "But I don't know how."

"Dr. Weiss isn't in the castle. He's in that long low building at the base of the cliff." Nick frowned as he sought more information with his finder's talent. "It might have been a hospital. Now it's a combination of prison and laboratory. I think he lives and works there along with some other captive scientists."

"Are you sure, Nick? That building doesn't seem quite as impossible as the castle." Allarde studied the laboratory, which had barred windows and its own barbed-wire fence within the larger enclosure. "Though bad enough."

As they watched, a motorcar came sweeping through the darkness to stop at the main guardhouse. Two guards emerged immediately and saluted the passenger before opening the gate to admit the vehicle.

"That's an SS vehicle," Nick said softly. "The *Shutzstaffel*. Hitler's protection squad. They're known for ruthlessness and absolute loyalty to *der Führer*. A nasty lot. The officer in the car is probably the commandant of this camp." The motorcar cut through the village and onto the road that climbed up and around the escarpment.

Tory studied the fences. The laboratory enclosure was at the far right end of the compound, not far from the main fence. "I can get inside. I've been counting the seconds between sweeps of the spotlights, and I could float over the fences and get to the laboratory without being seen."

"No!" Both her companions spoke so quickly they sounded like one voice, Allarde's louder than Nick's.

Allarde continued, "If you safely reach the laboratory door, you might be able to unlock it, but you'd have trouble finding Dr. Weiss without Nick. If you find him, you'll have to get him out of the laboratory and over both fences. Can you lift a grown man twice your size and carry him that far in the interval between light sweeps?"

She frowned as she calculated. "You're right. Carrying a person bigger than I am would be slow and difficult and dangerous. So much for that idea."

"Nick, have you thought about how you'll convince Dr. Weiss to leave with a sixteen-year-old stranger?" Allarde asked. "A scientist will have trouble believing in magic. And he might not speak English."

"Which is why I'm grateful you volunteered for this mission. You'll have to come with me to do the talking." Nick sighed. "I have thought about this. Dr. Weiss will certainly be startled, but he'll want to escape. Performing some simple magic, like mage lights, should be enough to persuade him. I hope."

"Then what, assuming you convince him?" Allarde asked. "Did you originally plan on cutting through the fence wire? You don't have the tools."

"I thought I'd be better prepared," Nick admitted. "I didn't expect to come tumbling through the mirror so soon. Luckily you're here. With your talent for lifting heavy weights, we won't need wire cutters."

"My skill is best at lifting inanimate objects. Tory is better at living beings," Allarde said with a swift glance at her. "If we blend our powers, we should be able to lift several people and move them fairly quickly."

Tory winced as she thought of how they'd shared energy when they danced on air at Kemperton. It had been joyous. Intimate. How could she bear to allow him in her mind again? How could either of them bear it?

She turned her gaze back to the compound. "With several of us together, I doubt we could move fast enough to avoid the spotlights. If we're seen leaving, they could shoot us out of the air like pheasants."

"So we can't do anything even though we're so close," Nick said tautly. "I have an itchy feeling that we must work fast because Dr. Weiss's situation might change. If it does, it won't be for the better."

"Think of this as a scouting expedition," Allarde said. "We need as much information as we can gather through observation if we're to have a chance of success when we make our move."

"The voice of reason speaks, and is right," Nick said. "Once we know what we need, we can send a message stone to Lackland for supplies. Since flying would make us easy targets, we'll need those wire clippers. Powerful ones."

"You won't find those in our time," Tory said.

"I can get cutters from Polly. She promised to check the mirror every day I'm gone." He frowned. "I can get a message to her, but I don't know if she has the mirror magic to send something back."

"Since you have mirror magic, there's a good chance she does also," Tory said. "It would be more reliable if you or I went to Lackland in person to get what is needed, but who wants to do that if it can be avoided?"

"Magic is wonderful, but it doesn't remove all obstacles." Nick frowned at the compound. "If the fence is electrified, cutting it won't work because anyone trying would get a dreadful shock. Likely an alarm would go off, too."

"Going over the fence would be best if we can manage it safely. I wonder if it might actually work better in daylight, when there aren't any spotlights. The laboratory is in a fairly isolated corner of the compound." Allarde's gaze methodically scanned the area. "I've only seen two guards patrolling. They should be easy to avoid, especially with our stealth stones. A gray, rainy day would be ideal."

The rain had slowed, but thunder boomed nearby and the rain increased. Tory jumped at the sound. The guns of Dunkirk had made her skittish about loud noises.

Thunder. Lightning.

An idea struck. "Nick, where does the electricity for the spotlights and the military facilities come from?"

He scanned the compound, then pointed. "The power lines come in through that pole over there."

"If the pole is destroyed, would the electricity fail long enough for us to get in and out again?"

"That depends," he said, looking intrigued. "If they have an emergency backup generator, the lights would come back on almost immediately."

"Then we call down lightning and blast that pole to tinder!"

"Interesting thought," Allarde said approvingly. "Do any of us have enough weather magic to direct lightning like that?"

"Nick isn't as strong as Jack, but he has some weather power. We can increase that by working together. We couldn't call a storm very far, but this one is right on top of us," Tory replied. "If we can knock out the electricity, how long will it take to restore?"

"Hard to say. At least half an hour, I think. Probably longer. Maybe much longer." He glanced from Tory to Allarde. "Shall we try?"

"We'll have to move quickly before the storm passes," Allarde said. "Which means going down this hill and moving as close to the laboratory as we can. Then we try to channel the lightning."

"With the help of you two, I think I can do that," Nick said. "If we fail, we're no worse off than we are now."

"If the power goes out and stays out, Nick and I will go over the fences with Tory's help," Allarde said. "I'll unlock the laboratory door and Nick will lead us to Dr. Weiss. God willing, we persuade him to leave before the power is restored. If we all make it out, we head back to the cave as quickly as we can."

"They probably won't realize Dr. Weiss is gone till tomorrow, and we'll be back in Lackland by then," Nick said. "Let's do it!"

"A good plan, except I'm going with you two over the fence," Tory said. "Don't protest, Allarde. My ability to lift people is strongest if I'm touching them. We'll have the best chance of getting in and out again if we hold hands when we go over."

"You make me long for the days when a duke could just lock an unruly wench in a tower!" Allarde said with exasperation.

"But she's right," Nick pointed out.

"I know," Allarde said glumly. "Very well, let's get moving. If this is to work, we'll have to move fast."

He caught Tory's hand and headed down the hill. She felt a shock as intense as the lightning they planned to bring down. Reminding herself that he just wanted to help her over the rough ground, she matched her pace to his.

She'd known they must join hands if they traveled over the fence, but this felt dangerously romantic. Fiercely she reminded herself that nothing had changed. She cared too much for him to ruin his life.

Better to concentrate on her breathing and her footing as they raced down the hill.

CHAPTER 23

The ground had been cleared for several yards around the fence, but they found a concealed position in dense shrubbery just outside that area. The storm was already moving off. After Tory caught her breath, she said, "Nick, you have the most weather magic and you understand electricity best, so you lead."

She took his hand and let her energy flow into him as he turned his face to the sky. Allarde joined hands with Nick and poured his smooth, deep power through their connection. Tory was far too aware of him whenever they touched and this was much, much worse. The passion and deep understanding hovered so close . . .

Focus on the job that must be done. Shutting out her personal feelings, she blended their power into one powerful force. "We're ready, Nick."

Nick stared at the power pole. "Now!" He sent his energy into the heart of the storm, and he carried the other two with him.

Giddily Tory soared into that raw, exhilarating power as Nick sought the lightning. They were one with the fierce winds, slanting rain, bone-shaking thunder.

There! For an instant, Tory *was* lightning, a searing energy that destroyed all in her path. A volatile force that coalesced, struck, *transformed*. White sparks exploded into the sky on the far side of the compound. The power pole shattered and she sensed power lines melting away in white hot coils.

All the lights vanished, leaving absolute darkness. As they waited to see if power would be restored, another slash of lightning illuminated the faces of her companions. Allarde was calm, Nick excited. "Ready to jump, Tory?" Allarde asked.

"Nick, you be in the middle since you haven't done this before. I'll take your left hand, Allarde your right. You don't have to do anything but make your power available to us. We'll take care of the rest." As they positioned themselves to enter the compound, Tory rebalanced their energy, then changed the focus from weather to flying. When the energy was right, she gathered it together. "Now!"

They rose swiftly into the air. Nick made a strangled sound and his grip became bruising, but he didn't falter even though wind and rain tore at their clothing.

Supplementing her power with Allarde's allowed her to manage their combined weight handily. They should be able to add a fourth person and escape with Dr. Weiss.

The main fence was barely visible with the spotlights off. They skimmed over. Wise of Allarde to choose dark clothing for the three of them. In the middle of the storm, they must be almost invisible. Plus, she and Allarde had stealth stones that were spelled to make people's gazes pass by them.

In the distance voices called out in German. Though Tory didn't speak the language, the tone sounded like furious curses.

They moved silently over the empty ground between the outside fence and the laboratory fence. The laboratory was light-colored, easy to see in the dark.

"Down now," she murmured, and brought them down in front of the building's main entrance. Unused to flying, Nick stumbled but recovered immediately.

There were no signs of life, only wind and rain. Anyone imprisoned in the laboratory was in his bed unless woken by the storm.

Dropping Tory's hand, Allarde stepped forward and placed his palm over the door lock. After a long buzz of magic, he opened the door. Its faint squeal sounded painfully loud, but probably couldn't be heard more than a few feet away.

Allarde stepped back and gestured the other two inside. Tory's saturated clothing dripped on the cold tiled floor, but it was good to be out of the pounding rain. The chilly air contained odd, medicinal scents.

When they were all inside, they waited to see if their entry had been noticed. All was silent except for the rain pounding on the roof. When he was sure they were unobserved, Nick created a very faint mage light and aimed it at the floor. Then he started off without hesitation, leading them down the long corridor until they reached a set of swinging double doors.

Cautiously Nick opened them. Ahead was a shorter stretch of corridors with the medicinal scent diminished.

Once again Nick led the way. The corridor ended in a tee junction. Nick turned into the short passage on the left and stopped in front of a door. Carefully he tried the doorknob. Locked.

Allarde was about to step forward when Tory raised her hand to halt him. She moved up to the door and placed her hand over the keyhole. Then she guided her magic into the components of the lock, puzzling out how the mechanism worked. Ah, *there*. A quick, sharp effort moved the latch and unlocked the door.

She stepped back and waved Nick in first. He opened the door and stepped inside. The small, spare room contained a narrow cot that held a sprawled sleeper.

Nick increased the power of his light. "Dr. Weiss?" he asked in a quiet, unthreatening voice.

The sleeping figure rolled over and sat up. Speaking in weary French, he said, "Have you come to drag me from bed and execute me for insufficient progress, *mon colonel?*"

Allarde said in French, "Not at all. We're here to rescue you, Dr. Weiss."

In the brighter light, Tory saw that the scientist was a lean man in his forties with dark hair and haunted gray eyes. The room itself was stark as a cell. Besides the bed, there was a battered metal desk covered with books and paper and a door that must lead to a closet or washroom. The high, narrow window was covered with a heavy curtain.

As the scientist blinked in confusion, Allarde asked, "Do you speak English?"

"Yes, and also German, Russian, and Greek," Dr. Weiss said tartly in fluent, French-accented English. "Which you should know since you're figments of my imagination." He pulled a pair of spectacles from his desk and slid them on. Frowning, he added, "Wet and very young figments of my imagination."

He removed the spectacles and lay back on the bed, pulling the blankets over him. In French, he muttered, "Fairly benign as nightmares go."

Thinking a female voice might be more soothing, Tory stepped forward and laid a hand on his shoulder. "We're not figments of your imagination, Dr. Weiss," she said, speaking in English so Nick could understand. "We came here at considerable risk to take you to England where you can continue your research without having to worry about being shot in the middle of the night."

Dr. Weiss stared at her hand, then reached for his spectacles again. "You certainly feel real, but you look younger than my daughter! Have the British started sending children to war?" His gaze moved to the door. "If you're real, how did you get in here? I heard the click when they locked me in for the night."

The three mages exchanged a glance. "Allarde, you explain," Nick said. "You have more gravitas."

The scientist smiled. "Gravitas? You're well-educated children, but you boys don't look much older than she is. Is this some kind of bizarre joke?"

"It's no joke, sir," Allarde said.

Tory noted that Nick was right: Allarde had gravitas, which gave him the best chance of convincing the scientist that they were serious. Persuasion needed to be quick, because she was itchily aware that the lights could come on again at any time.

Allarde continued, "The three of us have magical powers. I understand how difficult this is to believe, especially for a scientist. But there have always been people with magic, and we can prove we have it." He snapped his fingers. Another globe of mage light appeared. He tossed it into the air and it hovered above them.

Dr. Weiss stared at the light. "That . . . that has to be some kind of secret British scientific discovery. Just a different type of torch."

Which was exactly what Nick said when Tory first met him. Impatient and very aware of time passing, Tory used the same proof she'd used on Nick: She floated up to the ceiling.

"You can't explain this away, Dr. Weiss," she said briskly. "Nick used magic to call down lightning to destroy the power pole, I used magic to float us over the barbed-wire fences, and Allarde used magic to unlock the laboratory door."

Seeing the scientist's baffled expression, Nick said soothingly, "You don't have to believe that magic is real, sir. Just trust us to get you out of here safely. You can argue about whether it's really magic when we're a safe distance away."

Dr. Weiss ran trembling fingers through his unkempt hair, then swung from the bed and passed his hand through the air under Tory. Allarde obligingly floated his mage light higher so it was clear that no wires supported her.

The scientist tried the light switch. The electricity was still out, which might be considered proof of their claims.

Turning to face the Irregulars, Dr. Weiss said, "The two logical hypotheses are that you have magical abilities, or I am mad. I rather think it's madness."

"You're not mad, sir," Nick said. "We are not here as official Allied agents. My father works in British intelligence. I learned of your work when a scientist from Oxford, Dr. Florey, pleaded for my father's agency to rescue you. He said he needed you for his research."

"Howard Florey did that for me?" Dr. Weiss said, surprised. "We have met at scientific meetings and he said he would like to work with me someday, but I didn't realize he was this serious."

"He's very serious, but he was refused because British intelligence consider rescue impossible." Nick hesitated as if wondering how to explain this rescue attempt. "I had a very strong intuition that your work was vital, and that with magic I could bring you safely out of France. So I collected some friends and here we are."

"But we must leave as soon as possible." Allarde's face showed tension. "We don't know how long the lights will be off. When electricity is restored, escape will be far more hazardous."

"Assuming I'm not mad," Dr. Weiss said flatly, "I would like nothing better than to leave this damnable place. But I can't go with you."

CHAPTER 24

The scientist's words silenced Tory and the others until Nick exclaimed, "Sir, why can't you come with us? Surely you don't want to work for Hitler!"

Dr. Weiss spat on the floor. "I wish him to die an ugly, painful death. But my wife and children are held captive in the castle above. They are—how you say?—hostages for my cooperation. If I am not here in the morning, Colonel Heinrich, the truly evil commandant of this installation, will see them dead by noon. I cannot leave."

Nick caught his breath, his expression startled. Something about the scientist's words struck an intuitive chord, Tory suspected.

But it was Allarde who spoke. "The Sword of Damocles hangs over your head," he said gravely. "But surely you know there is a terrible likelihood that if you stay, all of you will die. Wouldn't your wife and children want at least you to escape?"

The scientist's face twisted in agony. "Perhaps they would. But I would never be able to sleep again for visualizing them being dragged screaming into the castle courtyard and being shot. Or . . . or worse."

"Then we shall have to rescue them at the same time as you," Nick said.

Tory gaped at him. "Nick, you've seen the castle! Even magic can't get us up that cliff and back with Dr. Weiss's family! Not with Nazi soldiers all around us."

"I can try. I may succeed." Nick's gaze met that of the scientist. "I will be back for you, Dr. Weiss, and on the same night I will also rescue your family. I swear it."

The scientist sighed, his face haggard. "You are a brave young man, or I am mad. Once again, I incline to believe it's madness. I shall not expect to see you again. If you are real . . . do not risk your life or that of your friends on me. Nothing can be done."

"Perhaps not," Nick said stubbornly. "But if we do return, how large is your family? How many children?"

"My wife, Sarah. My daughter, Rebecca, who is fifteen. My son, Joel, is eleven." Dr. Weiss sighed. "One reason my work goes slowly is because my wife was my research partner. Her training is the same as mine, she is as good a scientist as I. But the colonel refused to believe a woman could be equal and necessary to my work."

"Then he's a fool," Nick said. "You may doubt that I'm real or that I can do what I say, Dr. Weiss. But just in case, be ready. If you have notes or personal possessions, keep them close. Just in case."

"Almost you convince me," the scientist said sadly. "I have no hope for myself, and my family's situation is even worse than mine. But I wish you brave young people Godspeed. Leave now and save yourselves." He gave a twisted smile. "If you are real."

"I am real." Nick offered his hand.

Dr. Weiss returned Nick's firm handshake. "Indeed you feel substantial. Go now, and swiftly."

"He's right," Allarde said, his voice sharp. "We must *move*." He

180 · M. J. Putney

opened the door and peered out. Seeing the way clear, he beckoned to his companions. Catching his urgency, Tory darted through, closely followed by Nick.

Allarde took a moment to lock the door behind them, then set off swiftly down the corridor. "My foretelling sense says we're cutting this very close," he said in a nearly inaudible voice. "The sooner we get out of here, the better."

They hurried to the entrance as quickly as they could while making minimal noise. Again Allarde checked for danger outside before they left the building. As he locked the laboratory door behind them, the rumble of a motorcar sounded nearby. The compound might be dark, but there was activity.

Tory stepped out into the rain and caught Nick's hand. "Everyone ready?"

Allarde took Nick's other hand. "Ready!"

"I'm looking forward to flying again." Nick's voice was jaunty, but his hand clamped tight on Tory's.

She closed her eyes and cleared her mind to find the stillness needed for her floating magic. Power shared among them, take it slowly, visualize rising in the air . . .

Click!

As they began to lift, lights blazed on through the compound. Allarde swore under his breath and poured more lifting magic into the link. The rush of power helped Tory speed up their flight.

Over the laboratory fence. Over the bare ground between fences.

They were soaring over the barbed wire when the glaring beam of a spotlight slashed over them. Its brilliance almost blinded Tory. A guttural shout rose, followed by the ear-piercing rat-a-tat-tat of a machine gun.

As bullets whizzed by, Tory swooped them down into the shrubbery so fast they risked sprained ankles. As soon as everyone was on solid ground, they bolted into the woods. Tory prayed she wouldn't run into a tree or step into a rabbit hole.

No shots followed them. After they'd run perhaps a quarter mile,

Tory gasped, "Enough! I need to rest." She leaned back against a wet tree trunk, not daring to sit because she'd have difficulty getting up again. "I think we got away safely."

"I doubt anyone saw us clearly," Allarde halted, breathing hard. "And if someone did, he probably didn't believe what he saw. The machine-gun fire likely came from someone who thought we were a pair of geese flying into the woods so he shot after us on general principles."

"Three geese, not two," Nick panted. "Unless you consider Tory gosling size."

As Allarde chuckled, Tory said sternly, "You'll pay for that, Nicholas Rainford!"

"Yes, my lady," he said with exaggerated deference. "But not just yet."

Allarde glanced skyward. "Nick, can you guide us back to the cave before daylight? The rain is clearing and it won't be long before the sky lightens."

"We should just make it." Nick set a brisk pace up the hill in the direction they'd come from. Tory followed, Allarde bringing up the rear.

As Allarde had predicted, the rain clouds moved on and the sky was lightening fast. Better visibility helped with their footing but made Tory feel vulnerable as they made their way along twisting lanes and minor roads.

Though they avoided farmhouses, once a farmer driving a horse-drawn wagon passed them coming from the other direction. He looked at them curiously, but only nodded when Allarde greeted him in French.

Later they had to move off the lane while a shepherd passed with a flock of sheep. The countryside was getting busy.

Tory was relieved to enter the woods at the foot of the hill that concealed the cave. As she trudged doggedly along behind Nick, she prayed she'd be able to make the last stretch without dropping in her tracks.

She squeaked when Allarde's arms came around her. "You look ready to collapse," he said as he swept her from her feet. "You've had a stiff hike as well as burning a large amount of power getting us in and out of the laboratory."

After an instant of shock, she tried to struggle free. "You shouldn't have to carry me!" she protested. "You burned a lot of power, too."

"You hardly weigh more than a sparrow." He smiled with intimate mischievousness. "Or a gosling. Relax and enjoy the ride." He resumed his uphill climb, moving faster now that he wasn't matching her pace.

Surrendering, she closed her eyes and relaxed against him, her muscles shaking from fatigue. His warmth and strength were so familiar, so painfully welcome. When her forehead rested against his cheek, she felt a tingle of whiskers against her skin. The sensation was startlingly sensual.

She bit her lip. How fortunate there was still enough rain dripping from the trees to disguise any vagrant tears.

They reached the cave just as the sun came over the horizon, splashing the top of the hill with golden autumn light. Allarde set Tory down just inside the entrance.

"Thank you," she said as she forced herself to let go of his arm. "I'm sorry you had to carry me, but I'm just not as strong and fast as the two of you."

She thought Allarde murmured, "I'll always carry you if you need me, Tory."

His words were drowned out by Nick saying, "Pound for pound, you're probably stronger than either of us, Tory. You just don't have many pounds."

"More pounds than a gosling!" She gave him a withering glare, then sat down against the wall and wrapped her tattered blanket around herself. The blanket offered warmth, but didn't do much to soften the hardness.

Allarde and Nick also retrieved their blankets and settled down in the cave's antechamber. The space was about six feet wide and not much more than that high. Allarde had to be careful not to knock his head on lower sections of the ceiling. He sat a couple of feet to Tory's right while Nick sat opposite, next to their small store of food.

Not exactly luxury quarters, but there was enough natural light so mage lights weren't needed. Tory was so drained that even that much magic would be too much.

"We all burned a lot of power." Nick produced his folding knife and opened the paper-wrapped chunk of cheese. "We're lucky your shopkeeper was so generous, Allarde." He cut slices of cheese and bread and passed them across the cave.

Tory wolfed down the remaining food with a haste that would have shocked her mother. The others were equally ravenous. The wine had been finished off the night before, but Allarde had refilled the bottle with clear spring water from a pool farther back in the cave. Tory tried not to think about how lovely hot tea would taste.

With hunger slaked, she felt much stronger. Ready to think about the future. "Nick, I'm sure you haven't given up hope of rescuing Dr. Weiss."

He smiled ruefully. "It was disappointing to make heroic efforts, use masses of magic, find our man, and then have him refuse to leave. But yes, I do have another plan."

"We'll have to perform two rescues the same night, and the castle would be much, much harder to enter and escape. Particularly with three people," Allarde remarked.

"A pity there are no true invisibility spells," Tory said wistfully.

"My plan is mostly nonmagical, actually." Nick cleaned his knife on the paper that wrapped the cheese, then tucked it away. "Remember that Jack mentioned Castle Bouchard having hidden tunnels? If we can find one, that might overcome the chief difficulty. If we can get up to the castle without being seen, magic should make it possible to do the rest."

"Is it even possible that a tunnel runs all the way from the bottom of the escarpment up to the castle?" Tory asked.

Allarde nodded. "There are castles in England that have medieval tunnels like that. Nottingham Castle has a famous tunnel called Mortimer's Hole."

"If Castle Bouchard has a similar passage, we could enter that way rather than risk flying so far, and we could save our magic for other things," Tory agreed. "But if there's a well-known tunnel, it might be guarded. And if it isn't well-known, that could mean it has collapsed since our time."

"Can your finder talent locate the tunnel so we could see if it would suit our purposes?" Allarde asked.

Nick hesitated. "That would take time. I'm better with finding people. As soon as Dr. Weiss said his family was in the castle, I knew exactly where they were. I could go right to them. But I don't have any sense of a tunnel."

"When he mentioned his family, I saw your face change. Was that because you knew where to find them?" Tory asked.

Nick nodded. "In my mind, there's a glowing light that shows where they are. It was the same with Dr. Weiss. As soon as he mentioned his family, I realized they're an essential part of this intuition that has me by the throat. I must free them all."

"If his wife is his research partner, I can see why." Allarde's voice became brisk. "We have the start of a plan. Now we must make it more specific. I hope the three of us have enough weather magic to get inside the camp again. Nick, will they be able to repair the pole so that lightning can't destroy it in the future?"

"They might install a big lightning rod that would ground the energy so the pole wouldn't be damaged. In that case, we could hit the generator shed nearby and take out the generator itself. That would give us more time."

"We'll need a real weather mage like Jack, though," Tory said. "We're not likely to get another such storm at exactly the right time."

"A good thing Jack volunteered to help," Nick said.

Tory groaned. "I'll need to go home to guide him through the mirror. I'm not looking forward to that."

"Let's not get ahead of ourselves," Allarde cautioned. "First we need to find if there's a tunnel up to the castle. We can do that by sending a message so Jack can get the information we need from Comte du Bouchard."

"*If* we can get a message to Jack, and he can get one back to us," Nick said pessimistically. "It could take days."

"Maybe, but surely the Irregulars are keeping a close eye out for messages," Allarde said. "It's worth trying this to spare the strain on Tory." He gave her one of those unsettlingly intimate smiles that made her bones feel like melting.

Looking away, she said, "Assuming a tunnel leads up the castle, we'll have to stage two rescue missions at the same time. Who do we need besides Jack?"

"If Jack joins us, we'll have two teams of two," Nick said. "I need to go to the castle to find the Weiss family."

"Maybe you can go to the castle and I can go to the laboratory since Dr. Weiss will recognize me," Allarde said. "Tory and Jack can stay outside the compound. No sense in them risking themselves unnecessarily."

"Nick needs someone to unlock doors," Tory said. "Plus, I may be needed to speak French to the Weisses."

Allarde said reluctantly, "I suppose you're right. Maybe Jack can stay outside in case he needs to do more with the weather."

"Jack won't want to stay in safety and work weather again," Nick said. "He can go with you and work weather on the run."

"Of course, all of this is tentative," Tory pointed out. "If there's no tunnel to the castle, we may have to accept that rescue is impossible." Nick's jaw set. "Never."

"Has anyone ever said you're pigheaded?" Tory asked pleasantly.

Nick relaxed into a grin. "Many have. Most often, my mother."

"Who, as we all know, is a remarkably intelligent woman," Allarde said with a lurking smile as he got to his feet. "Let's take this one step at a time. First I'll check the mirror to see if there has been a response to our message. If so, we'll know that communication has been established."

"I'll go with you." Tory also stood, needing to stretch her aching muscles. "If a rock arrived when we were out, I wouldn't have felt it."

"If we send another message, ask for food," Nick said as he rose. "Another foraging trip might not be so successful."

They headed toward the mirror single file. Tory wrinkled her nose when they hit the repulsion spells designed to send casual cave explorers in a different direction, but they weren't too bad since she knew what they were.

A paper-wrapped stone awaited them when they reached the widened area of the cave where the mirror energy simmered just out of sight. She scooped it up and read the terse sentences. "Jack says they're glad we're alive, and he's ready to come after us if we don't send another message within two days."

Allarde scanned the paper, then handed it to Nick. "I'll write a note asking for tunnel information and food supplies. Now that the connection has been established, we should hear back fairly quickly."

After Nick read the note, Allarde printed their message on the back of Jack's note. Tory tossed it through the mirror and wished that she were the one going home instead of this piece of rock.

CHAPTER 25

As Cynthia and Elspeth entered the corridor that held Merlin's mirror, they discovered that Jack had arrived there first, and he'd found a message stone. He looked up from the paper with a grin.

"They're safe, they've located Dr. Weiss, and they want information from Comte du Bouchard on any tunnels into the castle." He glanced back down. "They also want food since they're living in a cave and have to be careful about going out."

"Jack, shall we take a trip through time once we have the castle information and supplies?" Elspeth asked.

"My thoughts exactly," Jack said. "I've already had the count map the tunnels. I can be back here in two hours with the map and supplies so we can leave."

The matter-of-fact words jolted Cynthia. Jack was going to travel through the mirror to heaven only knew where or when? "All they want now is information. If they can't use the tunnels, they'll have to come back, so there's no point in making a blind jump that could take you somewhere unexpected." And be really uncomfortable in the process. And dangerous! "Tory is the one with mirror talent and experience."

"It's not a blind jump." Elspeth's eyes narrowed as she regarded the invisible portal. "I'm reasonably sure I can get us there, Jack. I'll go back to my room and get anything that might be useful and meet you back here in two hours."

"Are you two *mad*?" Cynthia exclaimed. "Wouldn't it make more sense to wait and find out if another mirror passage is even necessary?"

"It's necessary," Elspeth said grimly. "I've known that ever since Nick came back. Time is of the essence and I don't want to wait any longer."

"We'll be all right, Cynthia." Jack smiled cheerfully. "Probably. I agree with Elspeth, we're needed, and waiting is making me twitch. You don't have to go. Covering up the absences at the abbey is important, too."

The thought of him going off to war without her made her pulse spike. The idiot needed her, even if he didn't realize it. He'd get himself killed, or he'd fall in love with Elspeth as they shared excitement and danger.

She wasn't sure which fate was worse.

"If you think I'm going to let you go jumping into this particular fire without me, you're even madder than I realized," she snapped. "I'm going with you. Besides weather work, I've been practicing my illusion magic and I've learned a few useful tricks."

Her companions looked interested. "What have you learned?" Elspeth asked.

Cynthia closed her eyes and concentrated on the illusions she wanted to create. Then she laid one hand on Elspeth's arm and the other on Jack's. *Jack's strong, warm arm that felt so good when he'd held her . . .*

Mentally slapping herself, she created her illusions, then dropped her hand. Jack and Elspeth both gasped. "What do you see?" Cynthia asked.

"Nick," Elspeth said. "I see Nick."

"And I see Tory." Jack sounded like Nick. He studied his hands. "I see myself as I am, but Elspeth looks just like Tory. Amazing, Cynthia! A very useful skill for an undercover mission into occupied territory."

"Illusion magic might help us, but going through the mirror almost killed you before," Elspeth said, frowning. "I was able to revive you then, but what if I couldn't this time? I'll have to burn a great deal of magic to get us through the mirror. I might not have healing power available at the other end."

Wishing she didn't have to explain this, Cynthia said, "I've been holding illusion magic on myself for so many years that it's automatic." She snapped her fingers and the illusions vanished, including the one she held on herself. "When Tory realized that, she guessed that if I wasn't using illusion power when going through the mirror, the passage might not be as hard on me."

"Perhaps, but we won't know until you try, and I don't want to take that risk," Elspeth said firmly. "I'm a healer. I do not want to kill a friend."

Elspeth thought of her as a friend? Cynthia found that cheering. "You said yourself that this mission is necessary. Isn't that worth some risk?"

"It's not me I'm risking, but you, which is quite another matter," the other girl said acerbically.

"I think you'll be all right." Jack took Cynthia's hand in his. "You'll be between Elspeth and me. We'll get you through safely."

His warm, confident smile lifted Cynthia's spirits even more. "Two hours then." And she hoped to heaven she was doing the right thing.

Tory jolted from sleep into full wakefulness. "The mirror! Something large has come through!"

Nick, who had also been drowsing, became alert. "Food?" he said hopefully.

190 · M. J. Putney

"Let's find out." Allarde had been standing in the cave entrance admiring the afternoon sunlight on the brilliant autumn foliage, but he turned and joined them as they headed into the cave.

Tory led the way, her pace quickening as she neared the mirror. The disturbance she'd felt in the energy seemed too great for a rock or even a bag of food.

She wasn't surprised to burst into the mirror chamber and see her friends sprawled on the floor. "Elspeth! Jack!" But then she blinked in shock to see her roommate. "Cynthia? Are you all right?"

Cynthia pushed herself up blearily. For an instant, the scar on her cheek was visible. Then her image shifted and her face was flawless again. She muttered, "It looks like your theory about my mirror travel was correct."

Jack and Elspeth were also sitting up and taking stock. Jack carried a sizable knapsack while both girls had smaller ones. Nick stepped up and offered Jack a hand. "I'm even more interested in the tunnel information than the food, cousin."

Jack laughed as he got to his feet with Nick's help, hanging on until his balance steadied. "I have both."

Allarde knelt so he wasn't towering over Cynthia and Elspeth. "You did well with the mirror magic."

Elspeth made a face. "Sending the messages back and forth created a sort of trail of breadcrumbs that I followed here. It burned a lot of magic, though. I'm not going to be good for much until I've had some rest."

"And some food." Jack shrugged out of his knapsack and opened it, removing a lumpy packet from his knapsack. He poured a pile of brightly colored balls into his other hand. "Marzipan sweets," he explained. "My mother thought these would be good for helping recovery from a mirror passage." He offered them to Elspeth and Cynthia. "Take several. Nick doesn't get any until the three of us are recovered."

"I'll behave," Nick promised. "But I do hope some are left over."

After the new arrivals had consumed enough to regain some energy, Jack gave the remaining half dozen pieces of marzipan to Tory and Allarde and Nick. They were delicious, and a nice change from bread and cheese.

Twitching from proximity to the mirror, Tory said, "If everyone can walk, let's move toward the front of the cave. It's more restful there."

Elspeth made a face as she stood with Allarde's help. "Guiding us through the mirror has made me more sensitive to the energy, so I'll be glad to move away."

Jack offered Cynthia a hand. "You came through better than on your other passages, but you still look a bit gray."

"You are so flattering," she grumbled. "At least I'm breathing."

She wavered when she stood and Jack put an arm around her for support. Tory blinked as subtle energy shimmered over the two of them. There was definitely something going on there. Though slowly, given the way Cynthia broke away after a few moments of leaning into him.

Allarde and Nick scooped up the backpacks and carried them forward until they reached the front section of the cave they'd dubbed the drawing room. Once there, Nick almost jumped on Jack. "The map?"

Jack pulled a folded paper from inside his coat and handed it over. "There's a long tunnel up through the rock to the castle and several shorter ones under the castle only, but since I haven't seen the terrain, I don't know if they'll suit your purposes."

Nick opened the paper. "Allarde, take a look with me while we try to match this to the landscape." Allarde joined him and created a bright mage light over the paper while the two of them studied the drawing.

As Jack unpacked more food, he asked, "What's happened so far?"

Tory gave a brief summary of the compound and their visit to the laboratory. She ended with, "You can see why we hope there's a secret way into the castle."

Cynthia shivered as she listened. "I do hope this is worth the risks."

"I don't know if Nick's dream will come true, but I'm absolutely sure that this drug will change the world. I'm glad we're working to save lives rather than taking them," Elspeth said pensively. "I would have been less comfortable if he was working on some evil new weapon, even if the Allies need that."

Tory felt the same. "What does the map show?"

"The main tunnel just might work," Nick said, his voice hopeful. "Assuming that it's still open and isn't situated in the middle of the military camp. Allarde and I will have to scout it to see."

"I'll go with you. I want to study the site, too." Tory said. Seeing the expressions on the newcomers, she added, "You three should get some rest. Once we know more about the tunnel, we can make plans."

Jack smiled ruefully. "Much as I'd like to go, I'm not sure I could walk there and back in my present state. I'll stay here and guard the womenfolk." Ignoring Cynthia's withering glare, he added, "I'm guessing that a night raid would be aided by some weather work to cover up what you're doing. With Cynthia and me both here, we should be able to conjure up any kind of storm you want."

"We're counting on it," Allarde said. "As soon as it gets dark, we'll be off to see if we can find the tunnel entrance."

"Which should give us enough time to eat," Nick said with a grin. "What else do you have in there, cousin?"

CHAPTER 26

Lying on her stomach between the two boys, Tory studied the square towered church of Notre Dame du Lac. The ancient structure was tucked between the lake and the escarpment at the west end of the village. Perhaps in deference to the church's age and beauty, the handsome old trees surrounding it hadn't been cut down.

The road to the castle ran a couple of hundred yards or so behind the churchyard, and the barbed-wire fence was about the same distance in front. The vicious fence skirting the lakeshore was an ugly reminder that this was a war zone. There were no signs of life around the church. With all the villagers removed from their homes, it must be closed now.

She and her companions had followed a narrow lane through a wheat field and now lay on the edge, where they had a clear view of the church. The ripe golden stalks should have been harvested by now, but farms would be short of labor if most of the men had been sent to Nazi labor camps.

What had become of the villagers who had been driven from these homes when the soldiers took over? Tory guessed they had moved in with nearby friends and relatives and were living in cramped misery.

"The Comte du Bouchard said the tunnel ended in the church-yard, and that it was well hidden," Allarde said quietly. "Nick, can you tell exactly where?"

Nick narrowed his eyes as he gazed at the church. "I wish he'd been more specific. I think it comes out by the farthest stone buttress on the left side of the church, but it's hard to be sure from this distance."

"Even if we find the entrance, we don't know if it's clear all the way to the castle. Anything could have happened over the years." Allarde frowned, his face faintly illuminated by reflected light as the spotlight swept to the end of the fence, then away.

Tory shifted, removing a rock from under her stomach. Nick lay on her right, but he was merely there, her comrade. Allarde was on her left, and she was acutely aware of his long, powerful body. He seemed less distracted by their proximity than she. Of course, he was a master at concealing his emotions.

"Someone will have to go up through the tunnel," Nick agreed. "But it will be dangerous getting into the compound to look for the entrance. We haven't got a convenient thunderstorm to call on this time."

Having studied the ground carefully, Tory announced, "I think I can get to the church without being seen."

Allarde flinched noticeably at that. "It's too dangerous! I'll go."

She laid her hand over his. "Justin, it's gallant that you want to take all the risks, but I'm better suited to this particular task. There are small patches of shadow and cover between here and the church. I can conceal myself much more easily than a great strapping fellow like you."

He rolled his hand upward and laced his fingers between hers. "You're frightened, I can feel it. You don't want to do this."

She pulled her hand away, unable to deal with the surge of emotions between them. "Of course I'm frightened," she said irritably. "I'd be a fool not to be. But I'm still the best person to look for the tunnel. If Nick is right that it ends on the lake side of the church, I'll be in the shadows most of the time. This is only a little dangerous."

"I'll be able to find the tunnel more quickly," Nick said. "So I'll go."

"You, like Allarde, are not easy to conceal," she pointed out. "Look at that little gully on this side of the fence. If I lie down in it, I'm not likely to be noticed when the spotlight moves over me. Either of you would. If I am seen, I'll probably look like a little boy. Whoever is behind the gun might hesitate a moment before shooting a child."

"Maybe not." Nick glanced across at Allarde. "But mostly Tory is right."

"It's her most irritating quality," Allarde said dryly, but there was an undertone of humor in his voice. "Be careful, Tory. If it looks like you're in trouble, I swear I'll pull boulders down the mountain as a distraction."

"Better to save your ability to move mountains for later. We might need it more then." Tory laid a hand on Nick's shoulder. "Let's see if my ability to enhance other mages' power can give you a clearer sense of where to look for the tunnel."

Nick closed his eyes for the space of a dozen heartbeats. "It ends inside that last buttress," he said finally. "On the back side, the fourth stone up from the bottom on the outer edge is a lever that opens into the tunnel. I think. It will probably be hard to move and will need to be pushed and kind of twisted toward the back at the same time."

"The lock-opening magic I learned from Allarde should help there." She glanced toward Allarde. "I'll need your help getting over the fence as quickly as possible."

He nodded. "This time you really will fly, not just float."

"If I find my way into the tunnel, I'm going to follow it all the way up to the castle if I can, so don't worry if I'm gone for a while."

"I'll know if you're distressed or in danger," Allarde said tersely.

He would, too. She turned her attention to the path of the spotlight. The huge light fixture was located toward the center of the camp, and it covered the western half. Light swept along the fence, past the church, and continued left to the edge of the lake. Then it swung back to the right. She would have more time to get over the fence during the long sweep to the right.

She was all set to leap up when a huge black motorcar roared around the corner on the road to the castle. Her muscles spasmed as her reflexes instantly ordered her body to freeze. Feeling like a rabbit hiding from a fox, she watched the vehicle slow for the turn up toward the castle.

His voice a bare thread of sound, Nick said, "That's the commandant's Mercedes again. See the SS insignia on those pennants? It looks like a pair of lightning bolts."

"He's probably quartered in the castle," Allarde said just as softly. "So he can look down in disdain on the country he helped conquer."

The returning spotlight struck the car and for an instant the commandant was silhouetted against the light. He had the ruthless profile of a bird of prey.

The moment passed and the motorcar continued up the road, the menacing throb of its engine fading as it rounded the escarpment to the side that was less steep. Tory was pleased at the steadiness of her voice when she said, "After the next sweep, I'll be off."

Allarde gave her hand a quick, hard squeeze. "I shall be extremely irritated with you if you let yourself be captured."

Or shot. "I'll bear that in mind." She drew herself up into a crouch so she could take off quickly. The seconds dragged, and then suddenly it was time to go.

She sprang up and raced full speed toward the fence, tracking the spotlight out of the corner of her eye. It swung back toward her, moving swiftly along the line of barbed wire. The distance to her hiding place seemed much longer than it had been when she was in the field.

Just before the light beam struck her, she reached the shallow depression she'd noted earlier. She dived into it and flattened herself, heart beating. She felt terrifyingly exposed as the blazing light passed over her.

But no alarm was raised. No shots were fired.

By the time she caught her breath, the light was returning from the lake. She spent a moment focusing her magic, then reached out to Allarde. He enhanced her power with a deep rush of his own. When the light passed over her again, she scrambled to her feet and put all her energy into getting over the fence.

The addition of Allarde's magic swept her over the barbed wire faster than she'd ever flown on her own. In seconds she was over the fence and running toward the church. Dancing on air with Allarde had been much more enjoyable.

She reached the shelter of an oak tree by the time the spotlight returned. Her heart hammered as she pressed her back into the trunk, which was wide enough to conceal her, but not Allarde or Nick.

The light passed to the lake. From this angle, she saw how it shot over the water before disappearing into the distance. After the beam passed her on the return swing, she bolted toward the church, hoping there was no one close enough to hear the crunch of dry autumn leaves under her feet.

Then she was alongside the church and safe from the relentless spotlight. The church was at the far west end of the village so there was unlikely to be anyone around to see her at the moment. Guards patrolled the compound, but one had been by here recently and wouldn't return soon.

The church was large for such a tiny village. The structure must have been built as a testament to medieval faith, or perhaps to reflect glory on the noble family who lived in the castle high above.

She passed a side door and on impulse tested the heavy latch. Though the door was locked, the simple mechanism opened easily with a touch of magic. The door squealed as she inched it open. She froze, but the interior remained silent. The Germans must have driven out even the church mice.

When she was sure no one was near, she closed the door behind her and created a mage light. The sanctuary contained stacks of rough wooden cases of different sizes. A case near the door was open so she moved closer. Inside were smaller boxes of cardboard. She lifted one, surprised by the weight, and opened it.

Ammunition. They had turned the house of God into a storehouse for weapons. Disgusted, she closed the box and left, locking the door behind her.

A dozen more paces brought her to the last buttress. These were not the elegant Gothic arches of the late medieval cathedrals, but tall pillars of solid stone built to support the church walls.

She circled to the back of the buttress and counted the fourth stone up from the bottom. Pushing and twisting as Nick had described didn't shift the stone. She guessed that it hadn't been opened in many years. Mentally she felt her way into the mechanism, pushing what would move. Abruptly the outside of the buttress swung away, revealing steps going into the earth.

She stepped back, wrinkling her nose. The air was dank and earth-scented. The Labyrinth had given her plenty of experience with underground passages, but this tunnel was less welcoming than Lackland's, and not as well kept. There were cobwebs. Ugh!

Reminding herself that an unused tunnel was far safer than a Nazi military camp, she stepped inside and pulled the massive stone door shut with an iron handle mounted on the inside. Despite its weight, the door was well balanced and moved easily.

Feeling the pressure of the darkness, she quickly kindled a mage light, making it extra bright to drive away her fears. Then she cautiously descended the uneven steps.

Fifteen steps down, the tunnel flattened out and she followed it far enough to be under the escarpment. Then more steps, this time ascending. The walls looked as if they had been formed by running water and later shaped and enlarged by human hands. Sometimes the shaft narrowed or dipped so low even Tory had to duck. There were no railings, but occasionally the steps flattened out for a few feet before rising again.

She climbed and climbed and *climbed,* stopping for breath several times. Once she halted to press her hand against her side because of a painful stitch.

The tunnel walls changed from raw stone to brick before ending at a heavy, ancient wooden door. The door was unlocked. She froze as the hinges squealed when she inched it open, but no one seemed to hear in the dark space on the other side. She lit a dim light and saw a cluttered, windowless cellar.

She cautiously stepped inside. Her door was set almost invisibly into a rough paneled wall. There was another door opposite, so she crossed the room, doused the light, and peered out. Beyond was a door-lined corridor. Hearing heavy footsteps and German voices, she hastily closed the door to the corridor and retreated to the tunnel.

Only when the door was safely closed behind her did she allow her excitement free rein. There was a way to get the Weiss family safely out of captivity! Nick could use his finder ability to locate them and the doctor would be whisked away at the same time. Within hours, they would all be safely back in England.

Heart light, she descended the steps much faster than she'd gone up them. The trek was still a long one and she had to be careful of her footing where steps were wet, but it was far less tiring that the climb to the castle.

It was a relief to emerge from the smothering confines of the tunnel and into the fresh night air. The area was as quiet as when she'd gone down. Closing the stone door, she headed back toward the fence. Though she knew where Allarde and Nick must be, they were so well concealed that she couldn't see them.

She was checking the position of the spotlight when she stepped beyond the church wall and smacked hard into the gray-clad body of a towering soldier. She gave a squeak of shock while he swore in German. A patroller!

Allarde's emotions flared with concern so intensely that she hurled her own emotions back to reassure him. *Relax, I was startled, not in danger. Do nothing!*

At least, not yet.

While sending her emotions to Allarde, she also flung herself away from the soldier, but to no avail. He grabbed her arm in an iron grip. He was scarily large—as tall as Allarde, and much bulkier.

She'd told the boys that she could pass for a child, and now was the time to find out if that was true. Pitching her voice higher and thinking herself young, small, and harmless, she said in French, "Excuse me, *monsieur*. I meant no harm!"

The soldier squinted down at her face. "Why are you here?" he said in badly accented French. "It is forbidden!"

She shrunk back from his menacing expression. *"Le cimetière."* She gestured toward the graveyard. "I came to pray for my father's soul. I meant no harm, *monsieur!*"

"You might have been shot!" He shook her arm angrily. "How did you get into the camp?"

"Under the fence." She pointed to a spot beyond the church, then mimed wiggling under the wire.

"Tomorrow I will look for that hole so it can be stopped up." He hesitated, indecision on his face. Finally he released her shoulder. "Return to your mother and never do such a stupid thing again! If you come here again, I will shoot."

"Oui, monsieur," she gasped, having no trouble sounding terrified and obedient. He might not want to shoot a child, but he knew his duty.

"Go!" he barked.

"Oui, monsieur! Merci, monsieur!" She scooted into the shadows below the trees. As the guard resumed his patrol, she moved toward the fence.

When he was out of sight, she waited for the spotlight to pass, then launched herself over the fence. An extra rush of Allarde's energy whisked her over. She landed and took off running for the wheat field.

As she entered the field, Allarde rose and swept her into his arms. Enveloping her in his embrace, he pulled her to the ground before the spotlight could reach them.

She began shaking from reaction as she burrowed so close it would take a chisel to separate them. She felt the quickened beat of his heart against her cheek. "We shouldn't be doing this," she whispered. "We are not together anymore."

Nick murmured, "You certainly seem together," in an amused voice.

Ignoring that, Allarde cradled Tory close, his warm hand cupping her neck and head comfortingly. "What happened? I felt such fear from you that I was ready to start throwing boulders."

"I was caught by a guard who was patrolling," she explained. "I said I'd come to pray at my father's grave behind the church, so he let me off with a stern warning."

Allarde's embrace tightened even more. "A reminder that not all Germans are monsters. But dear God, that could have been a disaster!"

"The tunnel!" Nick asked urgently. "Is it open all the way to the castle?"

"Yes," she replied. "It's narrow and not pleasant, but it goes all the way to the castle cellars. I'll tell you more when we're farther away."

Allarde released her with great reluctance, and she moved away with equal reluctance. It was easier to keep her distance when they were in their own world.

In this time that was not their own, only the moment seemed to matter.

CHAPTER 27

Cynthia slept all day after arriving in the cave. She didn't even say good-bye to the scouts as they went off. When she finally awoke, she was stiff from sleeping rolled up in a blanket on hard stone, but felt otherwise refreshed.

The soft glow of a mage light revealed, among other things, that Jack had rolled his blanket up next to hers. Now he slept beside her. And was holding her hand. That was the source of her well-being, and the gentle desire pulsing through her.

Since he was asleep, she didn't feel compelled to yank her hand away to demonstrate that he wasn't supposed to touch her. She liked holding his hand when there were no complicated emotions involved.

When he shifted a little closer to her, she decided it was time to get up. She stood and stretched her sore muscles. Though she was in no hurry to go through the mirror again, she was glad to know that temporarily dropping her illusion magic had spared her from being almost killed by the mirror passage.

Since it took more than one meal to rebuild the energy lost in mirror passage, she was ravenous. Creaking in every joint, she investigated the pantry area that Jack had set up with their supplies. The first requirement was tea.

Jack had brought a lightweight pot that held enough water to make half a dozen cups of tea, and he'd filled it the night before. A blast of hearth-witch magic brought the water to a boil. She wrapped tea leaves in cheesecloth since straining would be difficult, then let the tea steep while she piled ham and cheese on a piece of bread.

She couldn't toast the sandwich without an open flame, but it was easy to heat the sandwich till the cheese melted. Delicious!

The scent of warm food awakened Jack. He sat up and covered a yawn. "Could you make one of those hot sandwiches for me, Cynthia?"

She supposed he was entitled since he'd brought the food. She assembled one and heated it for him. Her father, the most noble Duke of Branston, would be horrified to see a daughter of his preparing food like a scullery maid, much less sleeping in a cave with a young man of inferior birth. But then, everything she did horrified him.

Smiling to herself, she handed Jack the sandwich. She enjoyed watching his appreciation when he bit in. Though she didn't much like sleeping on rock, the rest of this little adventure was rather amusing.

Jack swallowed a bite and sighed blissfully. "Thank you. Where's Elspeth?"

"Just outside the cave," she called back. "The others are almost back."

"Just in time for tea," Cynthia observed. Jack had also brought a set of light mugs that nested together, so she used one to scoop tea from the pot. A pity there was no milk, but with a chunk of sugar added, it would do.

Tory bubbled into the cave, flanked by Allarde and Nick. Cynthia felt deep envy. Tory might not be beautiful and she should look absurd dressed like a boy, but her warmth and vitality and vivid prettiness drew eyes no matter where she was. Even Allarde, who had ignored all the other girls at Lackland, hadn't been able to resist her.

It was hard to blame everyone for liking Tory. Even Cynthia did, though she had tried not to. Jack liked Tory a lot, but then, he liked everyone. He seemed to like Cynthia even when she was at her bad-tempered worst. There really must be something wrong with him.

Maybe his judgment was weak where she was concerned . . . but she did like him back. She always had a weakness for handsome young males. Once she'd been attracted to Allarde, whose rank matched her own, and heaven knew he was good-looking. But he was far too serious. Jack was much more amusing.

She also recognized with a start that because he was impervious to her barbed tongue, she could relax with Jack as with no one else. A pity he was such a flirt.

All of those thoughts passed through her mind in an instant. Aloud, she said, "I just made a pot of tea if you'd like some."

"Splendid!" Nick poured cups for all three returnees. "It's chilly out there."

Tory took a swallow of tea. "Heavenly! I have *longed* for tea!"

"Tell us what you discovered," Elspeth said impatiently. "Will we be able to rescue Dr. Weiss's family?"

"The tunnel is open!" Nick said jubilantly. "Tory hiked all the way up to the castle cellar. It's time to make final plans."

"But first, we eat," Allarde said firmly. "Wisdom is scarce when one is hungry. I'm glad you brought such good supplies."

"I brought some clothing, too." Jack opened his knapsack. "Lovely as you ladies are, it might be safer to have the freedom of trousers. I have small sizes for Elspeth and Tory. Since Cynthia is taller, I brought an old pair of mine for her. I also have coats and shirts. The styles are plain and shapeless enough that they shouldn't look too out of place in 1940. The fit won't be wonderful, but they're good outfits for midnight raiders."

"That was really clever of you, Jack!" Tory said. "If Allarde hadn't visited a used clothing shop, I'd have needed the trousers. I found how useful they were when we sailed to Dunkirk."

Elspeth nodded agreement. "I would have brought trousers if I owned any. Thank you."

"I will not dress like a hoyden!" Cynthia said flatly. Not to mention that she found the idea of wearing Jack's nether garments *appalling.*

Tory laughed. "I quite like being a hoyden."

Jack's eyes sparkled mischievously, but he contented himself with saying, "You don't have to wear my old trousers. I brought them just in case."

"You're a good planner," Nick said admiringly. "What kind of food did you bring to go with the tea?"

They were all hungry, and getting everyone fed took several minutes. Cynthia heated up ham and cheese sandwiches for the others. It was nice to have a skill everyone appreciated so much.

Then it was time for their council of war. Allarde sat next to Tory, and Cynthia was pleased when Jack oh-so-casually sat next to her. Nick remained standing, almost vibrating with intensity.

"It's too late to start tonight, so we'll have to rescue the Weisses tomorrow night," he said. "Before the three of you appeared, we'd decided Tory and I would go to the castle, and Allarde would collect Dr. Weiss, with Jack's help if he joined us."

"That seems like a good plan," Jack remarked. "There's no need for Elspeth and Cynthia to go to the military camp. They can send us energy as needed without going into the line of fire."

"I'll go with Tory and Nick," Elspeth said in a voice that brooked no disagreement. "A healer might be needed, and hands-on healing is more effective than working from a distance."

As everyone nodded, Cynthia considered kicking Elspeth. Staying in the cave was a *lovely* plan. The two of them could easily send their power the short distance to the military camp. But no, Elspeth the Fearless wanted to make a target of herself. Which meant that Cynthia would look like a coward if she didn't do the same.

Worse, she'd be left out while the others developed a battlefield bond. Jack envied that bond because he'd stayed in Lackland rather than sailing to Dunkirk. His decision had been the right one, but ever since, it had bothered him. Which was why he'd been determined to join Nick on this mad mission.

Cynthia had no desire to prove her courage. She was a *girl,* for heaven sakes! She didn't have to be brave. Tory and Elspeth were setting a terrible example.

Jack turned to her. "We need someone to hold our base here. You and I can easily work together on the weather over such a short distance."

Perversely, when Jack said that, she immediately wanted to do the opposite. "I think I should be there, too. If there's a crisis, response needs to be immediate. Magelings have already been in and out of the compound a couple of times, so it's not like leaping into the unknown."

Tory made a face. "I ran into a guard, but he let me go. We've been so lucky till now that it seems time for something to go wrong. Rescuing Dr. Weiss should be fairly straightforward, though. We've been into the laboratory, and we know exactly where he's being held. Getting his family out of the castle will be more complicated."

"Once I'm there, I can locate them," Nick said confidently. "They're on the lowest level of the castle. We go up the tunnel, I find where they're being kept, you unlock their door, and we leave. Simple."

"Optimist," Cynthia said tartly. But he was right that the tunnel would make all the difference in achieving success.

"We'll need weather magic to shut down the power again," Nick continued. "On our first entrance, we destroyed the power pole. This time, we need to take out the whole generating shed since that will take longer to repair. Can that be done, weather mages? It's a building about the size of my family's henhouse, only taller."

"Not a problem," Jack said. "I've been herding a North Sea storm in this direction. I'll time it to strike about midnight tomorrow. Cynthia is good with lightning and can annihilate the shed with a cluster of strikes." He raised his brows questioningly.

Cynthia reached out to the oncoming storm and tested its shape and power. Its energy made her smile. "This should be easy. It's de-lightfully vigorous."

"Does it have powerful winds?" Allarde asked. "Rather than burn huge amounts of magic flying in and out of the compound, I'd like to knock down sections of fence so we can enter and leave on foot. That will be faster and we won't be such easy targets."

"This storm has plenty of wind to work with," Jack replied. "Do you want me to blow something into the fence, or would you rather do it with your magic?"

"I'll do it with lifting power. More precise than wind."

There were nods of agreement all around. Cynthia was relieved. Flying didn't interest her, not when the magic wasn't under her own control. Much better to go into the compound on her feet. "After, will we meet up outside and return here together?"

"The castle rescue will take longer, so we should probably go separately," Tory said, her brow furrowed. "Smaller groups are less likely to be noticed as well. After we're all safely back here, we'll take everyone to present-day Lackland. That shouldn't be difficult since we've all been there."

"Will it be a problem taking nonmages through?" Jack asked.

"I don't believe so," Tory said. "All people have at least a spark of magic. I think it will go smoothly. At least as smoothly as mirror pas-sage ever goes."

"We'll need to obscure people's memories of their rescue," Allarde said. "Does anyone know the forgetting spell used by Miss Wheaton and Mr. Stephens?"

Cynthia hadn't thought of that. In Nick's time, magic was largely unknown and considered mere superstition. The Weisses would be grateful for rescue, but the magic was going to be a shock.

"I can't do quite what Miss Wheaton does," Elspeth said. "But I should be able to blur their real memories and give them impressions of confusion and perhaps a vague belief that they crossed the channel in a small boat."

"And were seasick so they didn't remember much. That should work," Nick said with a grin. "Easier to believe in a boat ride than the truth."

"I hope all will go smoothly tomorrow," Elspeth said. "But what if soldiers catch us and point guns in our direction? Magic won't stop bullets."

"I've got a pistol," Nick said. "It was my father's when he was in France and he isn't using it now, so I borrowed it."

Cynthia felt chilled. Talk of guns and the chance that they might be needed was sobering. They were taking a deadly risk.

Her face showing a similar reaction, Tory asked, "Do you know how to use it?"

"Yes," Nick said tersely.

"What about the laboratory raiders?" Cynthia asked. "Will we be unprotected?"

"We're less likely to run into armed men," Allarde said. "But if we do, I'll pull down roofs or throw things."

"I can do the same." Tory glanced at Allarde, her expression unreadable. "Since Allarde and I have somewhat similar abilities, it's easy for us to share power in an emergency."

Other possibilities were tossed out and discussed. By the time they were ready to sleep, they'd considered all the problems they could think of and discussed possible solutions. They were as prepared as they could be.

When Cynthia rolled up in her blanket again, she felt more confident about what they would be doing. They were mages with powers the Germans had never imagined, and their dual raid was completely unexpected. They would be in and out before the enemy knew what happened.

But when Jack's hand reached out to her in the darkness, she was glad to clasp it. Even though they were both awake.

CHAPTER 28

After the war council broke up, Tory was too restless to sleep. Rather than go into the dark woods, where cold autumn rain was falling, she decided to explore the cave a bit. With luck, she'd leave here the next night and never return. If the mages who'd created the mirror portal had left anything else interesting, now was the time to look.

She retraced the path to the mirror, brushing off the old spells meant to dissuade nonmages from finding it. She didn't expect any messages, since almost anyone who could send one was already here. But she wanted to pay her respects.

The mirror was its usual self, an ancient vortex that throbbed with deep power just out of sight and sound. She had the odd sense that it silently acknowledged her presence. She touched it with her own magic in an equally silent greeting. After thanking the mirror for bringing them all here safely, she said that soon they would be in urgent need of its power again. The mirror felt—cooperative.

Feeling vaguely foolish for conversing with an invisible magical space, she withdrew and headed off to explore other passages. One led to a small chamber with the pool of springwater they'd been using for drinking and washing. Others ended in blank stone or became too small to use.

Aware that it would be easy to get lost if she wasn't careful, she tried one last branch. To her surprise, she saw a glimmer of light ahead as she traveled deeper into the hill. One of her friends was also exploring?

She reached the end and caught her breath. The water that had formed the cave had created a gallery of treasures. Stone pillars and curtains and lacy threads glimmered in the reflections of her mage light. She smiled in delight as she drifted among the stone icicles and frozen fountains and clutches of sparkling crystals.

"Beautiful, isn't it?" Allarde's deep voice was soft behind her.

She turned with a feeling of inevitability. Awareness caught fire between them as their gazes met.

Even in ill-fitting clothes and with dark bristles on his chin, Allarde was as handsome as a prince from legend as he moved toward her through the magical stone formations, his strong features and broad shoulders barely brushed by light. The sight of him would live in her heart forever.

She'd avoided being alone with him because she didn't want to talk about their separation. Her head knew that she had done the right thing, but that knowledge was a frail barrier against the power of Allarde's presence. Trying to be sensible, she said, "Let's not speak of impossible things, Justin. Our world is too far away to worry about."

"Indeed it is." He reached Tory and put his arms around her. Before she could point out weakly that this was a bad idea, they were embracing and he was kissing her with crackling intensity.

Passion, magic, and need blazed between them, burning away all her reservations. The longing that had been building since Kemperton Hall shattered in a firestorm of heat and magic that flooded her senses and burned away the world. When they broke the kiss, she said dizzily, "When we kiss, it feels like I can move mountains. Literally."

He laughed. "Small ones, perhaps."

She gave him a crooked smile. "Are we kissing to increase our shared power? That will be useful on our raid, I think."

"No." Tenderly he brushed a strand of hair from her brow. "It's because I don't want to die without kissing you again."

She froze. "Does your foretelling talent see disaster ahead?"

"Not exactly, but something unexpected will happen tomorrow night. A great complication that we haven't anticipated." He shook his head, frowning. "I'm not sure how much trouble we'll be in. Because this concerns me so closely, I don't have a clear sense of how it will work out."

Guessing at what he wasn't saying, she said, "But it could be bad."

"Perhaps," he agreed. "But I think we must go ahead. Lives are at stake."

"We have our magic. We can do things the Germans won't expect."

"That's our greatest strength." He kissed her again, his hands roaming in delicious ways. "*You* give me strength, Tory."

"And you make me weak," she said shakily. "Common sense goes out the window when you touch me. But you can't choose me over Kemperton! Life is uncertain. What if I die? Then you'd have nothing. Choose Kemperton and it will be yours as long as you live."

"So practical," he murmured before he kissed her forehead. "But as you say, life is uncertain. One or both of us might die. We might become trapped in a time not our own. There are a thousand other possibilities beyond our imagination. Which is why I don't want to waste what time we have to be together."

She let her eyes drift shut as her head rested against his chest. "You make it very hard to be practical," she sighed. "But I've thought of a solution. You can marry a girl with no magic and I'll be your mistress."

"That is nonsense in so many ways that I'll ignore it," he said firmly. "Now let us sit on that lovely stone formation that is rather like a bench, and we will discuss possibilities for our missions between kisses."

Eyes bright, she took his hand and led him toward the stone bench. She suspected there would be more kissing than discussion. And that was fine with her.

A day of rest and mental preparation left the Irregulars as ready as they could be, but the journey to Castle Bouchard was silent even with six people. Jack's storm was moving in. Though he was holding back the full fury, heavy wind and rain had already arrived. Cynthia offered to keep the rain off them, but was told to save her magic since it might be needed later.

There was something unreal about the fact that she was heading off to war. She, Lady Cynthia Stanton, the most beautiful debutante of the season she'd never had! Though she'd refused the trousers, she had traveled through the portal wearing a plain warm dress and her best pair of half boots for walking.

She did wear the coat Jack had brought for her. Old and comfortably worn, it was broad of shoulder and fell past her hips. It also carried the irresistible scent and feel of Jack, not that she'd tell him that.

As they walked, much of her attention was on the weather as she gradually gathered the wild lightning energy. She had her hands full with it, too. It was good she and Jack were both here, since controlling the storm and so much lightning would have been difficult for one person.

They crested the hill opposite the escarpment and Cynthia, Jack, and Elspeth got their first view of the castle and the military camp. Cynthia's pulse accelerated and she lost hold of a lightning bolt when she saw the great height and sheer cliff face. No wonder the castle was considered impregnable!

If she and Jack hadn't rescued Comte du Bouchard and learned of the tunnel, they could never have attempted this mission. She gave private thanks that she was a member of the laboratory team. She'd let Tory and Elspeth scale the castle heights from within.

Allarde studied the scene with narrowed eyes. "I can use that tall elm to take down the fence near the church. There aren't any trees near the laboratory, but I should be able to roll that motor vehicle through the fence."

"With luck, we'll be at the cave with the Weisses in a couple of hours and back in Lackland by morning," Nick said cheerfully, but Cynthia suspected he was less confident than he sounded.

"Are we ready to go our separate ways?" Tory asked. "Allarde and I can communicate emotions well enough to synchronize the actions of our two groups."

"One last thing." Jack stepped up to Cynthia, took hold of her upper arms, and gave her a kiss that should have made the rain steam.

She clung to him, knees weak, heart hammering, and brain stunned. He was *outrageous*! But . . . *but* . . .

Her arms slid around his neck as she dizzily kissed him back. The embrace under the mistletoe had startled her with its intensity, yet by comparison, that had been a mere breeze. This kiss was hurricane force, with wind and lightning and rain going sideways.

She might have fallen when he ended the kiss if he hadn't held her steady. She managed a strangled "What was *that* for?"

"I didn't want to head off into danger without giving you a proper kiss," he explained.

Cynthia slapped him hard on the check. "Don't you dare talk about getting killed!" She glared at him, on the edge of tears. "You need to survive so I can torment you about your utter lack of manners."

He grinned, unabashed despite the mark of her hand on his cheek. "I'd like that."

The others had been watching in fascination. "Now that that has been taken care of," Nick said, "shall we carry on with our mission?"

Allarde said quietly, "Be careful, Tory."

"We will," she replied in a steady voice.

Cynthia realized that the two of them had been holding hands. So much more genteel than Jack. She smiled involuntarily. Though Jack was outrageous, he did keep her intrigued.

The two groups split and headed in opposite directions. Nick and the other girls disappeared almost immediately in the rain and darkness. Allarde led the way toward the laboratory since he'd been here before.

Cynthia had underestimated the difficulty of walking on rough ground in the dark and increasingly heavy rain. When she stumbled going down the hill, Jack caught her arm. "Hold my hand," he said. "The ground is only going to get worse."

"I'm going to make an exception to my usual rule and actually do what you suggest," she returned, trying to sound flippant. Heaven forbid he realize how much she welcomed the excuse to hold on to him.

Not only for help in walking, though that was much appreciated. She also needed him to bolster her fraying nerves. From the top of the hill, she had seen the barbed-wire fence, the massive motor vehicles. Men with rifles patrolled the compound. She should have stuck to her original plan and stayed safe at home.

But she had wanted to be with Jack, who made so many things seem possible.

Since they were holding hands, she felt him marshalling his magic to bring the storm in at exactly the right time. As they neared the compound, he said under the sound of approaching thunder, "Do you have enough lightning, Cynthia?"

"As much as I can handle. I need to use it before I lose control."

They reached the place of concealment near the fence. As spotlights hunted back and forth, turning the perimeter from night to day, Allarde said, "The laboratory is that long, light-colored building."

"That will be easy," Jack remarked. "Where is the generator shed?"

"On the other side of the compound. Can you see it, Cynthia? There's a tall pole running up above."

She followed the direction of Allarde's pointing hand. "That small gray building? That shouldn't be much of a problem. Is it time?"

"The other team has farther to walk and they aren't in position yet," Allarde said. "Another few minutes."

Cynthia asked, "Can you and Tory read each other's thoughts?"

"Not thoughts, but we can sense each other's emotions," Allarde explained. "When Tory and the others are in place, she'll send a feeling of readiness. Completion."

"Amazing." Cynthia wondered what it would be like to have that connection with J . . . with a male. "Are you two back together? You seem to be."

Allarde gave her a freezing look that made it clear the subject was not open for discussion. Turning his gaze back to the compound, he said, "They're almost in place. Loose your winds, Jack!"

Like Cynthia, Jack had been working hard to control the storm so it would worsen at exactly the right time. Now she felt his exhilaration as he slammed together the powerful winds he'd been holding separate.

Within moments, hurricane-strength winds roared between the escarpment and the hill behind them. Cynthia was almost knocked from her feet and a tree crashed behind them with no help from Allarde.

Allarde was too busy concentrating to notice. A vehicle that had been parked on the other side of the fence flipped over with a crash and continued rolling with the sounds of crunching metal until it smashed both fences flat. He turned left, his concentration palpable. A huge tree crashed with a boom audible over the storm.

"Now, Cynthia!" Jack's grip numbed her hand.

She gazed at the roof of the generator shed. Coordinating lightning wasn't easy, but she almost had it. Almost . . .

Blinding white light illuminated the sky as an annihilating bolt slashed downward. The shed exploded and sparks blazed halfway up the escarpment. Every light in the camp vanished, plunging the compound into suffocating darkness. *Yes!* She felt exultant. A pity the camp was too wet to burn.

"Now!" Allarde ordered. "We need to cross the gap in the fence and get inside the laboratory while they're still shouting and running into each other."

Allarde focused a barely visible mage light at the ground in front of him and sprinted toward the flattened fence. Jack and Cynthia followed a little more slowly over the sodden ground, still holding hands.

She was glad she'd decided to go to the laboratory with her companions rather than stay alone outside. Underneath her excitement she was tired—herding lightning was hard work—but everything was falling into place just as they'd planned. Now she understood how sharing danger strengthened bonds between comrades.

They jumped over the barbed wire flattened by the weight of the truck, crossed the ground between fences and leaped over that as well. It took less than two minutes to reach the entrance to the laboratory. Shouts and curses came from the direction of the generator shed, but there didn't seem to be any Germans near the laboratory.

Allarde opened the door so smoothly that she barely saw how he unlocked it. Then they were inside dripping on the tiled floor and listening hard. There were no sounds of life in the building.

When Allarde judged they were safe, he strengthened the mage light a little and headed down the corridor. Double doors, more corridor, a turn before he stopped in front of a door. Once more he unlocked it and motioned Cynthia and Jack inside.

When the door was closed behind them, he brightened the light. "Dr. Weiss, we've returned," he said quietly. "Are you ready to escape?"

The lean, dark man on the narrow cot awakened immediately and swung his feet to the floor. He'd been sleeping in wrinkled trousers and shirt and socks, Cynthia noted. "Have you freed my wife and children?" he asked urgently in French-accented English. He frowned. "Where is the other boy, the one who made all the promises?"

"Nick is even now leading a team to the castle to rescue your wife and children," Allarde replied. "His ability to find people was needed there, which is why I've come here with two other friends."

"It is truly possible to free them from that place?" the scientist said with narrowed eyes. "You aren't merely saying that to placate me so I'll come with you?"

"We located an ancient tunnel that runs up through the rock from the base of the escarpment to the castle cellar," Allarde explained. "Nick and the others will be rescuing your family within minutes. Now it's time for us to go."

Dr. Weiss shoved his feet into shoes that had been tucked under his cot. After dragging on his coat and hat, he slung an improvised knapsack over his shoulders. "I'm ready. But I have one more plea to make." His dark gaze moved from one face to another. "There are others imprisoned in this building who also need to be rescued."

Cynthia's stomach clenched. Just like that, their neat plan had splintered out of control.

CHAPTER 29

Nick was taut as strung wire when Tory led the way down to the field opposite the church. Even Elspeth, usually the calm, still center of any group of Irregulars, was tense.

Having been raised in the country, Tory was pained to see the ripe stalks of wheat being flattened by the fierce rain. France would be a hungry country come winter.

When they were in position, Elspeth removed her shapeless hat and shook water from it. Like Tory, she'd braided her hair to keep it out of the way, and the braids were now saturated. "Weather mages are wonderful for covering our nefarious activities, but the results do make secret missions uncomfortable."

Tory chuckled. "I suppose we should be grateful snow wasn't required."

She scanned the area around the church, which seemed deserted. No sign of a patroller. The elm tree Allarde had tentatively selected

220 · M. J. Putney

to flatten the fence looked like the best choice for what they needed. "Are you both ready?"

After they murmured agreement, she said, "I'll let Allarde know it's time."

She concentrated on sending him a sense of preparedness. This was one time the connection between them was useful rather than a source of worry.

The rainstorm transformed into a violent tempest. She kept her attention on the tree. Since they were pooling their talents, her concentration should help him bring the tree down in the right place.

As the spotlight swung in their direction, the sky exploded with eye-searing white light. They all ducked instinctively as thunder rattled their bones.

Cynthia's lightning triggered an explosion as the generator shed disintegrated. All the lights in the compound vanished, leaving blackness and pouring rain and screaming winds.

Tory heard a metallic rumble and crunch to her right and guessed that Allarde had rolled a large motor vehicle to take out the fence near the laboratory. She felt him gather his power again. When he was ready, they channeled their combined magic into the towering elm in front of her.

The tree made an eerie groaning sound as its roots were wrenched from the earth. It toppled straight at Tory, smashing into the ground with shattering branches and fence-flattening force.

She sent a silent apology to the tree, destroyed for the purposes of humans who lived only short years in comparison. But it was needful. "Time to go!"

With a tiny mage light in hand, she raced for the fence, Elspeth and Nick behind her. A long swath of fencing was down, but the wire was still barbed. She scanned the fallen section and saw that on the left side of the downed tree, the strands had snapped and were curling up. That left a narrow passage where she could walk without the risk of stepping on barbs.

As Nick moved through, he ordered, "Wait!" Bending, he pulled the broken wires back to create a wider path.

When he was finished, he straightened and Tory resumed her run to the buttress. Memory of having been caught by the patroller before made her skin crawl as she darted toward the church and the concealed tunnel.

By the time Elspeth and Nick caught up with her, she had the hidden door open. It moved much more easily this time. "Careful," she said softly as they passed her. "There are steps going down."

Elspeth entered without hesitation, followed by Nick. After Tory closed the door, she demonstrated how to open the door from this side. Then she led the way downward. "Watch your step. The footing can be treacherous."

"At least we're out of the rain here," Nick said philosophically. "How long a hike do we have?"

"I'm not sure," Tory replied. "But think how high the castle is."

Nick shuddered dramatically. "I hope Mrs. Weiss and the children are in good condition for the hike out!"

"They might not be," Elspeth said. "Which is why I thought I should come."

Tory hoped her friend's healing skills wouldn't be required. But Elspeth, like most magelings, has some intuition about future events. If she felt her talents would be needed, she was very likely right.

Mostly they climbed in silence, though once Nick said, "Is it my imagination, or is the ceiling of this tunnel leaking?"

They stopped, taking the opportunity to catch their breath. Drops of moisture were coalescing on the pale stone above, then falling. "Definitely leaky," Tory said. "They just don't make tunnels the way they used to."

"This escarpment is made out of limestone, which is porous, if I remember my science classes correctly. Water like that created the natural cave that was the beginning of this tunnel." Nick turned sideways to edge through a particularly narrow section: "I hope none of the Weisses are claustrophobic."

"What is claustrophobic?" Elspeth asked.

"Someone who is terrified of tight spaces," Nick explained. "I'm not fond of them myself, so I'm not enjoying this tunnel. If I were a true claustrophobe, I would have sent the two of you in without me."

"And I'd have dragged you along because we need your finder skill," Tory said with a glint of amusement. "Time to get moving again. Allarde and the others probably already have Dr. Weiss safely away."

It was a relief to finally reach the landing outside the door that led into the castle cellars. Tory leaned against the wall, panting. Her companions were in no better shape.

"I tell myself it will be easier going down," Elspeth said as she gulped down air.

"Heroism is a lot of work," Tory remarked. "Nick, are the Weisses nearby?"

He closed his eyes and concentrated. "They're very close. On this level, I think."

"Good. The less we have to move about the castle, the better chance we have to get out without being noticed," Tory said. "Let's hope any Germans quartered here will have returned to sleep after the fireworks below."

Nick pulled a handgun from a holster under his coat. Tory hadn't even known it was there.

"This is my father's service revolver," he explained as he checked it. "A Webley Mark IV thirty-eight caliber. I can fire six bullets in a row without having to stop and reload after every shot like the pistols in your time."

Tory stared at the lethally efficient weapon. "I'm not sure if I find that reassuring or terrifying."

"Both," Elspeth said succinctly. "I hope you don't have to use it."

"So do I. But since we may run into armed men, I feel better for being prepared." He lowered the revolver at his side, relaxed but ready. "I'm glad I decided to bring it through the mirror with me. Intuition, I suppose. Any special tricks to this door, Tory?"

"Push this lever, but first lights off. The door opens to a storage room and it's probably empty, but we can't count on that."

After the mage lights were all doused, she opened the door, keeping it just slightly ajar while she listened. Darkness and silence on the other side. Opening the door wider, she lit another mage light and slipped through, followed by the others.

In a voice less than a whisper, Nick said, "Elspeth, I'm the finder and Tory unlocks doors, but I think you should stay here. Our reserve if something goes wrong."

"I can just see myself rescuing you from a platoon of Nazis," she said dryly. "But you're right. There's no need for me to go with you. I'm here if healing is needed."

Mentally girding herself, Tory dimmed her light and adjusted it so it pointed only downward. She had been skulking around so much lately that she'd become really good at calibrating lights that were the next thing to nonexistent.

They reached the door to the corridor. "Lead on, Nicholas," she said softly.

He stepped into the corridor, Tory right behind him. Quiet and confident, he led the way along one corridor, through a door that Tory unlocked, down another passage. She guessed they were traversing the full width of the castle. The cellars were shabby, but in regular use for storage. And if Nick was right, for prisoners.

Once they heard heavy footsteps directly overhead. They froze and Tory turned off her light until the steps moved unhurriedly away.

She told her pulse to slow down, created another light, and they continued on to another locked door. As Tory opened it, she sensed Nick's excitement. They must be getting close.

Her nostrils flared when they moved into the next passage. There was a sour smell of people crowded too close together. Nick stopped in front of a massive door with a small barred slit toward the top. His gesture said, *This is it!*

The old door had a new and challenging lock. Tory closed her eyes and concentrated on shifting the tumblers to the open position. Ah, *there!*

She opened the door and Nick stepped inside, Tory right behind. She was startled by the number of people crowded into a small space. Ten or twelve, all women and children, all staring fearfully at the newcomers.

"Mrs. Weiss?" Nick asked uncertainly.

Several people caught their breaths anxiously. Then a thin, dark-haired woman with resignation in her eyes stepped forward into the light. "I'm Dr. Sarah Weiss," she said in French. "Have you come to take me to my execution?"

CHAPTER 30

Cynthia cringed internally when Dr. Weiss said there were others in the building who needed rescuing, but Allarde merely said, "I knew there would be unexpected events tonight. How many and where are they?"

"My two colleagues are here," Dr. Weiss explained. "We worked in the same research laboratory before the war and were arrested at the same time. They are also Jewish. I fear for their safety. Can you rescue them also?"

Allarde glanced at Jack and Cynthia. She gave a small nod while Jack said, "I don't see why not. It will be more complicated, but not impossible."

"Then let us find them and release them quickly," Allarde said.

Dr. Weiss adjusted his improvised knapsack, which looked heavy. "I have my research notes and materials here." He hesitated. "Their families were imprisoned with mine. Will your colleagues bring out everyone as you are doing?"

"If they can, yes." Allarde headed to the door. "But I can make no promises. Are any guards stationed in this building? If so, how likely are they to wake up? The more of us who are moving around, the more likely we are to be noticed."

"Only one man sleeps here," Dr. Weiss replied. "A sergeant whose hearing was damaged by shell fire. He has a room by the front door, but does not wake easily."

"I hope you're right. Lead us to your colleagues."

"I'll use some illusion magic to age us," Cynthia offered. "It will save having to explain how young we are."

Jack grinned. "A good idea. There will be time enough for them to be disbelieving about that later."

Cynthia laid a hand on Jack's arm and channeled the magic to add eight or ten years. She was unsettled to realize that he'd look even better in the future than now. Turning, she did the same for Allarde and then herself while Dr. Weiss watched in amazement.

Nerves twanging with tension, she followed the others from the cell and down the corridor opposite to free the other two scientists. Mr. Stein was a young assistant, Dr. Heller older, with salt-and-pepper hair. Allarde didn't attempt to explain that they were being rescued by mages. That could also wait until later, when there was more time.

For now, Dr. Weiss explained to his colleagues that these were British agents come to free them. With luck, their families would be freed at the same time. That assurance meant both men were more than willing to leave.

The handful of minutes the researchers took to collect the few items they could carry with them seemed to take forever. How long would the power be out? Now that she'd seen the camp, Cynthia was painfully aware of how visible they would be if they didn't have darkness to cover their escape.

Six people made noise when they were walking, even though they were all trying to be silent. Cynthia gave a sigh of relief when they reached the front door. Allarde was opening it when a yawning soldier swung open a door on the left. He was half dressed, but carried an electric torch in his left hand and a pistol by his side.

The beam of light swept over the magelings and escaping prisoners. After a moment of shocked disbelief, the sergeant swung his weapon up and barked, *"Achtung! Halt!"*

Jack leaped forward and knocked the weapon from the soldier's hand, but it fired before spinning into the darkness. No one was hit, but the shot was horrifically loud in the confined space.

As the guard raised a shout, Jack slammed his fist into the man's jaw, knocking him down, but the damage had been done. The camp had been alerted.

"Go!" Allarde snapped. "Left toward the fence!"

The scientists ran. Jack grabbed Cynthia's arm. "I'm wishing you'd worn my trousers! Full speed, Cynthia!"

She didn't need urging. They were barely out of the building when a hair-raising siren wailed across the camp. The gunshot had been heard.

The power station was still out, but a nearby motor engine rumbled to life and the beams of a pair of headlights blazed past the laboratory. Another engine roared to life and more headlights slashed the darkness just behind Cynthia and Jack as they slowed to pick their way over the flattened laboratory fence.

Once they were out, Cynthia did her best to run, but her corset constricted her ribs so she couldn't breathe deeply, her wet skirts tangled around her legs, and the continuing rain had turned the ground into a muddy swamp. Even with Jack half-carrying her, she was moving too slowly. "Jack," she gasped, "go ahead without me!"

"Be damned if I will!" he swore. "Keep going, sweeting, it's not far now!"

Ahead of them, Allarde was shepherding the scientists over the outer fence. Another engine growled behind Cynthia and Jack, and new headlights nailed the pair of them with ruthless clarity.

Shouts sounded as German soldiers came in pursuit. Then the shooting began.

As bullets whizzed by, Cynthia tripped and fell, crashing hard into the muddy ground. Weeping, she cried, "Jack, *go!*"

He shouted, "Allarde, help Cynthia!"

Then Jack turned to face the oncoming German soldiers.

"We're not here to execute you, Dr. Weiss," Tory said in French, thinking her female voice would be less threatening, and besides, Nick's French wasn't good. "We are English agents here to help you escape to England. Another team is freeing your husband as well."

Sarah Weiss gasped. In English, she said, "This is the truth? You are not SS agents who are tormenting me?"

Tory smiled and brightened her light. "Do we look like the SS?"

The scientist looked Tory and Nick over. "To be honest," she said, still in English, "you look like friends of my children."

"We are young," Nick said, "but young agents are effective because we don't know enough to be afraid."

"That sounds . . . real," Sarah Weiss said. "If you have a way out of this castle, I will gladly risk it. But . . ." She gestured at the others in the crowded room.

A young dark-haired boy came to stand close and she wrapped an arm around him. Her son, presumably. A baby coughed wearily in its young mother's arms. The oldest person was a white-haired, grandmotherly woman.

A girl about Tory's age moved forward into the light. She had dark hair and riveting gray-green eyes. "All here are family members of other scientists working with my father," she said in English. "We will be shipped to Germany within a matter of days. Can you free us all?"

Tory realized three things simultaneously. The girl had magic, Nick was staring at her as if she were an angel descended from on high, and this must be the complication Allarde had sensed. Though they'd considered different possibilities, having to rescue more people hadn't been one of them.

Sarah Weiss gasped, as did several others who must understand English. "Rebecca, what makes you say this?"

Rebecca dropped her eyes. "I heard the commandant speaking outside the door, Mother. I didn't mention it because I didn't want to upset anyone."

Rebecca was lying, Tory realized. Not about the commandant's intentions, but how she'd learned them. It would be interesting to know why.

Her mother turned to Tory and Nick. "Can you take us all out?"

"A secret tunnel runs from the cellars down to ground level. After that, we have to walk a couple of miles." Nick's gaze moved over the captives, lingering on the white-haired woman. "It is not a great distance, but it might be hard for some."

The old woman said in German-accented English, "Don't worry about me, lad. I am stronger than I look."

"Good. We don't want to leave anyone behind."

The young woman who held the coughing baby asked, "Will the other men be rescued with Dr. Weiss? We were told they were all imprisoned in the laboratory. My husband . . ."

"As we are willing to help your fellow prisoners, our friends will surely do the same for the other researchers if they can," Nick said to them all, but his gaze returned to Rebecca Weiss. Tory suspected that Rebecca had much to do with the fierce intuition that had driven Nick to risk his life on this mission.

Sarah Weiss turned and spoke to the others in French. The crowded room surged with excitement and people moved to the door. They had few if any possessions to collect. A young girl moved to the side of the white-haired woman to help her. The old woman might be frail, but her expression was grimly determined.

As the room cleared out, Tory saw a door in the opposite wall with a large window in it. Curious, she crossed the cell and opened the door, then gasped with shock. It opened onto a narrow balcony on the face of the cliff with a sheer drop below.

As the wind whipped around her, she instinctively stepped back. Far below, an eerie siren began to wail. She prayed that Allarde and his team had escaped with the scientists by now.

Sarah Weiss joined her, laying a steadying hand on Tory's arm. "You see why Rebecca didn't reveal that we were about to be shipped to Germany," she said quietly. "One of our number might choose to end it all here in a moment of despair."

Tory stepped forward, gripping the balcony railing with both hands. Even for someone who could fly, the drop before her was unnerving. "Did anyone jump during your imprisonment?"

"No, but I'll wager that most of us at least thought about the advantages of a quick end," the older woman said bluntly. "Conditions have been difficult. If we were shipped to Germany, I doubt any of us would survive this cursed war."

Chilled, Tory sensed that Dr. Weiss was right. This war had just begun, and unimagined horrors lay ahead. "Do you think you were all locked up in this particular room to encourage suicide?"

The other woman's mouth twisted mirthlessly. "It was Colonel Heinrich's little joke. He said that we weren't imprisoned, we could leave whenever we wished."

A vehicle's lights sprang to life in the camp below. Time was passing. Tory said, "Then it's fortunate that we arrived when we did. Soon you'll be safe in England."

"Safer, anyhow." Dr. Weiss left the balcony and headed toward the corridor. "England may fall. But for at least a little while, we will be free. And God willing, I shall see Daniel again."

In the corridor outside, Nick had created a moderately bright light. No one seemed to notice that it didn't come from an electric torch.

Tory did a head count. Ten people: Three adult women who were wives of the imprisoned scientists, one grandmother, and six children ranging in age from the babe in arms to Rebecca Weiss. Most of the children were old enough to walk on their own out of the castle, though the smaller ones might need to be carried part of the way to the cave.

"Move quickly but quietly," Nick said in a low voice. He scooped up the smallest toddler. "We saw no one coming here, and with luck we'll see no one leaving."

Turning, he led the way back with Tory bringing up the rear with another light. The group was halfway down the last stretch of corridor that led to the storeroom when a side door swung open and a German soldier carrying a rifle emerged from a stairwell.

The soldier flipped a switch by the door, and the tunnel lights sprang to life. The camp's generator had been repaired.

As Tory blinked from the sudden glare, the soldier stopped at the sight of the fugitives, then jerked his rifle to his shoulder and barked, *"Achtung!"*

"No!" Nick snapped his revolver up, holding it with both hands to steady his aim, and fired. The gunshot was deafening in the narrow passage.

As the soldier pitched to the floor and Nick watched, aghast at what he'd done, Elspeth burst from the storeroom. "Is anyone hurt?"

In the same instant, a little boy screamed and raced past Tory back along the corridor. She made a grab, but he was gone before she could stop him.

"I . . . I may have killed this soldier, Elspeth," Nick stammered.

As the group churned in confusion, Rebecca pivoted and bolted after the little boy. "Aaron is running off! I'll bring him back."

Sensing possible disaster, Tory sprinted after them. "Nick, Elspeth, get everyone away!" she called. "I'll collect Rebecca and the little boy and follow. If we're separated, I'll meet you back at the cave!"

Elspeth knelt by the fallen soldier. "Be careful, Tory."

She laid a hand on the man's bleeding side. He moaned and rolled his head, his helmet falling off. He looked little older than Nick. "This wound isn't mortal," Elspeth said. "I'll stop the bleeding and then we're gone."

Tory reached the first set of doors, cursing herself for not locking them behind her. If she had, the boy couldn't have run any farther.

She flung the doors back and followed Rebecca, catching up with her halfway down the corridor. Ahead, their small quarry disappeared around a corner. He seemed to be running back to the familiarity of his cell. "What frightened Aaron so badly?" Tory asked between gasps for breath.

"Nazis, the SS, broke into his home and murdered his family," Rebecca said grimly. "Aaron hid and they didn't find him, but he saw his parents and brother die. Gunshots and German uniforms panic him." Rebecca was visibly tiring, worn out by imprisonment and not enough food. "His aunt and uncle, the Hellers, took him in. She's the redheaded woman. I often rock Aaron to sleep when he cries at night."

"Soon he'll be safe," Tory said reassuringly. Privately she qualified the statement to *if* they managed to get away from the castle and back to the mirror.

The child had run almost all the way back to the room where he'd been imprisoned by the time they caught up with him. Rebecca swooped him up in her arms, crooning reassurances in French.

At first Aaron sobbed frantically, but his tears diminished as they headed back toward the storeroom at a fast walk. Since it would be slow going to get the whole group through the tunnel, they should easily catch up.

Tory opened the doors to the last corridor just as armed troops poured out of the stairway used by the single soldier earlier. She gasped and instantly retreated, but it was too late. She had been seen.

A shout was raised and several soldiers began pounding down the corridor after them. Tory slammed and locked the doors, giving thanks that the soldiers didn't seem inclined to shoot two girls and a little boy. Yet.

Expression terrified, Rebecca said, "Is there another way out of the castle?"

Tory's heart sank. There was no good place to hide, and she didn't know how to get up to ground level and out of the castle, much less down the road that ran up the back of the escarpment. "Yes," she said reluctantly. "But it will be frightening."

She would have to take Rebecca and Aaron off the balcony and down the cliff.

CHAPTER 31

When Allarde raced back in swift response to Jack's call, Cynthia gasped, "Please, help Jack! He's committing suicide!"

Cynthia struggled to regain her footing, her gaze on Jack. He looked horribly vulnerable silhouetted against the headlights with his hands raised in surrender as a dozen armed soldiers charged at him.

"I can't!" Allarde said, agonized. "I have to get you and the scientists away, or we're all doomed." He caught Cynthia under her arms and lifted her to her feet.

She whimpered as the first soldiers reached Jack and threw him to the ground. But he wasn't helpless, she realized as Allarde pulled her toward the fallen fence. "Jack is doing weather magic! I think he's trying to raise a waterspout from the lake."

"Then help him while we run," Allarde said grimly. "He's sacrificing himself to give us a better chance to escape. Don't waste it!"

Cynthia turned and ran blindly, guided by Allarde's supportive arm while she concentrated on joining her weather magic to Jack's. The lake was nowhere near as good a source as the turbulent English Channel, but with Cynthia's help, Jack might be able to raise a waterspout.

She stumbled going over the fallen main fence, but Allarde's grip kept her upright. Lights flared behind them and she realized that the generator must have been repaired. They'd left the camp in the nick of time.

As Allarde steered her into the shadows where the scientists waited, she looked back over her shoulder. The spotlights were sweeping along the fence again, and every light in the camp was blazing, turning night into day.

The lights illuminated a massive tower of water rising from the lake like a mythic sea monster. She heard gasps from Dr. Weiss and the others as the column spun out of the lake and across the compound.

The spout fell apart quickly once it left the water, turning into a tidal wave that crashed along the line of the fence. Vehicles and buildings flooded, creating chaos. It would take time for the Germans to regroup and come after the escaped prisoners.

"They're going to organize themselves faster than we'd like, so we need to get away while we can," Allarde said sharply. "Staring at the compound isn't going to help."

Numbly Cynthia turned and headed west toward the point where they might meet up with the other group. If not, they'd proceed separately to the cave. "I should have worn the trousers," she whispered brokenly. "Then I wouldn't have fallen and Jack wouldn't have been captured."

"Perhaps. We can't know for sure."

Allarde's voice was expressionless, but she suspected that he agreed with her. She'd insisted on dressing like a lady instead of adjusting to circumstances as Tory and Elspeth had done. She was a *fool*.

And her foolishness might be the death of Jack.

"Cynthia," Allarde interrupted her lacerating thoughts. "Can your illusion magic make Jack look younger? Since he's in civilian clothes and obviously English, they'll probably consider him a spy. If you can make him look younger than his age, maybe fourteen or so, they may consider him a boy and treat him as a regular prisoner."

"Not shoot him, you mean," she said bitterly. "That's a good idea. I think I can manage it."

She stretched her magic out to Jack, once more barely aware of where she was walking. She trusted Allarde to keep her going in the right direction.

Though she and Jack didn't have the bond Tory and Allarde did, she found him easily. Giving thanks that he was still alive, she channeled illusion magic, adjusting his appearance so that he looked younger and more harmless than he really was. She tried to convey what she'd done, but didn't know if Jack was aware of her efforts.

They reached the rendezvous point, a small grove of trees between the lake and the wheat field. The others hadn't arrived yet. "Let's wait a few minutes," Allarde said. "The camp is still so confused that we can spare a little time."

Cynthia was glad of the chance to catch her breath, and she wasn't the only one. After months of imprisonment, the three scientists weren't used to strenuous exercise.

Allarde stood silently looking toward the church. She guessed that he'd be very relieved when Tory was safely out of the castle.

"They're coming," he said in a low voice. "I can see them leaving the buttress and waiting outside the range of the spotlight."

Cynthia followed his gesture and saw a ragged line of dark figures. "Look at all the people! They must have found the other families."

"Sarah!" Dr. Weiss started impulsively toward the compound.

"Wait!" Allarde grabbed the scientist's shoulder. "Let them come to us."

Cynthia held her breath, and she suspected the men did as well. When the spotlight swung away toward the center of the camp, the group from the castle surged toward the fence. They reached it as the spotlight returned, but the tree that had fallen earlier was large and bushy enough to provide cover for the fugitives, who dropped to the ground behind the tree trunk.

Cynthia's nails bit into her palms as she watched. Two or three of the group moved with excruciating slowness when every second counted.

"Tory's not with them," Allarde said tautly.

Cynthia didn't question his knowledge. "She'll be along soon," she said, trying to convince herself as much as Allarde.

The swinging light moved on, and the group bolted from the protection of the tree. After crossing the fence, they headed straight toward the grove that sheltered Cynthia and the others.

"Sarah!" This time Dr. Weiss would not be stopped. He lunged forward and grabbed his wife in a bruising embrace. They clung to each other, both weeping. The scene was repeated as the Steins and Hellers and their children were reunited.

Allarde allowed about half a minute before saying in a commanding voice, "There will be time to talk later. Now we must get out of sight of the compound."

The families obediently followed his orders, moving in groups behind Nick, who led the way with a child in his arms. As they headed away from the camp, Dr. Weiss looked behind, asking worriedly, "Where is Rebecca?"

Dr. Heller looked around then. "Aaron? Where is my Aaron?"

"And where is Tory?" Allarde said grimly. "Elspeth? What happened?"

Elspeth was a few steps away, carrying a baby and looking drained. "The little boy, Aaron, was frightened when a soldier discovered us leaving," she explained in a low, clear voice that carried to the others. "He ran and Rebecca and Tory went after him. They were cut off by the soldiers and couldn't rejoin us. They'll escape a different way and meet us at the cave."

Voice too low to be heard by the refugees, Allarde swore with soft, controlled violence. "Just how do you think that Tory and the others will escape?"

Elspeth's smile was brittle. "I have great faith in her talent and ingenuity."

Allarde swore again, but changed the subject. "How did the rest of you get away from the soldiers?"

"At first there was only one, and Nick shot him," Elspeth said wearily. "More arrived after we entered the tunnel. We heard them, but they didn't see us. They were probably chasing Tory and the others."

"So they might have been captured."

"They might." Elspeth pushed her wet braid back over her shoulder. "You would know better than I if Tory is safe."

Allarde closed his eyes and drew a deep breath as he cleared his emotions enough to seek Tory. "She hasn't been captured. I think she's safe. For now, anyhow."

"Good!" Cynthia said gratefully. She examined Elspeth with a frown. "You look exhausted. Did you have to do a lot of healing?"

"Enough to tire me out." Elspeth patted the back of the baby in her arms. "This little darling had pneumonia and was in serious condition, and Grandmother Stein has severe arthritis, but I was able to help them both. I can make it back to the cave, but I won't be doing any major magic for a while." She frowned, her gaze scanning the fugitives. "Where is Jack?"

"He was captured," Allarde said. "Now that our scientists and their families have been rescued, I'm going back for him."

"Into the middle of an armed camp?" Elspeth said, horrified. "It won't help Jack if you're captured or shot!"

"I'll think of something," Allarde said, his voice flat. "I'm not leaving anyone behind without trying to free him."

His words invigorated Cynthia. In a tone that didn't allow argument, she said, "If you're going after Jack, I'm going with you."

"Any way out is better than the SS," Rebecca said starkly. "Lead the way."

Tory did just that, racing back toward the prisoners' cell. With the corridor lights on, they were able to move faster than before, but the same was true for their pursuers, who could be heard not far behind. One last set of doors to lock behind them.

They reached the cell. Rebecca balked at the door. "Why do you bring us back to this vile place?"

"I'll explain, but first, come in." Tory ushered the other girl, who still held Aaron, into the cell. After swiftly locking the door behind them, she said, "I'm going to tell you incredible things. Please be open-minded."

Rebecca frowned, her dark brows a straight line. "I do not understand."

"There are people in the world who have magical abilities. I am one of them. The quickest thing I can do is demonstrate the ability that will get us out of here." A moment of hard concentration and Tory floated up to the ceiling.

Rebecca gasped and shrank back, clutching Aaron while the boy stared at Tory with huge brown eyes. "What *are* you?" she asked shakily.

"A girl much like you." Time travel could wait till later. Tory drifted back to the floor as she continued, "But I have some magical powers. Floating is my particular gift. There are many other talents. You have magical ability, Rebecca. I don't know what type, but haven't you ever felt different from others? Done things that are supposed to be impossible, and you're afraid to talk about them?"

Rebecca bit her lip. "Sometimes . . . I seem to know what people are thinking."

Tory's brows arched. "That's how you knew the commandant planned to send you all to labor camps in Germany?"

Rebecca nodded. "It was very clear in his mind. We'd be shipped out as soon as a lorry was available to take us to a train station, and good riddance. Heinrich feels that he is above being a jailer of women and children. But I saw no point in telling the others when we were helpless."

Impressed, Tory said, "If you can read minds, it should be easier to believe that I can fly. Going out that window with me carrying you two down is our only way out." German voices suddenly got louder and she guessed they'd come through the second set of doors and were getting close.

Rebecca opened the door to the balcony and looked down the cliff, the wind and rain tearing at her bare head and dress. One hand clamped on the doorframe, her knuckles white. "I'm taller than you, and there is also Aaron. Do you have the strength to carry all three of us down safely?"

"I think so, or I wouldn't suggest this," Tory said honestly. "Five other magelings came on this mission. If necessary, I can draw on their power if I need it. But there is risk. Even if I can carry you both safely, we might be seen and shot from the air."

"The camp is directly below and we'll come down in the middle," Rebecca said, her voice shaking. "We will be recaptured."

"I'll drift us to one side so we land outside the camp. Then we run." Tory glanced back at the door. They had only seconds left. "Please, trust me!"

The other girl looked toward the corridor, where guttural voices could be heard. Her mouth tightened. "Tell me what I must do."

Tory yanked off her coat. "We go out on the balcony and lock Aaron between us while I tie this around our waists to help us keep our grip. Then we go over the railing and descend to the ground fairly quickly so we won't be seen. I'll slow us down before we land." She didn't dare show her own fears. Rebecca was nervous enough already.

"Tie us together!" the other girl said shakily. "And may God protect us."

Tory stepped forward until she was pressed against Rebecca with Aaron between them. Using both hands, she wrapped the coat around their waists and knotted the sleeves behind Rebecca's back.

The other girl was taller, but mercifully slim so the coat sleeves reached far enough to tie into a hard knot. Though the garment wasn't strong enough to hold them together on its own, it would help.

Wrapping her arms around Rebecca, Tory said, "Can you put

one arm around me while keeping Aaron secure? He should be safe between us."

The little boy was supported on Rebecca's left arm, so she wrapped the right one around Tory. "Aaron, *mon petit chou,* close your eyes. We're going to get away from the bad men."

Trustingly the little boy closed his eyes and leaned his head against Rebecca's shoulder. When he was settled, Rebecca closed her eyes also. Her face was chalk white under her dark hair.

A rattle of gunfire blasted behind them. The soldiers were shooting off the lock of the cell door.

Invoking her magic with prayerlike intensity, Tory lifted the three of them from the floor of the balcony. Rebecca whimpered when her feet no longer had solid footing, but her grip never wavered.

Then they were over the railing and going down, down, *down.* . . .

CHAPTER 32

Cynthia had never seen Allarde lose his temper, but when she stated that she was going with him to rescue Jack, she half expected him to say, *"Haven't you caused enough trouble?"*

Instead, he said tersely, "That won't work. It will be difficult enough for one person to get into the camp. Two will be more conspicuous, especially when one is an attractive young woman. I'd have to look after you as well as look for Jack."

He was tactful even when refusing her—she wasn't attractive, she looked like a hag who'd been dragged through a mud wallow. Not that she blamed him for being skeptical. "I wish to heaven I'd been practical and worn trousers! But even in a gown, I believe I can lead you to where they're holding Jack."

Allarde frowned, considering. Beside them, Elspeth said quietly, "Since men are physically stronger, they've traditionally been the protectors of women and children. But among mages, female abilities match those of men."

Sensing that Allarde was wavering, Cynthia said coaxingly, "I can use illusion magic to help us get inside."

"That would be good," he agreed. "Helping us get out with Jack would be even better. Why, Cynthia? You've usually been more sensible than the other girls."

How polite of him to say "sensible" when the real word was "cowardly." Even to herself, Cynthia didn't want to admit the whole reason. She settled for, "It's my fault Jack was captured, so it is damned well my responsibility to get him out."

As they stared at each other, Dr. Heller spoke up hesitantly. "Jack is the blond young man who helped you to free us? He has been captured by the Nazi pigs?"

"I'm afraid so," Allarde said. "With luck, the camp is still in such chaos that it might be possible to get him out, so I intend to try."

"The young lady said she should have worn trousers," the scientist continued. "If it would help, I have a spare pair because I had little else to carry away." He smiled at Cynthia. "Your waist is much slimmer than mine, but we are much of a height. I shall be happy to give them to you if it will help you rescue your brave young man."

Cynthia wanted to protest that he wasn't *her* young man, but—he was. *He was.* "Thank you. That will be helpful."

Once they were decided on a plan, Dr. Heller sacrificed his only spare shirt and trousers. Cynthia kept her hat and Jack's saturated coat. Even heavy with rain, it gave her comfort. Then she and Allarde headed back toward the camp while the rest of the group started their hike to the cave.

Cynthia looked even worse in her oversized male garments. Dr. Heller hadn't been exaggerating when he'd said his waist was much larger. Her borrowed belt was cinched to the last hole. Her trouser legs had to be rolled up as well.

But looking like a beggar was worth it for the freedom of

movement she had now. Later, if she survived, she'd kick herself for having refused the trousers Jack had offered. If she had to wear male garments, much better she wore his.

She and Allarde retraced their steps to the end of the camp by the church, where the fallen tree and deserted buildings offered the best cover. When they reached the fallen tree crossing, she asked hesitantly, "Tory is still all right?"

"Yes, but in danger." He paused a moment. The flatness of his voice was alarming.

Cynthia asked reluctantly, "Do you want to go after her while I go into the camp for Jack?"

He hesitated a long moment before replying. "Jack is a prisoner and his situation is more dangerous. Tory is free and will make her way back to the cave, so she doesn't need the help as much."

Cynthia was relieved. While she'd go into the compound alone if necessary, success was more likely with Allarde.

The spotlight moved away and they darted over the fence and took shelter beside the tree. As they waited for the spotlight to move over them, Allarde asked, "Do you have some sense of where he's being held?"

Cynthia concentrated, reaching out to find the essence of Jack, then trying to read his circumstances. "He was taken to the camp headquarters. A building in the center of the village. The old town hall, I think." Pain stabbed through her belly. She moaned and pressed her hand to her stomach.

"What do you pick up?" Allarde asked sharply. "Is Jack . . . ?" He didn't complete the sentence.

"He's alive, but they're beating him!" she said in a choked voice.

Allarde shook her shoulder. "Pull back, Cynthia! You can't help Jack if you let yourself be crippled by his pain."

She knew he was right. Turning her face up, she let the cool rain wash over her cheeks and aching temples. After half a dozen heartbeats, she said, "Very well, I've pulled back. Not so far that I can't find him, but enough that I can function."

"Good girl," he said quietly. "Has anyone mentioned that you're at your best when the situation is worst?"

She smiled wryly. "Mostly they say how sharp my tongue is."

"Heroines are allowed a few flaws. Come along now."

His warm hand on her back was comforting. Silly of her to have fancied him merely because he was heir to a dukedom. His friendship was more valuable than that.

The spotlight passed over their heads and they ran into the compound heading for the shadows of the abandoned church. The rain made it a miserably, muddy night, but at least it helped conceal them.

They circled the church to the side that faced the village. Most of the military camp's lights were on, except where Jack's waterspout had wreaked the worst havoc.

The road that led up to the castle ran between them and the main village. They were about to cross when the throbbing engine of a powerful motorcar sounded, the noise increasing rapidly.

As they dropped back into the shadows, Allarde said under his breath, "I think that's the commandant's car."

An idea struck Cynthia. "Can you stop the car with a tree so we can catch him?"

He opened his mouth to question why, but there was no time to waste. Fiercely she said, "Just do it!"

He obeyed, pulling major power as the heavy Mercedes roared around the curve. A sharp crack split the air and a massive tree limb crashed onto the vehicle. It stopped dead in a crunch of metal and snapping branches. The Mercedes was pushed onto one side, its headlights shooting down at an angle.

They waited to see if the accident had been observed, but no one came. Though the crash sounded loud to them, the steady rain muffled the noise from carrying far.

"Now that I've crushed the car and possibly killed two people, would you care to explain your plan to me?" Allarde asked in a dangerously silky voice. "If you think we can exchange the commandant for Jack, I doubt the Nazis will cooperate."

Cynthia decided to overlook his tone of voice since his nerves would be on edge until he got Tory back. "Not a hostage exchange. If I know the commandant's appearance, I can make you look like him. If we move quickly, before they're sorted out, you could probably go into the headquarters and order them to release Jack to your custody. You speak German, don't you?"

"Yes, though there's more to an impersonation than appearance and basic language ability." Allarde's voice had turned thoughtful. "Your illusion magic. Is it strictly on the surface, or is part of it working on the mind of the viewer to make them believe in what they're seeing?"

"I . . . I don't know. I've only recently recognized what I'm doing." She frowned, thinking. "Mostly it's on the surface, but there might be an element of mental persuasion as well. Let's try an experiment."

She closed her eyes and concentrated on changing her appearance to that of Tory. Opening them, she said, "How do I look?"

He blinked. "That's remarkable. I've heard of high-price courtesans in London who can change their looks completely, but I've never seen it."

"A courtesan? Wonderful," she said caustically. "Still another way for me to support myself that would make my father insane."

Allarde grinned. "Weather working is a better career in the long run. Besides, a courtesan needs to be compliant. I doubt that's your strong point."

He had that right. "I'm going to try something more with this." She sank deeper into her magic, then projected that she didn't just look like her roommate, she *was* her.

Allarde gasped. "Good God, even though I know what you're doing, I can almost believe you're Tory! If I didn't know about illusion magic, I would never guess that you aren't her." After a moment, he added, "At least, until you opened your mouth and said something sharp."

She laughed, refusing to be insulted. "I think we've just increased the chances of persuading the soldiers in the camp headquarters that you're their commander. Shall we go take a look at him?"

As Tory and her passengers glided across the cliff face toward a landing spot well beyond the camp, she felt Rebecca shaking, but the other girl didn't make a sound. Aaron hummed with what seemed like enjoyment.

Though Tory had worried about carrying this much weight, she found that the increase in power that had occurred at Dunkirk made it possible. Her magic was strained to the limit and she couldn't have managed if she were carrying larger people, but at least she didn't have to pull power from her friends when they might need it themselves.

Before jumping, she'd scanned the area below the cliff and decided that traveling to the left would take them to safety most quickly. She felt horribly conspicuous in the air, but the continuing rain, not to mention the chaos in the camp below, must be keeping German eyes on the ground.

She sighed with relief once they were beyond the boundaries of the compound. "We're almost down if you want to open your eyes now, Rebecca."

"I'll wait till we're on the ground," Rebecca said, her eyes still firmly shut. "I'm terrified of heights. I have nightmares of falling from a high place."

Her words jolted Tory, reminding her that she'd had similar dreams. Tonight she'd lived it, but with a better outcome. Clear proof that she had no foreteller talent. She was glad of that. Allarde's ability in that area had made her realize how disturbing it could be to know some of the future.

When they drifted close to a hedge that was a safe distance from the camp, Tory said, "We're about to land, and you're less likely to stumble and pull us all down if you open your eyes."

Rebecca swallowed hard. "Very well."

When the other girl's eyes opened, Tory set them down as gently as she could manage. Her hovering was much better than it had been, but even so, it was good Rebecca was watching, or they might have fallen over.

When they were firmly on solid ground, Rebecca exhaled with relief. "Thank God! You are amazing, Tory, and I hope I never have to do anything like that again!"

"I shouldn't think you will," Tory said with a laugh as she set to work on the knotted sleeves of her coat. It came free, releasing them from their involuntary embrace.

Tory was going to put the coat on again when she realized that Rebecca was shivering still. The autumn night was chilly, and by now Rebecca was as soaked by the rain as Tory. She didn't have the hearth-witch magic to help warm herself, either.

Holding out the coat, Tory said, "Put this on. It will help a bit. Do you want me to carry Aaron for a while?"

Rebecca didn't argue about taking the coat. Setting Aaron on his feet, she said, "He'll walk for now. You saw how fast he could run." She stroked the boy's head. "We're away from the bad men, *mon petit chou*. Soon we'll be safe."

"Auntie?" he asked.

"Yes, we'll be with your aunt and cousins, and God willing, your uncle as well."

Aaron's face brightened and he took firm hold of Rebecca's hand.

"We have something of a hike ahead of us," Tory explained as she set off along the hedge away from the camp. "We're heading to a cave that's on the far side of the military camp, so we'll need to circle around the long way."

"Then we'd better get moving. My parents and Aaron's aunt and uncle will be worried about him." Rebecca's voice faltered. "Do you think they got away safely?"

"I'm sure of it." Tory didn't have to pretend conviction. "With Nick and Elspeth as guides and that nice, secret tunnel the Germans knew nothing about, they would have been clear of the compound before the electricity was restored. They're probably halfway to the cave by now."

"Grandmother Stein has arthritis and doesn't walk well," Rebecca said worriedly. "And the baby, Shoshanna, is very ill. Pneumonia, my mother said. We were terrified that she wouldn't last another day."

"Elspeth is a gifted healer." They reached a gap in the hedge that opened to a lane. Tory checked that it was clear, then turned into it. "She came to the castle because she felt her ability would be needed, so she would have cured the baby, then reduced the pain of Grandmother Stein."

"She can do that?" Rebecca asked incredulously. "Why do we need doctors?"

"Because healers like Elspeth are very rare, and magical power is limited," Tory explained. "Saving a baby from lung fever and easing arthritis will use up much of her power for several days. She'll keep some in reserve if she can, but you can see how physicians are still required."

"God willing she was able to fix Shoshanna at least!" Rebecca exclaimed. "After we reach your cave, then what? Will a British plane come for us? My father's work is important, but I wouldn't have thought the British would send agents and an airplane."

"They didn't." Tory smiled wryly as they walked away from Castle Bouchard. "We came because Nick had a powerful feeling that your father must be rescued and persuaded the rest of us it was necessary."

Tory felt the alertness in Rebecca when she asked, "Nick is the blond boy who was with you?"

"Yes, he's the savior of you and your family." Tory wasn't averse to matchmaking. She'd seen how Nick looked at Rebecca, and apparently interest was mutual. "Do you want to hear the whole long, unbelievable tale of magic and magelings and how we came to Castle Bouchard?"

"Indeed I do." Rebecca looked back at the looming cliff that still dominated the landscape. "Tonight has taught me that Shakespeare was right, and there are more things under heaven and earth than are dreamed of in our philosophies."

"Then prepare yourself to learn of wonders," Tory said. "A good thing we have a long walk ahead of us!"

CHAPTER 33

"You have good aim," Cynthia murmured as they approached the crushed Mercedes. "You hit dead center."

"Mostly luck." Allarde made a shushing gesture when Cynthia opened her mouth again.

A low moan sounded from the front seat, so at least the driver had survived. Though the front door was jammed, Allarde managed to yank it open.

The driver was slumped in his seat and bleeding from a gash in his forehead. He didn't react when the door opened, and Cynthia guessed that he'd be unconscious for a while. She created a mage light and used it to study his features and uniform.

Then it was time to look for Colonel Heinrich, the commandant. Allarde had to use major magic to wrench the back door open, and the commandant had received the brunt of the impact from the massive tree limb. "From the way he's breathing, a broken rib might have punctured a lung," Allarde murmured. "He might not pull through."

"Given what Nick has said of the SS, he's administered his share of death," Cynthia said callously. "Can you pull him out so I can see his uniform clearly?"

Allarde took hold of the colonel's shoulders and managed to pull him free, then lay him out on the muddy road. "He's about your height and build," Cynthia said. "Maybe you should put on his uniform. That would be really convincing."

"If you can create the illusion without me wearing his clothing, I'd really rather not put that uniform on," Allarde said with distaste. "Except for this." He knelt and unfastened the commandant's belt, which carried a holstered pistol.

As he buckled on the belt, Cynthia said, "Do you know how to use that?"

Allarde pulled the pistol from the holster and examined it carefully, testing the feel of the wooden grip in his palm, turning it over, examining the metal bits, and always keeping it aimed away from her. "I believe so," he said at length. "I've used firearms in our time and Captain Rainford showed me his service revolver, the one Nick is carrying. I think I can manage this if necessary. I hope it won't be."

So did she. She rose and conjured an image of the commandant over Allarde. Biting her lip, she circled him, making some adjustments in his appearance. The quality of her illusion magic could mean the difference between life and death.

When she finished her circuit, she gave a nod. "You look very commanding. Now it's my turn. I'll see if I can make myself look like the driver." She closed her eyes and visualized the man, pulling the image around her. "How do I look?"

Allarde whistled softly. "Incredible. We might actually bring this off."

She studied the harsh features of the unconscious colonel. "Just remember to act suitably arrogant."

Allarde gave a smile that showed his teeth. "I am heir to a duke. I have no trouble being arrogant."

They headed into the village, which was eerily quiet. "Where is everyone?" she asked softly. Power had been restored, but most of the houses that had been turned into barracks were dark. They saw no one else on the streets, though a lean cat crossed their path with a wary glance.

"They've sent out search parties for the escaped prisoners," Allarde said. "Both foot and motor patrols. It wouldn't surprise me if they enlisted the French police as well."

"Would Frenchmen obey the Nazis to capture their own countrymen?" Cynthia asked, appalled.

"Some would." His brows furrowed. "Will you have trouble maintaining two such complex spells while we're in the headquarters? It would be easier if you only had to keep the spell on me."

"And here I thought you weren't going to give your usual 'let the girl stay safely outside' speech again," she said dryly. "No, I will not stay outside. I need to be there to help deal with the unexpected."

Allarde smiled humorlessly. "You can't blame me for trying."

Under other circumstances she might, but she guessed that now his worry about Tory strengthened his need to protect any other girl around. Changing the subject, she said, "As we walked, I've added a persuasion element to your illusion to increase the likelihood that anyone seeing you will think you're the colonel. For me, I've added some 'don't see' magic so they'll be inclined to overlook me."

He nodded approval. "We should be in and out quickly."

"Either that or captured."

"Or captured," he agreed. "Try to walk like a soldier. Rigid. I'm sure you've admired handsome young officers in scarlet coats. Imitate them."

"So I should strut. I can do that." The trousers helped her get into the role. Shoulders back and head high, Cynthia marched two steps behind Allarde.

They reached the town hall and he swaggered toward the door

and its guard as if he owned the world. The guard had been sagging in the rain, but seeing his commandant, he straightened and saluted. *"Guten Abend, Herr Oberst!"*

Allarde snapped several menacing words. Cynthia didn't understand the brief exchange that followed, but it resulted in the soldier opening the headquarters' door. He also escorted them into the empty vestibule and down a passage toward the back.

The building was sparsely inhabited. Not only was it absurdly late at night, but as Allarde said, search parties must have sent most of the troops after the escaped prisoners.

The soldier opened another door. Inside a bleeding figure was tied to a chair, his head slumped and pain in every line of his body. Jack.

Cynthia choked back a cry at the sight. The two Germans in the room had been "interrogating" him even though her illusion magic made him look like a schoolboy. This close, his pain was so acute she couldn't block it completely. Her left eye ached in sympathy with his eye, which was badly damaged and swollen shut.

His left shoulder must be excruciating if the pain in her shoulder reflected that. There were other aches and wounds, but the shoulder was the worst. Biting her lip, she concentrated on maintaining her illusions, including an expressionless face for herself.

Allarde barked a question at the interrogators, wisely keeping his speech to a minimum to reduce the chance of mistakes. After the officer replied, Allarde gave an order, disgust in his voice.

The officer started to protest only to have Allarde repeat his order with throbbing menace. Angry but obedient, the interrogator unfastened Jack's bonds and hauled him to his feet.

Jack cried out and almost fell when the officer yanked on his left arm. Cynthia could see red agony flare in his shoulder.

As Jack stood swaying, Allarde said in German-accented English, "Come, spy. I will deal with you as you deserve."

Jack's head came up, but if he recognized Allarde, his bruised face concealed that. "Not a bloody spy," he growled. "Came here to find my French girlfriend."

Allarde snarled an oath in German, pulled out his pistol, and waved Jack toward the door. His glance and terse command to Cynthia made it clear she was to help the prisoner so he wouldn't fall over.

She moved to Jack's right side, the undamaged one, and took his arm. Jack's muscles spasmed under her grip. He knew who she was, but again he made no sign of recognition. Leaning hard on Cynthia, he stumbled from the room.

Allarde followed, his pistol ready. As they walked, Cynthia used what small amount of magic she could spare to dull Jack's pain. She hoped it helped.

The corridor seemed ten times longer going back, the vestibule much wider. The guard who had greeted them waited there, and he opened the door.

Down the front steps, Jack almost pitched to the ground. Allarde couldn't help because he was pretending to be Colonel Heinrich and commandants didn't help battered spies. The guard saluted again and took up his position outside the door.

Ignoring him, Allarde snapped an order at Cynthia, probably telling her to take the prisoner to his car. The medieval village streets were narrow and twisty, so within a few steps of leaving the small town square, they were out of sight of the headquarters.

Cynthia wanted to whoop with relief. They had done it! By Jove, *they'd done it!*

As soon as they were out of sight of the town hall, Jack lurched over to a wall and leaned against it, sweat on his brow. "Are you two *crazy*? You should both be dead or in chains by now!"

"But we're not," Cynthia pointed out.

"Thank God," he said with a crooked smile. "What the devil are you doing here, Cynthia? You're a lady, not a Nazi soldier!"

"I got you captured, so I had to help rescue you," she said tartly. "If anyone is going to murder you, it's going to be me!"

He laughed and wrapped his good arm around her, burying his face in her wet hair. "That's my Cinders," he said in a voice whose warmth ran deeper than even the best hearth magic. She clung to him, fighting back tears of relief as she hid her face in the curve between his neck and shoulder.

Jack crushed her close with his good arm, but kept his voice flippant. "Allarde, you are far too convincing as a Nazi colonel. It must be the ducal upbringing."

"I'm glad your sense of humor has survived," Allarde said. "We need to get you inside so I can see how bad your injuries are. I'll help you since you've almost dragged Cynthia down."

Reluctantly Cynthia stepped back so Allarde could assist Jack. Sentimentality could wait. Now they needed to complete this rescue. She scanned the nearby street. The rain had started to let up and visibility was now slightly better than midnight in a coal mine. "There's a garden shed down that alley."

Allarde helped Jack along the narrow passage that ran between two houses. The shed was small but sturdily built. Cynthia unlatched the door and moved inside, creating a dim mage light. When the boys were inside, she brightened it since the two small windows had blackout curtains.

A potting bench stretched across the end of the shed with two battered stools in front of it. Shelves of clay pots and well-used tools lined the walls. Cynthia could feel that the gardener had spent many happy hours here.

She pulled off her hat, relieved to be out of the rain. Though Jack's vicious early storm had passed, steady rain had pounded down on them for all this endless night.

As Allarde eased Jack down on a stool, Cynthia used hearth witchery to fill the small shed with warmth. Jack in particular was shivering, perhaps in shock. "My shoulder is dislocated," he said through gritted teeth. "Hurts so much I can't be sure what else is wrong."

"Then we need to put the bone back into the socket," Allarde said calmly. "I've dislocated my shoulder a couple of times in riding accidents, so I have a good idea of how to fix it. This will hurt like Hades, though."

"I know," Jack said raggedly. "Just do it!"

"How come girls don't learn useful skills like fixing shoulders?" Cynthia said, trying to joke because otherwise she might pass out in reaction to Jack's pain.

"Girls don't do the foolish things that cause so many injuries . . . Aaah!" Jack's comment dissolved into a gasp as Allarde gently peeled off his jacket.

Cynthia's nails bit into her palms at Jack's stifled moan when his shirt came off. She always admired Jack's fine broad shoulders, and he jolly well needed to have them both working.

Allarde glanced up. "Cynthia, if you drop the illusions, you should have enough power to reduce some of the pain." His voice was composed, but his pale face showed that he was also finding this upsetting. "You might want to close your eyes, though."

"Good idea." Cynthia released the illusions, freeing her remaining power. Then she rested a hand on Jack's bare right shoulder, trying to ignore the way awareness sparked between them even in these conditions.

Taking Allarde's advice to close her eyes, she channeled all the white healing light she could muster into Jack's battered body. Her healing abilities had always been modest, and they were even less tonight despite her best efforts. They were all becoming dangerously depleted, not only physically but magically.

She heard an appalling click, accompanied by a hair-raising muffled cry, then a sigh of relief. "Better," Jack said. "Much, much better."

Wishing she could do more, Cynthia asked, "Can we channel some healing energy from Elspeth? It's a long walk back to the cave."

Allarde shook his head. "She's already drained from the healings she did on the family members who needed it. We can't ask her to give more. We're going to need a lot of power to get so many people through the mirror."

It was hard to argue with that, so she didn't. Allarde continued, "Do you see anything here that could be used as a sling? Jack will need support for his arm."

She turned to examine the shelves, guessing that part of the reason Allarde had asked that was so she wouldn't have to watch his swift examination of other injuries. She couldn't block out Jack's gasps of pain, though. If only she could do more!

Back resolutely turned to the two boys, she said, "Here's a stack of rags, nicely washed and folded before the Germans arrived. And an apron, too."

The irregular pieces of fabric were worn and had probably been ragged even before being consigned to the garden shed. Giving thanks to the good French housewife who had washed everything before being driven from her home, Cynthia shook out the apron. "This one is large enough to make a sling," she said, passing it to Allarde. "The smaller rags might work for bandages."

"Of which we need a few," he muttered. After a few minutes, he said, "You can turn around now."

She did, and found Jack pale but dressed again with his left arm in a sling and a piratical bandage over his left eye. There were also crude bandages in a couple of other places. Allarde had obviously paid attention when people or animals needed treatment.

Jack managed a crooked smile despite his drawn face. "How did the rescue go? You must have got the scientists away or you wouldn't have come back for me. What about the families?"

"Success for both missions," Allarde replied. "Nick and Elspeth are guiding the scientists and most of the family members back to the cave."

"But Tory and two of the children were cut off in the castle and had to find another way out," Cynthia said glumly. "We don't know exactly where they are."

Jack swore under his breath. Cynthia had noticed that secret missions and danger brought out bad language even in those who generally never swore. Though she was concerned about Tory, she had reasonable faith in her roommate's abilities. It was Jack she was worried about.

Before his eye was bandaged, she'd seen how damaged it was. They needed to get him to Elspeth quickly, before inflammation set in. If that happened, he might end up blinded in both eyes. Or worse. After the beating he'd taken, inflammation was a lethal possibility.

"Tory will be soon back, Allarde," Jack said reassuringly. "And with the two children in tow. She's ingenious and multitalented."

"I hope so," Allard said, his expression shuttered. "But the countryside is alive with search parties. She'll have to be very, very careful."

"So will we." Jack levered himself up with his good arm. "Despite your excellent repair work, I'm going to need help if we're to make decent speed. Can I have your arm, Allarde?"

As Allarde silently offered it, Cynthia doused her light and opened the door. When and if they got safely home to Lackland, she promised herself a nice bout of weeping hysterics. She really was not cut out for heroism.

CHAPTER 34

"Are we lost, or should I not ask?" Rebecca asked in a weary voice.

Tory winced. "Not lost, I know the right direction. But I'm having trouble finding the way through this maze of hedges and lanes."

"Not to mention Nazi search parties roaring past on the roads. I thought that one pair would see us for sure. Did magic keep them from noticing?"

"Probably, but that sort of magic has its limits. We were lucky they weren't watching as carefully as they should."

"As long as you know we're heading in the right direction, we'll arrive there eventually." Rebecca sighed and adjusted Aaron, who was asleep in her arms. "Will you be able to take us to England if the others have already gone by the time we reach your cave?"

"That won't be a problem. I'm best in our group at mirror magic." Tory wiped water from her wet face. "Though I might need to rest for a few hours first, I can get us to England. Your family will be waiting for you."

"That's good enough for me." Rebecca's voice dropped to a whisper. "I didn't think I'd ever see my father again."

Rebecca's fear had not been misplaced. If she and her mother and brother had been shipped off to Germany, the family would have been broken forever. Tory really liked the other girl. She hadn't once complained and she accepted the explanations of magic with remarkable calm.

She insisted on carrying Aaron, too, saying that he felt safer with her and that Tory must keep her strength up. But she looked as if she badly needed a rest.

"I have an idea," Tory said. "There's a little barn ahead where you and Aaron can nap while I scout the best route. I'll climb that hill and float up to the tallest tree where I can get a better view."

Rebecca gave a sweet, tired smile. "That would be very welcome."

The barn proved to be an excellent choice, with several cows and goats warming up the atmosphere and a pile of clean hay for Rebecca and Aaron to rest in. "I won't be gone long," Tory promised. "Half an hour or less."

Rebecca settled back, the sleeping boy tucked under her arm. "If I weren't so tired, I'd worry about being separated, but at the moment, I could sleep on hot coals."

"I think we have only a mile or so more to go," Tory said. "After I pick out the best route, we'll join the others very soon."

Rebecca was probably asleep by the time Tory left the barn. Tory longed to join the others, but if she didn't keep moving, she'd never make it back to the cave.

The hill nearby wasn't steep, but floating up to the tallest tree on the crest gave enough height for her to get a better view of the landscape. Finally the rain had ended and a sliver of moon illuminated the ancient hedged lanes that wound through the patchwork quilt of fields. Dawn wasn't far away.

As Tory had guessed, the wooded hillside that concealed the cave was visible. From this height, she saw that there was a farmhouse near their barn with a lane ambling past. If they turned right into that lane, then left and right again, they should reach the hill soon and only have to cross one road.

Her vantage point also showed the lights of the search cars and foot patrols that were combing the countryside. There were so many searchers that she suspected the Germans had enlisted local policemen to join the hunt. The Nazis did not want Dr. Weiss to escape, and she feared they'd rather see him dead than with the Allies.

Praying that everyone else had made it back to the cave, she glided to the ground and headed down the hill. She could have floated, but using magic would tire her even more than hiking over the muddy ground.

The lane she'd seen started at the edge of the woods. Numb with fatigue, she followed it toward the barn. She was nearing the farmhouse when machine-gun fire blasted crazily from the upper floor.

Panic spiked through and she dove, glad the mud softened the impact. Fatigue vanished, replaced by fierce awareness. After taking cover under a hedge, she studied the farmhouse. A chill went through her when she saw that the weapon on the upper floor was aimed at the small barn where Rebecca and Aaron were resting. How to stop that rain of death? She was no warrior.

But she could call on the magical powers of the other Irregulars. A vague plan in mind, she quietly approached the back of the house. Since the rear door was locked, she floated to the upper story. She'd learned so many fine criminal skills lately that it wasn't hard to get inside.

One of the drunken Frenchmen made a sneering remark about killing the filthy Jews that had taken refuge in the barn. Her annihilating rage was swiftly followed by icy determination. She looked up and saw that the old cottage had gnarled beams running across the ceiling. Perfect.

She walked the length of the house to the open door of the room that contained the machine gun, three men in French police uniforms, and bottles of spirits. When she reached the doorway, one of the men turned and looked right at her. He blinked uncertainly, but the stealth stone wasn't enough to conceal a direct stare.

He lurched to his feet. "It's a little girl! Must have hidden here when the rest of the family ran."

A second man turned and smiled nastily. "Old enough that we can use her."

When he stumbled toward Tory, her rage flared again. These men were willing to shoot Rebecca and Aaron for sport. Drawing her focus to blazing intensity, she reached for power from her friends. Most of all, she drew on Allarde's special talent for moving large objects.

Brimming with power, she made a furious sweeping gesture at the beams. *"Enough!"*

Magic surged as she collapsed the massive beams that supported the front half of the roof. Even before the beams had smashed into the men and their horrible gun, Tory threw herself out the door in a rolling tumble.

The shouting ended with lethal suddenness, but the remaining roof beams began to groan ominously. *Devil take it!* The whole cottage was collapsing.

In a blur of motion, she dived out the window in the back bedroom and managed, barely, to land safely in the muddy yard. She was bruised and out of breath and her left arm had been damaged by flying debris, but nothing seemed to be broken.

She closed her eyes as she fought the pain and horror of knowing what she'd done. She had never imagined herself as a killer. She never should have come through the mirror.

Yet as she thought back on the events that had brought her to this moment, she didn't see how she could have behaved any differently. Nick had come to the Labyrinth seeking aid. She'd offered to help him survey the portals of the mirror, which had been triggered by Nick's intensity, and here she was. She couldn't *not* help when she might be able to save lives.

Wearily she struggled to her feet. God willing Rebecca and Aaron were all right, and soon this endless night would end in safety. As she circled the mound of rubble that had been a home, she thought of how it had sheltered families for centuries, and in an instant she had destroyed it.

Again, she didn't see what choice she'd had, so there was no point in berating herself. Opening the barn door, she called, "Rebecca? Are you and Aaron all right?" Terrified she might find their bleeding bodies in the hay, she created a light. "It's me."

"*Mon Dieu,* you are all right!" Rebecca emerged from the darkness, wild-eyed and with bits of hay clinging to her. "I was so afraid those swine had shot you and were now going to kill me and my boychik!"

"We're safe." Tory gave the other girl a twisted smile. "I pulled the roof down on the swine."

"So that was the crashing sound." Rebecca's gaze went to Tory's left arm. "You're hurt!"

"Nothing serious."

"Bleeding can't be good. I have a handkerchief."

"Yes, doctor," Tory said meekly as Rebecca pulled up her sleeve to reveal a laceration on her forearm. The other girl's handkerchief was large enough to wrap twice around the injured arm. "You're good at this."

"Both my parents are doctors, and I want to be one, too." Rebecca tied off the improvised bandage and gently rolled Tory's sleeve down again.

It still amazed Tory that in this century, girls could plan to become doctors. In her time, such a thing was unheard of. The twentieth century produced ghastly wars, but also more freedom and choices.

Aaron emerged from the shadows with a yawn. "Tory?" he said with a cherubic smile.

"Yes, I'm Tory." She smiled at the little boy, her regret over de-

stroying the cottage fading. If violence was needed to preserve innocent lives, she could and would do what was necessary.

"Time for the last short stretch of our journey." Remembering
what Rebecca had called him, she grinned and added, "Boychik."

CHAPTER 35

By the time they reached the cave, Jack could barely move. Cynthia couldn't even help on his left side because it would hurt him too much. She settled for keeping a hand on his back and channeling what pain relief she could manage. He seemed to appreciate the help, and touching him made her feel better. She was too tired to analyze why when the answer was so complicated.

Nick emerged from the cave just as they reached it. "Good God, Jack! The Nazis did this to you?"

Jack managed a twisted smile. "Of course not. This happened when Cynthia lost her temper with me."

She didn't dignify that with a reply. "Nick, take over from Allarde. He's pretty much carried Jack all the way from the camp and he must be close to collapse."

"Not quite," Allarde panted. "But I'm ready to deposit Jack on the nearest blanket."

Nick moved in and carefully took Allarde's place, causing only one strangled gasp on Jack's part. "I'm so sorry, Jack. If anyone had to be beaten, it should have been me."

"Nonsense," Jack muttered. "I volunteered because I wanted my chance to be heroic. You gave it to me, so I owe you a favor."

Males! Rolling her eyes, Cynthia entered the cave and folded a blanket into a pallet. As the boys lowered Jack onto it, Nick said in a low voice, "Each of the families has found a separate cave room where they can be together. By now, they're mostly sleeping. Where are Tory and Rebecca and the little boy?"

"On their way here," Allarde said wearily. "Not far. She needed to pull a lot of magic a short while back, but she's still free." Looking more tired than Cynthia had ever seen him, he folded down onto the floor, his face haggard. "After I catch my breath, I'll go out to her."

Elspeth emerged from the inner cave. "Even your energy isn't limitless, Allarde," she said tartly. Her gaze shifted to Jack. "Just what I need. Another patient."

Cynthia hadn't known Elspeth could be sarcastic. The strain was affecting all of them. She settled by Jack's side and took his hand. He squeezed her fingers, but was worrisomely weak. "Jack keeps saying he's fine. He's lying, of course."

"Of course," Elspeth agreed as she sat on his other side. She maintained her tartly humorous tone, but her face was grave as she removed the ragged bandage so she could examine Jack's damaged eye. "Remember the story of the Spartan boy who hid a stolen fox under his tunic and died rather than show pain when it was eating his innards?"

Cynthia shuddered. "If that's what one learns from studying Greek, I'm glad I never did."

The banter dropped off as Elspeth cupped both hands over Jack's injured eye and poured in her healing magic. Silently Nick laid a hand on her shoulder, channeling extra power. Cynthia and Allarde followed his lead.

In the distance, Cynthia heard motorcar engines. She wondered how long the Germans would search for the prisoners before giving up.

Elspeth sat back on her heels with an exhausted sigh. "I've done what I can."

Eyes closed, Jack said, "Will I lose that eye?"

Cynthia bit her lip. Of course he'd been aware how serious the injury was.

"I believe I've saved it," Elspeth replied. "But my healing power is just about burned out, so I can't do anything for your other injuries."

"None of which are anywhere near as bad as having a fox gnaw on my vitals," Jack murmured. "Thank you, Elspeth. I think I'd look rather dashing with an eye patch, but my mother wouldn't like it."

Allarde stiffened and turned his head toward the cave entrance. "Tory is almost back, and she's in trouble." As he vaulted to his feet, gunshots sounded outside, the sharp cracks alarmingly close.

The Germans were near, and they must have Tory in their sights.

Dawn was breaking as Tory and her companions crossed the small road at the base of the wooded hill leading up to the cave. She had just sighed with relief when she heard the screech of brakes and German shouts coming from the road only a hundred yards behind them.

Rebecca gasped. "They saw us!"

"We're almost there. Run!" Summoning the last of her energy, Tory took off up the hill. She'd be leading the Germans right to the cave, but where else could she go? Surely six magelings could hold the enemy off long enough for everyone to escape through the mirror!

She sent out a mental call for help. Allarde at least could hear. She sensed his instant response. He was coming to meet them.

Praying she'd not signed his death warrant, she said between gasps for breath, "Rebecca, keep going up the hill! Allarde will help you and Aaron. I'll stay here and slow the soldiers down."

"But . . ." Rebecca glanced over her shoulder, her face agonized.

"Go! I'll follow soon." If she survived long enough to run again.

"God bless you," Rebecca panted as she struggled upward, Aaron whimpering at how tightly she held him.

Tory turned, summoning all her remaining magic and tapping into Allarde's as well. His energy was down, but what he had was freely given.

Soldiers crashed toward her through the underbrush lower on the hill. At least three or four, perhaps more. She saw their dark shapes moving among the trees. They were charging straight up the hill, which would take them by a leaning tree. With the soil so wet, it wouldn't take much power to pull it down.

She forced herself to wait as they drew closer and closer. Just as they reached the tree, she crashed it down on them.

The shouts and curses that followed its fall were so vigorous that she realized few if any of the pursuers were seriously injured. Hoping it would take a few precious moments for them to recover from their surprise and get untangled, she spun around and continued up the hill as fast as her tired legs would take her.

She flinched as a burst of bullets snarled by. One of the Germans had a portable machine gun. Nick would know what it was called. She began to zigzag, taking advantage of the larger trees while she prayed that the soldiers' aim would be bad since they were running, too.

Allarde burst from the cave and charged down the hill like an avenging war god. Nick wasn't far behind. Both were firing hand-guns at the Germans.

Hitting a target was unlikely, but their bullets slowed down her pursuers. Allarde passed Rebecca, who was staggering toward the cave, but Nick stopped and scooped Aaron from her arms. Not missing a step, he pivoted and wrapped his other arm around her waist to haul her to the safety of the cave.

Allarde continued toward Tory, his face blazing with determination. She wanted to scream at him to retreat before the Germans could see him well enough for a clear shot, but she had no breath, no strength.

She tripped and crashed to the ground. Incapable of moving, she began to weep uncontrollably. So close, *close* . . .

Gasping for breath, she called, "Justin, go back! Don't commit suicide in a hopeless cause!"

"Steady, Tory!" Covering the last yards between them, he skidded to a halt above her and fired the last bullet from his handgun.

She could feel him gathering his magic as he shoved the empty handgun into his waistband. Then he flung up his hands toward the oncoming soldiers and power blazed from his palms like invisible flames.

The sounds of gunfire changed. Weapons continued their ear-numbing bursts, but they were joined by a hard, pattering sound like hail.

Tory gasped. Dear God in heaven, Allarde was creating a shield that knocked the bullets from the air!

His flinty gaze still fixed on the oncoming soldiers, he caught her hand and hauled her to her feet. His touch conveyed the enormous strain of blocking the fusillade of bullets, but he never wavered.

She managed to get her feet under her so she could move on her own. Her hand locked on his, she guided them up the hill. He continued to face the Germans, protecting Tory and himself from the gunfire by magic and fierce willpower.

Heart pounding and muscles near collapse, she forced herself to keep moving. The cave was only a dozen paces ahead. Half a dozen. Only another stride . . .

They staggered inside. Tory hadn't thought what would happen next, but Allarde had. "Get back!" he barked at the other Irregulars. "Move Jack deeper into the cave!"

They scrambled to obey. Nick heaved Jack to his feet, the girls helping. Agony flashed across Jack's face, but he didn't utter a sound. The four of them disappeared into the tunnel, leaving Tory and Allarde alone in the antechamber.

Tory numbly followed, her hand still clamped on Allarde's. When they were a dozen paces from the entrance, he said tautly, "I need all the magic you have, Tory!"

"It's yours." She reached into her deepest reserves, finding resources she didn't know she had, pouring the power into him.

Focusing their combined magic in an incandescent blast, Allarde collapsed the entrance to the cave in a deafening avalanche of stone and earth. The door between them and their Nazi pursuers was now closed and locked.

CHAPTER 36

As debris showered between them and the entrance, Allarde pulled Tory down to the floor and engulfed her in his arms to protect her from the hail of dirt and rocks. She clung to him as fragments bounced off her back, coughing from the dust and never wanting to let him go.

His face was buried in her wet hair when the cascade ended. The darkness was absolute. She said shakily, "I didn't know you could block bullets like that!"

His embrace tightened. "Neither did I."

"You didn't know if you could?" she exclaimed, aghast. "And you still ran straight into the gunfire? Justin, you're insane!"

"I couldn't bear the thought of losing you," he said simply.

She wanted to weep. "You could have been killed! You shouldn't have risked your life. We aren't even really together."

His voice deep and amused, he said, "Tory, my love, we've never been apart, even when you were at your most nobly pigheaded. I admire the nobility, and prayed that it wouldn't take you too long to recognize that the bond between us is too strong to be severed for logical, worldly reasons."

He was right, she realized. Their connection had stayed strong and undeniable even when she was trying her hardest to do the right thing. Even now, she had to try. "Stronger than your bond to Kemperton?"

"Stronger even than that." His fingers lifted her chin and he kissed her with dizzying intimacy.

Surrendering, she dropped her resistance and all pretense to nobility. She kissed him back with feverish need as relief and magic melded them closer than they'd ever been. With him, she felt *right*.

When they finally broke for breath, she whispered, "I wish you didn't have to choose between Kemperton and me."

"I will miss Kemperton terribly," he said, his voice grave. "But you are my heart, Tory. How can I live without my heart?"

"And you are my soul." She leaned against him, her eyes closed on unshed tears. "I have never been more tired, or happier, in my life."

He chuckled. "My sentiments exactly."

She smiled into the darkness. He was right. They'd always been together.

They always would be.

Their moment of privacy ended when Nick arrived with a light. "Well, that was exciting," he remarked. "Are you both all right?"

Tory laughed, euphoria bubbling up through her fatigue. "Never better."

Nick regarded them both with interest. "It's about time you two made it up. I should have organized a betting pool for how long you could manage to stay apart."

"A gentleman would never place such a wager," Allarde said in his most aristocratic manner as he got to his feet.

"You're the only gentleman here," Nick said cheerfully, "so the rest of us could have indulged."

Allarde laughed as he brushed dirt from his clothing, then offered Tory a hand up. "Your little holiday in France has been interesting, Nick, but I'm ready to go home."

"So am I!" he said fervently. "Come into the next chamber. We're figuring out what happens next. Cynthia just heated water for tea."

"Tea!" Tory was grateful for Allarde's hand as she stood, aching in every muscle. "The drink that built the British Empire."

"Tea is all we have left," Nick said. "The remaining food was given to the children."

Tory shivered as she looked at the mound of stone and debris that blocked the tunnel. If she and Allarde had been two yards closer to the entrance, they wouldn't be walking away. "Rebecca has mage power."

Nick blinked. "She does, doesn't she? I was so distracted by—everything else—that I hadn't consciously noticed."

He was too busy drowning in Rebecca's gray-green eyes, Tory suspected. That was no bad thing.

They moved deeper into the cave and emerged in a medium-sized chamber containing the other Irregulars. Elspeth and Jack and Cynthia were settled around a large mage light that had been shaped to resemble a campfire.

Jack lay on a folded blanket, battered but conscious. He and Cynthia were holding hands. Tory suspected that her roommate's snobbery had given up the fight in the face of Jack's charm and obvious fondness for her.

Elspeth scrambled to her feet to hug Allarde. "When you and I shared a nursery during family visits, who would have dreamed what we'd be doing now?"

He hugged her back with the arm that wasn't around Tory. "You always were my favorite cousin. But I certainly didn't foresee this."

Cynthia poured cups of steaming tea and handed them to Tory and Allarde. "Alas, no sugar."

"It still tastes like ambrosia." Tory sat by Allarde and sipped at the hot, fragrant beverage. "How long until we've recovered enough to take everyone back to Lackland?"

Elspeth settled back by the pretend fire. "We all need a good sleep. It's going to take me a few days to recover from burning so much power so don't count on me to contribute much. But I did stop short of complete burnout."

Tory frowned as she thought of the upcoming mirror passage. "How are our guests taking the idea of magic? Are they alarmed? Will they talk about us too much in the future?"

"While I was doing healing on family members who needed it, I did some gentle work on everyone to persuade them not to think too much about their escape." Elspeth covered a yawn. "And not to talk about it since doing so might get them sent to Bedlam."

"I haven't used as much magic as the rest of you," Nick said. "So I'll be full strength. Tory?"

She mentally inventoried her supply of magic. "Eight hours' sleep and I'll be able to do my share, I think. But what if the Germans try to dig their way in?"

"I'll listen for that," Allarde said, "but I don't think they'll try. With luck, they'll think we died when the cave collapsed. They only saw four of us. As far as they know, there are other fugitives to be hunted down elsewhere."

"Not that the Nazis will find them." Nick quirked a smile. "Rescuing just one man seemed like such a simple mission."

Thinking of Rebecca, Tory said, "Your compulsion to come after Dr. Weiss has more than one reason behind it."

"Are we going to run out of breathing air now that the entrance to the cave is closed?" Cynthia asked.

Allarde shook his head. "The cave is too large, and there are other entrances."

"Wonderful," Jack said with a touch of his usual wicked humor. "So we can return if we want another holiday in France."

"You'll have to make it a boys' holiday," Cynthia said tartly. "None of us girls are fool enough to do this again!"

Tory didn't bother to mention that they hadn't meant to do it this time, either. She got creakily to her feet. "Is there a blanket? Not that I need one. Bare rock will do."

"There's only one blanket left," Cynthia said. "Several went to the children, and Jack is hogging two."

He started to struggle up. "I'll give one of these up."

Cynthia put a hand on his good shoulder and pushed him flat. "No, you won't. I'll stay warm without one. Hearth-witch magic is so useful."

"Tory, we should sleep by the cave-in to listen for possible digging," Allarde said calmly. "So we don't need a blanket."

She gave him a slow smile. "Indeed we don't."

He took her arm and escorted her toward the collapsed entrance. He was right that a blanket wasn't necessary. When he lay on his side and pulled Tory against him spoon-style, she had all the warmth and comfort she needed.

"Sleep well, my darling," he murmured.

"I already feel like I'm dreaming," she whispered as she rested her head on his shoulder. A stony bed was more comfortable than her four poster at Fairmount Hall when she slept warm and protected in the arms of her beloved.

To Cynthia's annoyance, Nick moved off to sleep outside the entrance to the Weisses' room. Then Elspeth joined the Steins so she could sleep with the baby and let the exhausted mother rest with her husband.

That left Cynthia alone with Jack. He had two blankets, she had the last one. She dimmed the mock fire to a gentle glow and was about to wrap herself in the blanket on the opposite side from Jack when he said in a low voice, "Come here."

She tensed, thinking of his injuries. "Is something wrong?"

He extended his good hand to her. "I'm cold and need you to warm me up."

"I can do that from here with hearth-witch magic," she pointed out.

He wiggled his fingers coaxingly. "It's not the same."

"Idiot," she grumbled, but he was right. Body warmth had a quality that mere heat could never match. Though she was warm physically, the depths of her soul were still shivering from the long, horrible night. She moved across the chamber rather warily.

"We are both in dire need of rest," he said, "so make yourself comfortable. I'm softer than the ground."

She hesitated, thinking of the agonies he'd suffered. "You have so many bruises that any kind of pressure might hurt you."

"Not having you close will hurt more." He caught her hand and tugged her down. "As long as you're on my right side, I'll be fine."

Fear and exhaustion and being in a time and place not her own stripped away any other objections. She stretched along his warm, firm body, her head on his uninjured shoulder. "I suppose you're in no condition to ruin me, and being compromised in a different century doesn't really count."

His laughter warmed her even more. "You're right, there is no way I could ruin you. Not that I'd want to do anything to hurt you." His hand stroked down her arm. "You saved my life, Cynthia. Now it belongs to you."

She jerked awake. "Nonsense! I was just . . . fixing a bad mistake I made. I don't want your life!"

"That's unfortunate," he said softly. "Because I want to give it to you."

The words were bad enough, but it was the warm emotion he poured into her that broke her down. The worst had happened.

Fighting back tears, she tried to get away, but his good arm held her in place with more strength than he should have after that beating. "I don't understand," she gasped, hiding her face against his side. "You can't mean that. How can you possibly like a scarred, impossible girl like me?"

He kissed her forehead. "Because I love beautiful, gallant, wounded creatures."

She began sobbing uncontrollably.

"Am I that bad a bargain, Cinders?" he asked softly. "I know I'm a peasant compared to you, but I thought that didn't bother you as much as it used to."

Voice choked, she said, "N . . . no one has really cared about me since my mother died. And . . . she wouldn't have died if my father had sent for a healer like Elspeth. But because she had magic, he wanted her dead. And me, too." Her mouth twisted with bitterness. "I refused to oblige him."

"Oh, Cynthia." His arm tightened around her and he rested his cheek against the top of her head. "What a fool he was to throw away such a jewel of a daughter."

The vibration of his voice was soothing, like the purring of his silly cat back at Swallow Grange. Deep knots in her spirit began to unwind. "You wouldn't throw me away, would you?" she asked in a small voice. Jack was nothing like her father, but this was a question she had to ask. And an answer she needed to hear.

For once speaking with no trace of levity, he said, "Only a fool would throw away the most precious thing he's ever found. And I am not a fool."

Cynthia had closed her heart to love after her mother died, but she could no longer bear the loneliness. Gathering her courage, she dropped the barriers she'd built to protect herself from pain. Though she'd shared magic with him for their weather work, the rush of his emotions she felt now was like nothing she'd ever experienced. Love, respect, a fierce desire that he'd kept banked so he wouldn't frighten her.

Most of all, she felt his love. As joy blossomed within her, she began to laugh. "I'm joining your collection of damaged creatures, aren't I?"

"They're all special." There was a grin in Jack's voice as he traced the scar on her cheek that she no longer bothered to conceal. "And you're the most special of all."

CHAPTER 37

Despite the unorthodox night's sleep, Tory knew exactly where she was when she awoke. She and Allarde still lay spooned together, her head on his shoulder, his warm arm wrapped around her waist. Despite the darkness and stuffy air and cold stone beneath her, she had never felt happier in her life.

"You're awake, aren't you?" he asked softly as he created a mage light and tossed it into the air above them.

"Your shoulder must be numb since I've been sleeping on it." She rolled onto her back and trailed fingers down his cheek. "And your whiskers are getting serious."

He turned his head and kissed the center of her palm. "I hope you don't mind."

She gasped as desire flared through her. "We . . . we should be thinking about going home," she stammered.

"Soon." He bent his head and kissed her again, his warm body enfolding her.

The world dissolved as she wrapped her arms around him and kissed him back. There was only now, only this heat and hunger to merge with him body and soul. She wanted to close down her mind and luxuriate in his scent and warmth and touch.

But her mind would not quite depart. Gasping for air, she turned her head and broke the kiss. "We can't. This . . . this is probably a bad idea."

He rolled away and sat up, breathing hard as he ran stiff fingers through his dark tangled hair. "Why do so many bad ideas feel so very good?"

She laughed a little as she pushed herself to a sitting position. "Mr. Hackett at Lackland would say it's the devil's plan to lure us to sin."

"He might have a point. Certainly you are wickedly alluring." Allarde squeezed her hand, then stood. "How do you feel? You burned a huge amount of magic last night."

She stiffly got to her feet as she tested the wellspring of power deep inside. "Every muscle in my body aches, but my power seems surprisingly strong. How about you? You burned as much magic as I did."

"I feel fully restored. Sleeping together is good for both of us." He slipped an arm around her waist and kissed the top of her head. "We'll need every bit of that power to get this group home. Can we manage everyone in a single trip?"

She closed her eyes and thought about how this transit should be done. "I think so. We need to space the Irregulars out. I'll lead, Nick will be at the other end, you and Jack and Cynthia and Elspeth interspersed along the line. The hard part will be persuading everyone to go along with something so strange."

But persuasion was easier than she expected. She and Allarde rejoined the others, who had gathered in the largest chamber, sitting in small groups and talking quietly among themselves. The connection Tory had noticed between Cynthia and Jack had turned into a blaze. She'd never seen her roommate look happier.

"Everyone is here," Allarde said after scanning the stone chamber. Raising his voice, he called, "It's time for the next step, which is the journey home. Tory will lead the way. Here she is to explain what must be done."

As Allarde helped Tory onto a natural stone block so everyone could see her, she hissed, "You're the one with the gravitas! You should do the talking."

He grinned. "In this you lead, my lady."

She felt awkward telling so many adults what to do, but when she finished her brief explanation, Rebecca got to her feet. "I'll follow you anywhere, Tory."

Her father also stood. "You young people have already performed miracles. I shall believe you can perform this one."

His wife nodded and took her son's hand. "When do we go? We have no reason to stay longer in this damp cave."

Glad that Elspeth's persuasion was making everyone cooperative, Tory said, "Then we shall leave now."

She stepped down from the stone block and led the way back to the mirror, Allarde behind her. It took time for such an assorted group to make their way through the varying passages, and when they reached the mirror chamber, it took more time for Tory to arrange everyone to her satisfaction.

Mrs. Stein was holding her baby, so her husband took hold of one upper arm and Elspeth the other. Since Jack was still battered and limping, Cynthia insisted on holding his hand even though it meant two Irregulars were standing together. But after a few minutes of shuffling, all was in order.

Raising her voice, Tory said, "This will be very uncomfortable, but it will be over quickly. Hold tight to your neighbors' hands and soon we'll be safe."

She looked down the straggling line, checking that everyone was in place and holding on to the next person in line. Then she turned to the mirror and closed her eyes as she marshaled her magic, drawing from the others, equalizing and balancing.

Elspeth lacked her usual power, but the other Irregulars had clear, strong magical signatures. Tory was also able to draw on the sparks of magic everyone had. Rebecca had power that rivaled the Irregulars. If she received magical training, she would become a mage to reckon with.

Tory drew together all the magic and decided that she had enough to conduct the group through the portal. Then she visualized the mirror in the Labyrinth during Nick's time. When she was ready, she reached out mentally to touch the mirror, offering the combined magic of all of them.

The mirror shimmered into sight and someone behind Tory gasped at its quicksilver beauty. Then Tory touched the power. Silver turned to black and chaos consumed her.

The mirror passage was no easier this time than the last.

Tory gave a sigh of relief when she saw the sprawling old farmhouse that Nick Rainford and his family called home. It stood sturdily on the famous white cliffs above Lackland village, facing the English Channel and offering shelter to passing mages.

Everyone had made it through the portal, though she felt as if she'd been flattened by one of Nick's lorries. The nonmages had found the trip easier, which was interesting. Perhaps having magic made the passage more difficult.

It was a good thing the farmhouse wasn't too far from the ruined abbey. Tory was numb with fatigue. If she hadn't been holding on to Allarde's arm, she would curl up beneath a hedge and sleep for a week.

Just in front of her and Allarde, Nick led the way home through the darkness. As they approached the stone house, he glanced at the line of people following. "My mother didn't flinch when I brought five Irregulars home, but this lot might startle even her."

Tory smiled. "Your mother teaches school. Surely she has nerves of steel."

Behind her, Daniel Weiss said, "We shall not be trouble, Nicholas. An old barn will suit us well. Tomorrow I will contact Dr. Florey."

"We can do better than a barn, though it might be rolling up in blankets in the drawing room." Nick tried the door to his house. Locked. With a sigh, he dug into his pocket. "We didn't used to lock the door, ever."

Before he could find his key, the door flew open and his mother stood there silhouetted against the light. "Thank God you're here, Doctor . . . !"

She stopped, startled, then grabbed her son in a fierce grip. "Nick!" Her face was haggard. "You're not who I expected, but thank God you're home! Where did you go this time, you beastly boy? I've been half mad with worry!"

"I've traveled through the mirror to France, Mum." He gestured behind him. "And I've brought back three families from there as well as some old friends. But now we'd better get inside or the wardens will come around to complain about the light."

Anne Rainford pushed her hair back with a distracted hand. "Three families?" Her gaze sharpened as she studied the clusters of people behind Nick. "A good thing I made a great pot of bean soup today! Come in, please, and rest."

Tory moved forward. "Mrs. Rainford, it's wonderful to see you! But you were looking for a doctor. Is someone ill?"

"Tory!" Anne gave her a quick hug, then looked anxiously into the night. "Is Elspeth with you? Polly is dreadfully ill. I've sent for her father to come down from London."

Tory caught her breath, feeling Mrs. Rainford's fear. Anne Rainford would not have summoned her husband if Polly's condition wasn't dire.

"Oh, no!" Nick cried, his face anguished. "Not Polly!" He bolted toward the stairs and took them three at a time up to the bedrooms.

Elspeth joined Mrs. Rainford as the refugees streamed by into the house. Voice low, she said, "I'm here, but my power is almost burned out. Of course I'll do what I can, but that isn't much just now. What's wrong with Polly?"

"Blood poisoning," Anne said tersely. "She was scratched by a piece of debris thrown up by a bomb. A scratch, it was *nothing*. But now . . ." Her voice broke.

Sarah Weiss said in her softly accented voice, "My husband and I are both physicians, Madame Rainford, and he has been developing a medicine to fight infections like blood poisoning."

Daniel added, "There has been great difficulty manufacturing this drug in large quantities, but we are close to success." He patted the improvised knapsack he carried. "I have with me the small amount we successfully made in France."

"If you wish us to try it on your daughter, we will," Sarah warned. "But it is still experimental."

Anne said starkly, "Would you give it to a child of your own?"

Gaze holding Anne's, Sarah said gravely, "I would."

Anne nodded. "Then please do what you can. Otherwise . . ." She shook her head. "The local doctor spends much of his time at the military hospital and hasn't yet come. I don't think he could help her even if he came, but I had to do something."

"We are here and will do our best," Sarah said. "Where is the child?"

"Upstairs." Her expression lightened by hope, Anne turned to the others. "Tory and Elspeth, you come, too. If Polly is aware, she will be glad to see you." She glanced over the people crowded into her kitchen. "Allarde and Cynthia, you know the household, please make our guests comfortable. Jack, you look ready to fall over. Do sit down before that happens. We don't need another patient."

Tory almost laughed as she went upstairs in Mrs. Rainford's wake. There was nothing like a schoolteacher for organizing a group of people.

Her humor vanished when they entered Polly's room. Two years younger than Tory, Polly was taller and had been robustly healthy.

Now she looked like a wizened old woman on the doorstep of death. Her fair hair was drenched with sweat and her skin flushed with fever.

Nick knelt by the bed, holding his sister's thin hand. From his stark expression, he was remembering his funeral dream and wondering if it was already too late.

Polly rolled her head toward the door when her visitors entered. "Tory?" she said in a thin, dry whisper. "Elspeth? I'm glad to have a chance to say good-bye."

Chilled by the fatalistic words, Tory kissed her friend's forehead. The skin was fever hot. "Wait until you hear of our adventures!"

"It's good to be back." Elspeth patted Polly's hand, then withdrew with Tory to the other side of the bed so they'd be out of the way. But there was anguish in her eyes. If she'd had her full magical power, she would be able to drive the inflammation from Polly's fever-wracked body.

"Darling, I've brought you not one but two physicians," Mrs. Rainford said, her voice soothing. "Dr. Weiss and Dr. Weiss. This is my daughter, Mary Rainford, but we always call her Polly."

"It is my pleasure, Miss Polly," Sarah Weiss said as she began a swift examination, checking Polly's temperature and pulse and general health.

Tory and Elspeth clasped hands, silently sharing their concern. While Sarah performed her assessment, Daniel set his knapsack down and delved into the center, bringing out a flat metal case and a pair of carefully wrapped bottles.

When she was done, Sarah smoothed sweat-soaked hair from Polly's forehead with a cool hand. "We have a magical new medicine, you see. It is called penicillin and is made from something very simple, a mold found on bread."

Anne Rainford looked briefly appalled. Elspeth said, "Molds have been used for dressings forever, but have always been unpredictable. If Dr. Weiss develops a drug that is consistent and can be made in large amounts, it will change the world."

"That will happen, though not by one man alone," Daniel said soberly. "Miss Polly, I have here the medicine and a needle, but my wife will administer it because she is better with injections. You will hardly notice."

"It is good you are small, for we have only a small amount of penicillin. But for you, enough." Sarah rolled up the sleeve of Polly's sweat-dampened nightgown. Using another bottle and a ball of cotton, she cleaned a spot on Polly's upper arm.

Tory realized that the two doctors were deliberately keeping up the flow of soft, reassuring words as they explained. Probably it was as much to soothe the others in the room as for Polly.

Inflammation was one of the great killers. Tory had known people to die from wounds as simple as the piercing of a rose thorn. The only sure cure was at the hands of a powerful healer, and there were few as good as Elspeth. Truly it was a miracle to think that this medical magic might soon be available to everyone.

Sarah took the needle and delicately inserted it under the skin. Polly instinctively tried to pull away, but the doctor said soothingly, "This will be only a moment. Great magic requires a little pain, eh?"

"My magic is a lot of work!" Polly said fretfully.

"You are very brave, *ma petite,*" Sarah said as she withdrew the needle and blotted the small drop of blood at the site of the injection. "Sleep now, and by morning you will be better. We shall give you another injection later."

As Polly turned away, her eyes closing, Anne Rainford whispered, "Truly she will recover?"

Sarah hesitated. "We have had very good results in tests. I shall pray that the results are equally good now."

Anne took her daughter's limp hand. "I'll stay with her tonight. Nick, look after our guests."

He nodded mutely and led the others out of the room. As the Weisses headed down the steps, Tory moved to Nick's side and gave his hand a quick squeeze. "Your dream must have been a warning," she said softly. "A good thing you acted on it."

"To think if I hadn't gone! Or if we'd returned a day later." He shuddered.

"But everything worked out as it should," she said firmly. "Even Jack and Cynthia rescuing the Bouchards. I don't think that was a coincidence, Nick."

He frowned. "Do you think that if the mirrors were designed by Merlin or other British mages, they built in magic to encourage events that will benefit Britain?"

"Perhaps. Or maybe it's divine plan." Tory covered a yawn. "I'm too tired to make sense of what happened."

"I don't care if it was coincidence or divine plan," Nick said with a sigh. "I'm just glad all the pieces fell into place for us and we got home in time for Polly. The dream I had—no longer feels like it's going to happen."

As they reached the bottom of the stairs, the door opened and a tired-looking man in army uniform entered. Captain Thomas Rainford. He stopped and blinked behind his wire-rimmed spectacles at all the people moving around his home. "What the devil?"

Allarde stepped from the kitchen. "A temporary invasion, sir. The result of a successful mission."

The captain's brows arched. "Allarde. Are you here with all your trouble-seeking cohorts?"

"Indeed he is, sir," Tory said, looking as innocent as she knew how.

"Nicholas?" Captain Rainford asked in a dangerous voice. "What has been going on here? And what about Polly? Your mother's message said she was very ill."

"She has been, Dad. But her condition is looking better." Nick beckoned to the Weisses, who had turned at Captain Rainford's entrance. "Thanks to Dr. Daniel Weiss and his fellow scientists. This is my father, Captain Thomas Rainford."

Captain Rainford's brows arched so high they threatened to hit his peaked hat. "Dr. Daniel Weiss? And this must be your wife, Dr. Sarah Weiss?"

"We are in your debt for sending your son and his young friends," Sarah said gravely. "We owe you our lives. We have tried to return that gift to your daughter."

Tom Rainford swallowed hard, but like his wife, he was a schoolteacher with nerves of steel. "In these days, all men and women of good will must work together. Dr. Florey will be very pleased that you have escaped and can join him."

"Will he welcome the two colleagues who were rescued with me?" Daniel asked.

Tom blinked, temporarily distracted, as little Aaron dashed in front of him on some mysterious errand. "I should think so. He believes that science has grown so complex that teams must work together for the best results. He told me when he visited that he needs more researchers experienced in biochemistry."

"We shall all do our utmost to help Britain and her brave people." Daniel Weiss gave a short formal bow, then took his wife's arm as they rejoined their friends to share the good news.

Eyes glinting, Tom said, "Nick, join me in my office. I wish to hear what has happened. In *detail.*"

"Yes, sir." After a pause, Nick added, "Mum is upstairs with Polly."

"Then I shall see them first." As the captain headed upstairs, Cynthia poked her head out of the kitchen. "We'll put together a tray of tea and sandwiches to take in with you, Nick. That might soften your father's mood."

"That and the bottle of brandy he keeps locked in his desk," Nick agreed.

"He hasn't much to be upset about," Tory said. "You did something British Intelligence couldn't do. And it's not as though this was your first mad rush into danger."

Nick groaned. "I doubt that memory will make him any happier."

"As long as you always come back, he'll manage." Tory gave Nick a gentle push. "Why not find Rebecca and see how she's doing? She's about Polly's size and could use better clothing, so maybe you can raid Polly's closet."

"Rebecca." Nick brightened. "Yes, I'll talk to Rebecca until my father comes down." He set off purposefully to find her.

Tory joined Allarde in the doorway to the kitchen. "Is all well?"

"The guests are so grateful for soup, safety, and freedom that they really would be happy to sleep in the barn," he replied. "Most are eating bread and cheese and bean soup and starting to believe they have a future." He put a hand on her back. "I'm not needed now that Granny Stein has taken over the kitchen. Let's find some fresh air."

"Oh, *please*," Tory said fervently.

From the light in his eyes, she knew that he needed the private time together as much as she did. They left the house and headed through the dark garden to the cliff path where they'd first kissed. The night was cool, but within the circle of Allarde's arm, Tory was warm and at peace.

Gazing across the channel, she said, "It's hard to believe that just across the water France is in chains. How long will this go on, Justin?"

"Too long." He fell silent. In the distance, bombers could be heard crossing the narrow strip of water that protected Britain. "But someday it will end. How is Polly?"

Tory recounted what the Weisses had said about the medicine and its effect. Allarde gave a sigh of relief. "By morning, she'll be so much better that it will be hard to remember that tonight she was dying."

"Is that foretelling?" Tory asked hopefully.

Allarde nodded. "Polly will recover, and the Weisses are going to be a valuable part of making this miracle available for everyone." He tightened the arm wrapped around her shoulders. "And we helped, Tory. That makes the last few days worth it."

"I agree, though we still have to go through the mirror again to get home," Tory said with a sigh. "But though I didn't come on this journey voluntarily, I'm not sorry."

She leaned into Allarde. Even helping to save countless unknown lives paled next to the fact that this mission had brought her and

Justin together again. "I said I'd never go through the mirror again. I guess I learned one important lesson on this mission."

"And that would be?" he said with a smile.

Laughing, she tilted her face for a kiss. "I'll never say never again!"

AUTHOR'S NOTE

I've taken some liberties with the development of penicillin. Dr. Weiss is fictional and I know of no secret missions to rescue continental scientists vital to the work. But penicillin really did change the world.

Infectious diseases have been among humankind's greatest killers, and history is rife with plagues. The infamous Black Death pandemic of the fourteenth century is estimated to have killed more than a third of Europe's population. Infected wounds were another great killer. Even minor injuries might lead to blood poisoning and death.

The use of molds by traditional healers is an ancient practice. In Eastern Europe, cottages might have a loaf of bread molding in the rafters in case it should be needed for wound dressing. Warm soil containing molds was used in Russia. A healer who had good luck with a particular batch of moldy bread might feed the mixture more bread and water to keep it alive indefinitely, as is done with yeasts for bread making.

But results were erratic and impossible to standardize, which made bread molds of limited medical value. Developing an effective standardized drug began with the Scottish biologist Sir Alexander Fleming. In 1928, he was already well-known when he accidentally discovered that a penicillium mold was killing off colonies of bacteria in his laboratory. Fleming coined the name penicillin. (At first he called the substance mold juice, which is not a name that inspires confidence.)

However, culturing the mold, creating a purified strain, and isolating the active ingredient was difficult, and eventually Fleming put the work aside. Development of a usable drug was done by a team of scientists in Oxford. They were led by an Australian researcher, Dr. Howard Florey, who realized that increasingly complex science called for groups of trained researchers working together. Dr. Sarah Weiss was inspired by Ethel Florey, whom Howard met in medical school. She became his research partner as well as his wife.

Developing effective, standardized penicillin in large quantities was high priority in both Britain and the United States. The first production drugs were reserved for military personnel in need. By the end of the war, penicillin was saving countless lives.

In 1945, the Nobel Prize for Physiology and Medicine was awarded to Fleming, Florey, and Earnest Chain, a German-born Jewish scientist who worked with Florey at the Radcliffe Infirmary in Oxford. Chain left Germany for England in 1933 after the Nazis came to power since he knew he would no longer be safe in his native country.

Many other antibiotics have joined penicillin over the years, and they have changed the face of medicine. While they can't cure all diseases—for example, they're useless against the many viral diseases we suffer, starting with the common cold—they have become an indispensable part of medical treatment. Sadly, overuse of antibiotics may undermine their effectiveness as bacteria evolve that are resistant.

The human race and bacteria have been at war for a very long time. If we aren't careful, the bacteria may get the upper hand again!

Turn the page for a sneak peek of

DARK DESTINY

Coming in spring 2012 from St. Martin's Griffin.

CHAPTER 1

Lackland, England, Autumn 1940

A fighter plane roared menacingly over the farmhouse just as Tory bent to blow out the candles on her birthday cake. She froze—she would *never* get used to destructive flying machines!

But she could pretend to be brave. She drew a deep breath and blew. The seventeen candles for her years were easily extinguished, but the one added for luck flickered persistently before guttering out. She hoped that wasn't an omen.

Her friends around the table applauded. Those who'd come from 1804 with Tory were enjoying the twentieth-century birthday customs. The five of them would return to their own time in the morning. She was glad to be heading home, but she'd miss her other four friends.

"Did you make a wish?" Polly asked. The youngest Rainford, she belonged to this house and this time. Though she was still weak from a bout with blood poisoning that had almost killed her, her mischievous smile had returned.

"Indeed I did," Tory replied. "And it was hard to decide what to wish for!"

Her life had changed so much since she turned sixteen a year ago. Then, she had been the well-brought-up Lady Victoria Mansfield, youngest child of the Earl of Mansfield. Most of her thoughts had been turned toward her upcoming presentation to society, where she would look for the best possible husband.

In the year since, she'd become a mageling, an exile, and one of Merlin's Irregulars, sworn to use her magic to protect Britain. Not to mention being a traveler through time and an unsung heroine of Britain.

Best of all, she had fallen in love. Her gaze drifted to Allarde, who sat on her right, looking impossibly handsome. He gave her a smile full of the warmth and intimacy that had grown between them in the last months.

"Time to cut the cake!" Lady Cynthia Stanton, who was Tory's roommate back at the Lackland Academy, was eyeing the dessert hungrily. "Mrs. R., if I come back for my birthday, will you make me a cake like this?"

"I will," their hostess said cheerfully. "But give me some warning, please. This cake required almost a month's worth of our sugar rations. I'll need to save more coupons to create another cake this size."

"You won't want to take another beastly trip through the mirror jest for a cake, Cynthia." Tory got to her feet so she could cut properly. "But you can have the first piece of this one."

The round cake had a thin layer of white icing and HAPPY BIRTHDAY, TORY! was spelled out in rather uneven red letters. The same red icing had been used to draw little red rockets exploding around the edges.

Tory could have done without the explosions, but Polly had been pleased with herself for coming up with the idea. After all, war had drawn together this group of magelings from two different eras, and had forged lasting friendships.

Mrs. Rainford was sitting on Tory's left, and she held out a small plate to receive the first slice. "Here you are, Cynthia," Tory said as she set the wedge of dark fruitcake on the plate. Mrs. Rainford handed it across the table.

"I'm going to have trouble waiting until everyone is served!" Cynthia exclaimed. "I still haven't recovered from burning so much magic in France."

"As the birthday girl, I give you permission to eat now rather than wait for the rest of us," Tory said grandly. "We all need to eat to build up our strength for the return journey through the mirror."

Cynthia didn't hesitate to dig in her fork. After the first bite, she smiled blissfully. "This is wonderful, Mrs. R. If I didn't hate traveling through the mirror so much, I really would come back for my birthday. I'd even bring sugar so you could make the cake without using up your rations."

"That's not a bad idea!" Nick Rainford exclaimed. "Sending sugar, I mean. How hard would it be for you to throw sugar through the mirror?"

"We could do that," Elspeth replied. "Our sugar comes in big loaves that have to be broken into smaller pieces, but they'd throw very nicely."

"Tea and butter and bacon and all kinds of other things are also rationed," Nick said thoughtfully. "If you can send them through the mirror, we could . . ."

"I will not have a black market operation run from my house," Mrs. Rainford said firmly. She handed another plate of cake to Rebecca Weiss, who was staying with the Rainfords to study magic. "But some sugar now and then would be nice."

"We can arrange that," Allarde said as he clasped Tory's hand under the table. She could feel his amusement.

She bit her lip, thinking how much she would miss this freedom to be together when they returned to Lackland Abbey. Male and female students were strictly separated in the abbey. Only in the Labyrinth, the maze of tunnels below the abbey buildings, could they work together as they secretly studied magic. And only there could she and Allarde have the privacy they craved.

"What is a black market?" Tory asked as she cut more slices.

"Illegally selling rationed goods, and Nick would dive right in if I let him," Mrs. Rainford said with a laugh.

She laid her hand on Tory's, but before she could continue, magic blazed from Mrs. Rainford through Tory to Allarde, kindling another blaze of magic from him. Allarde's hand clamped hard on Tory's and he exclaimed, *"No!"*

"Justin?" Tory said dizzily, shaking as she channeled power and shock between Allarde and her hostess. "What . . . what just happened?"

He swallowed hard, his gaze unfocused. "I . . . I saw Napoleon invade England."

The Irregulars gasped with horror. The threat of invasion had been hanging over their heads for months as Napoleon Bonaparte assembled an army just across the English Channel from Lackland Abbey. Jack asked, "What makes you say that?"

Tory felt Allarde's effort to collect himself. "Mrs. Rainford and I both have foreteller talent, and Tory's ability to enhance magic seems to have triggered a vision of the future when the three of us were touching." He glanced at their hostess. "Did you see images of invasion?"

"I . . . I saw Napoleon in Westminster Abbey," Mrs. Rainford said unevenly. "But that was fear, not foretelling! We know from history that Napoleon never invaded."

Allarde shook his head. He was still gripping Tory's hand with bruising force. "I don't know about your history books. What I saw was an event that may well happen if we don't act. We need to return home immediately. If and when the invasion takes place, Lackland will be a major landing site." He swallowed again. "I saw French barges landing in Lackland harbor and soldiers pouring off. The village was burning."

Jack Rainford rose from his chair. "My family!"

"The French are *not* going to invade!" Mrs. Rainford repeated. "I'll get a history book and show you." She left the room, her steps quick.

Tory took a swallow of tea for her dry throat. Mrs. Rainford was a schoolteacher and well educated, but Allarde's magic was powerful. "Foretelling is what *might* happen, not necessarily what *will* happen, isn't it?"

Allarde eased his grip, though he still held her hand. "This felt very, very likely."

Mrs. Rainford returned with a textbook. As she thumbed through the pages, she said, "There's a chapter about how close Napoleon came to invading, but he didn't." She found the chapter she was looking for and caught her breath, her face turning white.

Tory peered at the book and saw that the letters on the page were twisting and flickering like live things. The words couldn't be read.

Mrs. Rainford said in a choked voice, "I remember what this chapter said, but . . . it doesn't say that anymore."

"The text being in flux suggests that the history isn't set," Allarde said grimly. "Perhaps Napoleon just made the decision to launch and that's why we had the visions. If the Irregulars can do something to prevent the invasion, that might be why history records that it didn't happen."

"If the past has changed, wouldn't the present also be different?" Rebecca, raised by two scientists, frowned as she tried to puzzle it out.

"Time travel is a mystery, and I don't pretend to understand how it works," Jack said, as grim as Allarde. "But there is danger at home and to my family. I can feel it like a gathering storm."

Elspeth rose. "We need to leave right away. Most of us are already packed."

Ever practical, not to mention hungry, Cynthia said, "We should take the rest of the cake. It will help us recover from the mirror passage."

Knowing that was true, Tory tried to eat her slice, but it tasted like straw. She and the other Irregulars had faced danger here in 1940, but her own time, her home and family, had not been threatened. Not until now.

"I'll pack the cake and some cheese," Polly said briskly.

As the party dissolved, Nick caught Tory's gaze and said with deadly seriousness, "You've done so much for England in my time. If there is anything, *anything,* that I can do to help, send a message through the mirror and I'll come instantly."

"You saved my whole family," Rebecca said in her soft French accent. "I have only just discovered that I have magic, and I don't know how to use it. But I pledge everything within my power to your service."

Tory thanked them, but she realized with cold foreboding that even if all the Irregulars and their 1940 friends worked together, they were few and the French were many. The Irregulars might not be able to save England.

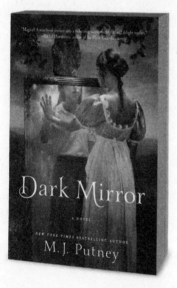